Bobbin's Journal

Waif to Wealth

by

Carol Jeanne Kennedy

Dedications

To all my wonderful friends and family who helped me along the way in writing my novels. This book is dedicated to Don Knight, Billy Miller, Jean Gess, Carol Silvis, and Mary Burdick. Also, special thanks to Hennie Bekker whose musical compositions *Algonquin Trails* and *Stormy Sunday* provided the creative spark for *Winthrope*, followed by the rest of my Victorian Collection.

Other Great Novels by this Author

Winthrope – *Tragedy to Triumph*
The Arrangement – *Love Prevails*
Bobbin's Journal – *Waif to Wealth*
Poppy – *The Stolen Family*
Sophie & Juliet – *Rags to Royalty*
The Spinster – *Worth the Wait*
Holybourne – *The Magic of a Child*

Visit the author's website for exciting new additions: Her *A Novel Victorian Cookbook* with authentic Victorian cuisine that her characters loved to eat; the author's **hand-painted slipcases** to house the collection of novels, and a gallery of **her own paintings** inspired by 19th-Century artists.

Links and Reviews

Visit the author's website: KennedyLiterary.com
Like on Facebook: caroljeannekennedy
Follow on Twitter @carol823599

Table of Contents

Chapter 1 – London, Beginning in the Year 1850

TO A CHILD
On parent's knees, a naked, new-born child,
Weeping thou saddest when all around thee smiled:
So live, that, sinking in thy last long sleep,
Thou then mayst smile while all around thee weep. [1]

Snowflakes floated down upon the raging inferno licking the flames like a hissing cat. Horrific pleas from neighbours to extinguish such a blaze fell numb on the frozen snow. Flames, in frenzied mass, burned everything up, burned everything down and the charred remains of the old Derby house crumbled upon itself—and atop all those within.

A few blocks distant, the vicar's voice rang out in the moist air, crystallising into words that floated cheerfully from his tongue, "Merry Christmas to one and all."

Unaware of the terrible fire that had claimed the lives of Bobbin Derby's family, the vicar closed the ancient iron-studded church door and forgot to lock it—again. He took his ailing wife's arm and helped her down the slippery church steps pausing only briefly to sniff the air. "It is a bit smoky this evening, my dear."

---

[1] Exact origin unknown. The poem was either composed or recorded by Kalidasa, 4th century China. Sir William Jones, (1746 – 1794) translated the poem from Sanskrit to English. The version quoted here is from Bliss Carman, *The World's Best Poetry*, 1904.

Had he looked up he would have seen an orange glow flickering on the church's grey stone spire; he would have seen the sparks circling, spiralling, and floating heavenward amidst the fire's updraft, but he continued along in careful and deliberate steps thinking only about the slippery places along the pathway home.

* * *

The centuries-old church, now dark and empty, held the close acrid smell of recently extinguished candles. Though Bobbin heard the vicar leave and the familiar dead thunk of the door as it closed, she remained hidden—too frightened to move. Finally satisfied that she was alone, she hugged herself in the numbing cold. "Mama," she murmured, "where are you, Mama? Oh, I am so cold."

In the sanctuary of her little heart, she heard a whisper. Feeling a great warmth move through her small naked body, she stretched out her little arms wide and smiled up at the cross above the altar. "Yes," she promised, "I will."

As if awakened from a dream, she felt the frigid wintry air move about her and rubbed her bare arms briskly. *Oh, the cloakroom, maybe I'll find a stray coat.* Shivering as she tiptoed along the back wall, she found the room's door slightly ajar.

Moonlight shined through the room's only window and shed its grace on a lonely shawl hanging still and lifeless on a wall peg. With a quiver of relief, she snatched up the old moth-eaten woolly and wrapped it tight around her shoulders, relishing its warmth.

When she bent down to rub her toes, she noticed alongside the mud tray, a pair of woollen socks. No matter that they were hard from filth and full of holes, she slipped them on and counted the find a miraculous blessing. To stop her teeth from chattering, she stuck her fingers in her mouth. Suddenly she heard the massive old sanctuary door open. In the dead of darkness she made out the shadow of someone creeping alongside the offering table, *but it is not the vicar, Mr Tillyard.* She backed up against the wall and held her breath. She watched the dark figure flip open the poor box's wooden lid and rummage for coins. There must have been a meagre few, for the stoop-backed shadow cursed and slammed the lid—it was a man's voice—gruff and mean. She closed her eyes, trembling.

"What ye doing in there hiding—shivering? Shivering like a mad dog. Come 'ere."

Bobbin obediently walked toward him, tugging her shawl tightly about her body. "Sir, I was searching for my mama."

He glanced around the sanctuary and then back at her. By the faint light that shone through a slice of the open door, he must have seen that she was nearly naked, but for the long wool stockings and raggedy shawl. "What's ye name?"

"I I cannot remember, sir," she whimpered.

Through one squinty eye, he looked her up and down. "Wait where ye are. Can't go outside with no shoes, you'd freeze your toes off. Stay here, I'll be back." He walked to the door and stopped. "Stay."

"Yes, sir."

She waited, shivering for a very long time when finally she heard the door open.

Tossing her a pair of boots, the old man said in a gruff tone, "Put 'em on. Best I could do. Least your toes won't fall off."

She found that the over-sized wool stockings filled up the toes of the boots and made them fit quite nicely. She took a few steps. "Oh, thank you, sir. They are very warm."

"Where's ye mother?" He looked her up and down. "Little girl, is it?"

"I don't know, sir."

"You know anythin' about that fire a little ways from here?"

She shrugged.

"What's ye mother and father's name?"

"I can't remember, sir." Trembling, she wiped her runny nose on the shawl.

He glanced up at the cross hanging askew on the wall and shook his head. "Very well then little girl, I'm gonna carry ye to an orphanage on the other side of the river."

He wrapped her tight within her shawl and threw her over his shoulder. She awoke when he stood her up on the sidewalk in front of the orphanage. It was early morning when she faced him, rubbing her eyes awake. "Happy Christmas, sir," she blurted.

He climbed three steps to the orphanage's door, turned the knob and pushed it open. "Merry Christmas, little girl." He patted her head with a smile. "Go in now, child." He turned and descended the snow-covered steps and never looked back.

Bobbin watched as he walked onto the bridge and slowly disappeared into the morning's snowy whiteness.

A sign above the door read: Newpark Institution, Charity School, London. It was snowing just a little, and as she stood in front of the open door, warm air moved slowly around her body. A shiver grasped her as she stepped across the threshold into the warmth of the room. Across from her was a blazing fire, four huge logs stacked atop each other in a frenzy of snaps and hisses. Red-hot coals smouldered amidst the grey ash beneath. The scent of the burning wood brought tears. It smelled like … she closed her eyes for she could not quite remember what it smelled like exactly. Her teeth began chattering again. *Mamma, I am so cold.*

Miss Susanna Neilson, a teacher at Newpark, was passing through the vestibule when she felt a cold draft. When she stopped to find the matter, she found a half-naked little girl standing in front of the open door.

Bobbin's spindly legs were knocking, rumpled socks bunched up over boots fit for a man, flesh bumps on her arms, and an old shawl wrapped around her. The child's hair was draggled, matted, and tangled.

"Dear me," said Miss Neilson, "who are you?"

Bobbin coughed, hugged herself, and glanced longingly at the fire.

"Well, then, come in, child, come in." Before she closed the door, Miss Neilson looked up and down the street. "Did you come here all alone?" She took her hand. "Why, child, you are cold as ice."

Miss Neilson wrapped the skinny, shivering little body within her arms and sat in the rocking chair next to the fire. She could feel her settle and thought the pathetically worn little waif's mind was confused. She rocked her to sleep and watched her tear-stained, black-smudged little face fade into a dream.

Miss Neilson was ten and eight, rather tall for her sex, with light blonde hair twisted and braided atop her head. Her clothes were of a modest grey, and everything about her was clean and neat. Her features were soft and warm; her kind smile invaded the hardest little hearts. Her soft blue eyes crinkled as if she found humour in all things, profound or lightweight. She kept a face that the children found comfort in.

On her desk, she kept Bulwer-Lytton's: 'The veil which covers the face of futurity is woven by the hand of mercy.' [2]

She had taught at the institution, a charity school for educating orphans, for several years now and developed a personal rule against favouritism. However, Bobbin proved to be the one exception; this orphan was somehow different, saintly in a way. Indeed she emanated an aura of goodness, certainly a destiny.

* * *

After waking that Christmas morning in the arms of Miss Neilson, Bobbin found that she could not speak and remained mute for many months. However, the patient teacher continued to nurture the child and wisely allowed her to find her own way. Bobbin had great difficulty in recalling her mother's name, thinking perhaps it was Mary—her father's name remained hidden in the deepest part of her mind.

The other children accepted little Bobbin's quiet ways. After all, she was not a crier. She dressed her own self and promptly. She rarely coughed at night, nor did she make trouble. And most importantly, thought the older children, she did not wet the bed.

One dismal February morning as the children sat in the refectory eating their porridge, Toby (the biggest boy) was told to fetch more firewood, for it had grown very chilly. At one end of the rectangular shaped room sat the hearth—a huge, charred and woefully sparse fire pit. This morning it held two pitiful logs that burned and sputtered upon the useless iron grate. Wet wood burns 'sizzly' remarked the children as they watched Toby carrying another armload. When he stooped to drop it into the woodbin, he slipped on a wet spot and fell hard onto the floor.

All the children laughed, except Bobbin. She stood. "My name's Bobbin Derby. I am nine years old; my Papa fell by the fire too." She dropped to the floor and curled into a little ball. "Papa, Papa," she cried over and over, "no, no, you must stop."

---

[2] Edward Bulwer-Lytton (1803 – 1873) English novelist, poet, playwright, and politician. Quoted from *A Dictionary of Thoughts*, by Tryon Edwards, (1908)

She curled tighter and tighter, writhing and shaking as she sobbed.

The children stopped eating and stared.

Miss Neilson picked her up wiping away her tears. "There, now Bobbin, there now."

But Bobbin would not stop sobbing, and the other children began to cry too.

Mrs Moll, the cook, came out of the kitchen. Wiping her floured hands on her apron, she saw Miss Neilson carry her from the room. "Well then, what could the matter be?"

"I dunno," said Toby with a shrug. "I fell, and it musta frightened her."

Tilley, one of the older orphans tugged on Cook's apron. "It's only that she finally remembered her papa, Mrs Moll."

"Oh, well then, yes. Now I understand."

"Miss Neilson will calm her," added Tilley confidently.

"Yes, she sure can do that." Mrs Moll offered rare second helpings of porridge to the orphans, and that soon settled them as well. They knew it was just a matter of time until the newest addition to their family would begin to speak.

"I like the name Bobbin," said Tilley.

One by one, each child began to laugh again. "Aye, Bobbin is just the name for her. She is so small. Little Bob Bob Bob Bobbin ..."

Their chatter and laughter again filled the glum dining hall, the crisis was over—Bobbin was finally becoming one of them.

When Miss Neilson and Bobbin heard them laugh, a certain calm settled over them as well. Holding tight to Miss Neilson, she closed her wet eyes. "I think my Papa is gone away forever, miss."

"Why is that?"

"He fell hard to the floor, miss, like Toby. One night Papa came home full of ale. It was very dark, miss. The fire was nearly gone when he fell. He called Mama a dog and spit on the floor. I told him Mama wasn't a dog at all and he got very angry at me."

There was a long silence. "Go on."

"Papa spanked me hard." She covered her eyes with her hands. "Papa took a burning log from the fire and threw it at me. He crawled after me laughing and spitting up heaps of ale. When he tried to grab my leg, he started to choke and cough, for the smoke was very thick by then. I ran and hid with our dog, Hester, and the others in the wood closet."

Bobbin wiped her eyes. "I heard someone outside shout: 'Fire, fire.' I crawled under the smoke to the door and unlatched it. Our landlady was screaming. 'Fire, fire.' She ran down the street holding her hands to her head.

"I heard Papa slam the wood closet and latch it. They were hidden in there. He tried to find me, but it was too thick with smoke. I could hear them shriek and beg to be let out, Miss Neilson. Hester was inside with them, barking and gnawing at the door to get out. I heard her whine. I could not find them. I covered my ears, miss."

Bobbin's hands were trembling. "Then the room was like that." She pointed to the fire in the hearth. "I ran away, fast as I could. I looked back, and it was burning; neighbours came running, shouting. I think my mother's name was Mary."

Miss Neilson patted Bobbin's head. "Perhaps it is, my child, perhaps it is, but you said you hid with the others? What others, dear? Where was your mother?"

"There were no others, miss, that I can remember, but only my dog, Hester. My mother ran away. Oh, I was so cold. I was so cold. I ran to the church to find Mama."

Bobbin's eyes clouded over.

"You must be very confused my dear Bobbin, but perhaps someday I shall understand." She rocked her back and forth, singing aloud a line from Dickens to which she added her own melody. She often sang to the orphans, *" 'I love these little people; and it is not a slight thing when they, who are so fresh from God, love us.'* [3] Let us not cry about yesterday, my dear sweet little Bobbin, rather, let us look happily for tomorrow."

★ ★ ★

The very next day Miss Neilson perused the month-old newspapers at the lending library for any news of a missing child. She found only an account of a bad fire in the poorer section of Squire Hill about the time Bobbin arrived at the orphanage. It was reported that a Mr Derby along with his son

---

[3] Charles Dickens (1812 – 1870) English Novelist. *The Old Curiosity Shop*, (1841).

and two daughters were found in a charred clump in their house on Long Sutton Street.

Further investigation indicated that the mother had run away with an unsavoury crowd of gipsies; then again there was a rumour she jumped in the Thames and drowned. The teacher had to assume that Bobbin was an orphan.

A few years later Miss Neilson learned that the church to which Bobbin had fled was St. Anthony's. When visiting there, she was shown Bobbin's baptismal entry and learned a little more about the family.

Mr Derby had been a drunk with a wife named Mary and three children. The family rarely went to church except for handouts. Because Bobbin could not or would not remember her family, Miss Neilson wisely decided to let the child remember on her own and gave her a journal in which to write her thoughts. Perhaps her memory would be restored naturally, in her own time.

Chapter 2 – The Year Being 1855

All the gestures of children are graceful; the reign of distortion and unnatural attitudes commences with the introduction of the dancing master. [4]

It was late spring in London, the sky was cloudy and grey. The trees were just beginning to bud—a touch of green against the winter's bleak swirl of sooty black and muddy brown. The streets shone from early morning misty fog. The rhythmic clop, clop of horses as they pulled wagons and carriages, echoed hard against the city's cold stone buildings. It was the beginning of a new day in London, the voices of street peddlers, greeters, and the ever incessant muffled drone of the rushing crowd moved along as precisely as a shop-clock. It was going to rain again, but then everyone was quite used to that.

In one home in particular, Mr John Philip Collier, wealthy and prominent Governor of the Bank of England, was discussing some important financial matters with his two sons. The lads were to accompany him to Liverpool that very morning. They had just sat down for their breakfast when the youngest of Mr Collier's three children, Maria, hurried into the room.

"Oh, Papa, why must I stay home again? When will I be able to go along as my brothers do?"

---

[4] Sir Joshua Reynolds (1723 – 1792) English portrait painter. Quoted from *A Dictionary of Thoughts*, by Tryon Edwards (1908).

"See here, Maria," replied her brother, Philip, "you must settle yourself. We are about important business. Women have no place in the business world. You are surely old enough to know that for you have been told many times." He snapped his napkin open, "Far too many times."

Even her favourite brother, Edward, just two years older than she, ruled in Philip's favour. "Now, Maria, we will not be gone so very long. When we return, I promise we will take you to a very happy assembly at Victoria Gardens."

Never lifting his well-trimmed, greying temples but once to look at his silly daughter, John Collier continued eating, pausing only to reprimand her. "Maria, sit still." Finishing the last of his revered coffee, he said in quiet exasperation, "Maria, I repeat, you must sit still."

She stuck out her lip and crossed her arms defiantly. "Why do I have to sit still, Papa, when they get to go with you every day?"

He sat down his cup. "Maria, I will explain to you once again that young ladies do not accompany their fathers and brothers when they are about business matters. We will return within the week. You must learn to entertain yourself. Read, walk, or go to a play. Does not your governess, Mrs North, have a plan for you? You are most annoying when you clamour about so—rather puts me in mind of a little ape."

She swallowed hard. "A little ape? Humph. I am an ape because I am alone so very much of the time, Papa. Mrs North is not such good company. Besides," she lowered her voice, "she is much too old. She has me reading silly, stupid books. I should like to read what I choose. I should like to walk in the park alone, if I want."

Collier shook his head. "Maria that will do, I will speak with Mrs North."

"Before you go, Papa?"

He glanced at the shelf-clock. "No, Maria, I do not have the time. We are to leave immediately after breakfast. I will speak with her when I return."

She glanced at Philip with a mulish pout.

Edward pinched her arm. "Maria, act the lady if you please. I shall be humiliated in public with your spoiled behaviour. You behave like a child."

"A child?" She took a penitent look. "Well, I am sorry if you think so."

Philip smirked. "Oh, my baby sister, Maria, you are a great actress. I know very well you are not sorry. You may fool Father, but you do not fool me."

"That is not fair, Papa, that he taunts me so. I was sorry. Indeed I was." Keeping a close eye on him, she sighed deeply.

Both brothers shook their heads.

Collier looked up at her. "Try another tactic, my dear, that one is wearing thin." Casually dabbing his lips with his napkin, he stood, excusing his family.

Knowing full well her charms had failed again she hastily removed from the table. Outnumbered and furious, she stomped out of the room. She was hurt more so since Edward was laughing, too. They had been close at one time, but lately, he was teaming more with Philip and her father.

* * *

Collier, feeling guilty over his daughter's behaviour, confided in his sons: "I must soon find a suitable school for your sister, she is growing quite wild. I do not believe Mrs North can handle her whims and trickery. I cannot imagine what must be going through your sister's head."

"Father," replied Philip, "she is a clever girl and needs a goodly portion of discipline. She needs a mother. Who else could reach her?"

"That is very true, Father," agreed Edward, nodding sympathetically. "Maria was always such a pleasant child, but, alas, to lose a mother and reach that particular age of," he hesitated, "age of transformation into a young lady must be horrid. It is obvious Maria has changed—and not for the better. No, I do not believe Mrs North is the one to help her. I agree the woman is simply too old."

Reaching for the door, Collier stopped. "Maria has been alone too much since her mother died. Perhaps I have not been as thoughtful of her as I should be." He sighed heavily. "She still misses her mother terribly."

"As we all do, Father," said Philip.

Edward smiled. "Father, what say we take her with us, then? What harm could come of it?"

Maria was eavesdropping and overheard her brother's words. She bounded up the winding staircase and into her room. She was confident a knock would come any moment, announcing that she was to go along. She rang for the housemaid in preparation for packing. Within those brief moments of anticipation, there indeed came a knock. "Come, I am ready," she called out in a happy tone.

Noticing her sunny countenance, Collier was surprised yet relieved at her mood change. "Maria, dear, your brothers and I shall be gone only one week. When we return, I have much I must discuss with you."

Her smile faded. "But, Papa, am I not to go along after all?"

Her disappointed air disturbed him; she was not acting now. "No, my dear," he kissed her forehead and glanced at the hearth, "I shall have Tessy tend your fire, it is beginning to wane."

"Indeed, Papa." Her face tightened. "Goodbye."

From her window, Maria looked down at her family's waiting carriage. Philip did not look up as he left the house, but Edward did. With a half-smile, he blew her a kiss. Collier followed and paused to exchange words with the footman. He briefly glanced up at her window, and without hesitation, followed his sons into the carriage.

Watching their vehicle jostle for position into the busy street, Maria sighed. Just as she was to turn away, she noticed a baker drop three hard-crust loaves of bread on the sidewalk strewn with house-slop and horse dung. He picked them up, wiped them off, and stuck them back into his basket.

She turned from the window. "How disgusting."

Leaving her room in a huff, Maria found one of the maids dusting the bannisters and flew past her taking the steps two at a time.

The maid shrieked and dropped her pail. "Oh, for my very life, miss, I thought you were falling, so I did."

Maria giggled. "Have you seen Mrs North?"

Resetting her day cap, the maid nodded. "Aye, Miss Maria, Mrs North is in her room."

"Humph, tell her I wish to see her. I will be in the study."

The maid found Mrs North. "Ma'am, Miss Maria requests your presence, immediately."

Raising her brows, Mrs North shook her head. "Immediately, is it?" Her lips pursed. "Indeed, one must be at her beck and call without a moment's rest." Closing her book, she exhaled heavily. "Very well, where is the little scrub?"

"In the study, Mrs North," she said with a deep sigh. "Aye, she's been a handful ever since her mum died. Indeed, the typhoid, ma'am, is a terrible thing. Miss Maria misses her so."

"Oh, that was over two years ago, she should be well recovered by now. The girl is simply melancholy for pity. Why, she has every single thing imaginable to make her light-hearted: money, prestige, a fine home, a distinguished family name, two handsome brothers, and a very fine father. What reason has she to mope about so?"

"I have no idea, ma'am."

"Of course you don't, nor will you ever."

* * *

When the governess came to her charge's summons, she found Maria in her father's study, sitting at his desk. The very desk she had been forbidden to even come near. Papers were lying askew, India ink spilt on the floor, and the rubbish bin tipped, but Mrs North knew Maria was in no mood to be reprimanded, so she listened patiently, as always, to her charge's complaints.

"Mrs North, as you must know by now, I have been left alone again." Knowing how the noise irritated her governess, Maria rocked back and forth in her father's squeaky leather chair. "And I hate being alone, the only relief being I will read and read, becoming swept up in someone else's happy life rather than my own stupid one."

"Well, now, Miss Maria, your life is not a stupid one. Perhaps a walk in the garden would occupy your idleness. Certainly the air would do you good."

"No, Mrs North, that simply will not do. I must have something else to 'occupy my idleness' as you call it. Come now, surely you can think of another." She continued rocking.

Anxious to quell more temper tantrums, Mrs North replied in a happy tone, "Well, Miss Maria, perhaps then we shall visit More Towns End Bookstore, if that pleases you."

Maria paused. "Yes. Yes, that shall please me. And, Mrs North," she lifted her chin, "I shall find my *own* books to read, without your help."

"Very well, miss. I will arrange that with your father."

"That shall not be necessary, Mrs North. Papa does not care one straw what I read. After all, I am ten and four you know. I am perfectly able to select a book of my choice." She stood abruptly. "Let us be done with it, Mrs North. I shall be in my room until we leave."

Maria ascended the long winding staircase, but instead of turning left toward her room something pulled her toward the right—her mother's bedchamber. Not having been there since her mother's death, Maria did not know why she now wanted to go into her room. Turning the crystal doorknob, she slowly entered. Her mother's scent yet lingered.

The room was warm; a fire burned softly. She walked reverently over the beige floral rug and passed her mother's bed without looking directly at it. She moved methodically to the long oval mirror, closed her eyes and breathed in deeply. Slowly opening her eyes, she pondered her reflection for a few moments. "Mama, I do not think that I look like you."

Leaning into the mirror, she fingered the soft blonde curls dangling deftly about her face. "My hair is much lighter than yours, Mama; my eyes, like Papa's, are dark brown and piercing." She glared at her reflection. "My, but I can look quite spiteful when I wish it." She pinched her cheeks, fluttered her eyelashes and then stepped back. "I am taller than you, Mama—by a head at least. I am most certain of it, though not as slender, perhaps." She went to her mother's wardrobe and brought out one of her gowns. Holding it up to herself she smiled. "You see, Mama, it is much too short."

Maria sensed the presence of an observer and froze. Turning, she found Mrs North staring from the open doorway. She dropped her mother's gown. Kicking it aside, she slowly walked toward the dour-faced woman. Holding a frosty glare, Maria moved past the governess and closed the door behind her.

* * *

Later that afternoon as the two were travelling to Maria's favourite bookstore, More Towns End Bookstore, she had a wish to break the monotony by admonishing her governess. "Why must you always twiddle your thumbs so, Mrs North?"

Being a nervous twig of a woman, and very much removed from the whimsical, naughty side of a young girl ten and four, the governess straightened. "I have no idea, Miss Maria. It is just a habit, I suppose." Irritated at her snippy mood, she added, "Yes, I suppose very much a habit, just as you swing your legs in idle motion, I choose to twiddle my thumbs. With no consequence at all, I would imagine." She lifted her chin.

Smirking, Maria looked out the window. "Boredom being the consequence, Mrs North."

The governess did not know what Maria meant and said nothing more. She dabbed at her upper lip, occasionally meeting Maria's gaze. The carriage remained quiet.

Maria read the expression on Mrs North's face. *Oh, but she is dull. In a short while, though, she shall be very entertaining.*

Mrs North caught her smirking. "Miss Maria, I would wish that you stay near me this afternoon and do not wander away."

"Oh, but of course, Mrs North."

* * *

The sudden familiar jostling of the carriage signalled that they had arrived at the bookstore. While Mrs North conversed with the footman, Maria noticed a brick wall being erected that adjoined the bookstore. Curious, she inspected the bricks and suddenly discovered that she was well hidden behind the newly erected six-foot wall. She peeked through a bit of misplaced mortar to watch Mrs North turn this way and that, obviously searching for her.

"I am over here, Mrs Grundy," [5] whispered Maria with a giggle.

When Mrs North spied the brick wall, Maria thought the game had come to an end. However, the governess immediately turned and headed in the opposite direction, toward the bookstore.

"Good for me, then," laughed Maria. *I shall just follow her now and look quite dismayed that she would walk ahead and not wait for me.* When she turned to leave, she stumbled over something. Regaining her balance, she found a book lying at her feet and opened it, but found no name.

"Excuse me, miss," said Bobbin Derby, "I dropped my journal, and I see that you found it."

---

[5] Mrs Grundy, a prude with a moralistic voice of disapproval-19th Century England.

Maria looked down her nose at the little dormouse of a girl. "Indeed, I almost tripped over it and fell. I could have injured myself, you know."

"I am sorry for it, miss." Bobbin's large brown eyes lowered out of respect for the obviously wealthy young lady.

Maria was intrigued with the very poor and was close enough to smell her. Oh, the poor seemed so hideous to her. With all the books she read, never were they nearly as descriptive as the real adventure of standing within touching distance of one of them. When she should walk along the avenue with her father or brothers, she was always spoken to with polite words by gentlemen and gentlewomen. White gloves, clean teeth, and smiles—tired of all that, Maria became fascinated with poor, destitute people.

And she paid particular attention to their rotten teeth, often thinking, to her amusement, that they were piano key beige with ebony edges. That always brought a laugh from her friends. Next, it was their hair she inspected, for not being covered with a proper cap left it filthy, matted, and frizzy. Her nose wrinkled as she envisioned little bugs nestled deep within the follicles. She shuddered at the thought. And now this girl, much her own age, with simple clothes, though Maria noted they did not stink, stood before her, hinting that she, Maria Collier, should hand over a book. "Humph, maybe I shall keep it." She casually thumbed through it, but soon became bewildered. "This is not a book."

"No, miss. It is a journal," replied Bobbin in a soft voice.

"A journal?"

"Yes, miss. I began writing in it when I was ten. There were things my Papa said that I do not want to forget. I try to write down his spoken words so that I shall always remember."

"You read and write then?" Maria looked at the little dormouse in doubt.

"Yes, miss. I work in the bookstore just up the street."

Maria eyed her suspiciously. "But you are too little to work."

"I am ten and three, miss, soon to be ten and four. I am little, yes, I have been told, but I must work, miss. My father died, and I now live in an orphanage." Bobbin respectfully added, "I must pay for my keep for soon I shall be sent out."

"Out?" responded Maria, "Out?"

"I am old enough now that I must soon go. And so I help teach in the orphanage. I scrub the floors, and then I come to the bookstore."

Maria was mesmerised by the little girl's story. "And then what do you do in the bookstore?"

"Oh, miss, I return books to their proper place. I clean them, too, and I wipe the floors, and whatever Professor Halliwell-Phillipps desires of me. He, of course, owns the store. ... "

"Of course he does, Dormouse," interrupted Maria, rolling her eyes. "I know him quite well, but I do not recall ever seeing you there."

Bobbin ignored her and went on. "And then I am allowed to read whatever books I wish."

Mindful of the girl's gaze upon her, Maria continued to thumb through Bobbin Derby's journal. "Well then, I suppose you may have it back. There is certainly nothing in it I should want to read."

"No, miss, I should think not."

"Very well, then, you may have it back."

Mrs North rushed up all a flutter. "Miss Collier, I must insist that you do not bolt from me again. I lost sight of you, and I am of a mind to have a word with your father over the matter."

Bobbin thought the governess was going to pop a button, for the veins on her neck were throbbing, spittle sprayed from her mouth. "Excuse me, madam, but the nice young lady found my journal after I accidentally dropped it. She kindly returned it to me. I am sorry if I made her tardy."

The governess looked down her nose at Bobbin. "Journal? What journal?"

Bobbin held it up as proof.

Maria's chin came up in indignation. "Yes, Mrs North, I nearly tripped over it after leaving the carriage. You were busy conversing with the footman, so I looked a little distance at who would own such a book."

"This wall probably blocked your sight," said Bobbin, "but I am very happy now. I would not want anyone to be out of humour for my mistake."

Mrs North's nerves were now calmed. "Well, certainly not, then." She looked Bobbin up and down with a wrinkled frown. "And what is your name, little girl?"

"Bobbin Derby, madam, I live there." She pointed to the orphanage two doors down in the alley.

"Newpark, then?" said Mrs North.

"Yes, madam."

"Well then, Miss Collier should be commended for returning it to its rightful owner. I shall inform her father of her most excellent deed."

"Thank you, madam." Bobbin curtsied.

Maria looked smug. "Bobbin, tell me, since you work in the bookstore, do recommend a book I would read."

"Oh, yes, miss. I have recently read ..."

"Come, Miss Collier." The governess took Maria's arm. "It is not a wise thing to ask a mere orphan what one should read or not read." She sniffed the air. "Come along now, it is beginning to rain."

Bobbin lowered her head, her face coloured. After a respectful, safe minute from Mrs North's rebuke, she lifted her gaze and watched them walk up the street toward More Towns End Bookstore.

It was raining harder now, and Bobbin knew she had to hurry. She ran through the alley, jumping puddles and garbage heaps. Her flimsy boots were now water-soaked. When she started up the narrow grey, slippery granite steps to the orphanage she glanced up at the bookstore window, Miss Collier was watching her. Bobbin smiled and waved, but Maria sneered and moved quickly away.

Staring at the empty window, Bobbin felt sad at the rebuff. She was lonely with no one her own age to talk to. She had no one at all except Miss Neilson and a few other teachers, and the very young children who would constantly come and go. Though she cared very much about everyone there, she wanted a friend, someone her own age.

Bobbin was under no illusions, though. Certainly the wealthy Miss Collier would never seek her out as a particular friend, but perhaps one day, if she should see her at the bookstore, she would make herself available for polite conversation regarding books.

Bobbin sighed. Her little shoulders drooped, and she went inside to begin her chores.

Chapter 3 – Bobbin Comes into her Own

Some of the domestic evils of drunkenness are
houses without windows, gardens without fences,
fields without tillage, barns without roofs, children
without clothing, principles, morals, or manners. [6]

The Newpark Institution had once been the grand,
fashionable home of Lady Newpark, now deceased by twenty
years. Since there were no heirs when she died, the mansion
was acquired by a London society and made into a school for
orphans.

It was stripped of its grandeur. Out came the chandeliers,
mahogany panelling, mirrors, stained-glass windows—and was
left cold and destitute. After many years of neglect, it was in
need of a great many repairs.

But the naked and once beautiful and stately old mansion
still held fast to its dignity: the steps refused to squeak, the
chimneys refused to fill with soot, the windows would not
rattle, and the doors stayed snug and fit as the day they were
hung. But in the attic, the grand old dame could not vouchsafe
for an airtight compartment. And that is where Bobbin Derby,
with five other little girls, slept. Though in the summer the
holes in the walls were welcomed, in the deepest part of winter,
they were not.

---

[6] Dr Benjamin Franklin (1706 – 1790), American inventor, author.
Quoted from *The world's Laconics* by Tryon Edwards, (1872).

Bobbin's chore was to scrub the attic floors every day, and today, while she was mopping, Miss Neilson came in search of something.

While moving things about, she came across Bobbin's journal, the one she had given to her on her tenth birthday. "Bobbin, look here, at your journal." She squinted up at the ceiling, thinking perhaps a leak in the roof caused the damage. "Child, it is wet and muddy."

Bobbin was ashamed that she found it so dirty. "Miss Neilson, I dropped it earlier today on my way from the bookstore and did not have time to clean it."

"Bobbin, have you been writing in your journal?"

"Very little, ma'am. I carry it with me to the bookstore and back every day, but when I try to write in it about Papa, oftentimes I cannot remember one thing."

She put her arm around Bobbin's shoulders. "You spoke of your Papa as being very wise, kind, and happy—rather tall, with a very long beard. Cannot you write that in your journal?"

"Oh, yes, Miss Neilson, I have written that already, but I cannot remember more. I try to think back, but all I can see is darkness and fog."

"Well then, Bobbin," she said reassuringly, "write other things and perhaps from those words you shall find the key that opens more to you."

"Write other things, Miss Neilson?"

"Well, I suppose you could make up rhymes or sweet little stories. Like the stories you tell to the other children when you calm them before bedtime."

Bobbin stood with her head down, her brow furrowed, thinking. "Yes, I suppose so, Miss Neilson."

Often times Bobbin thought of her dear papa and his words; words she tried to remember when he died near five years ago. Some of his words, though, and those blurry scenes she dared not write. She wondered why she could not sing aloud the songs her Papa used to sing as he sat in front of the fire.

In frustration she blurted, "Oh, why can I think precisely the lyrics, sing the melodies in my head, but they will not roll aloud from my tongue, Miss Neilson?" Wiping her leather-covered journal, Bobbin sighed. "This is a dilemma, miss." Her head began to throb, and she closed her eyes from the bright light that came from the attic's lone little window just above her bed.

Miss Neilson hugged her. "This will pass, Bobbin, and I am sure the words you write will someday contain the key that sets your mind at ease, perhaps no more headaches, Bobbin." She kissed her brow and left.

Bobbin sat on her bed and turned to the first page.

April 10, 1851, my journal, Bobbin Derby.

My father, William Derby, London, born in the month of March and died in December 1850. I cannot remember exactly my mother's name; maybe it was Mary. My name is Bobbin Derby and I was born in July 1841. I wish I had a dear sister or brother to love. My teacher, Miss Neilson, told me to write every day in this journal the very words I have spoken to her about my dear Papa. This then is my journal.

It was a kind face, I remember. He had brown eyes and brown hair and a very long beard.

It is raining this morning, there is very little light and it is cold, very cold. I put my fingers in my mouth to keep my teeth from chattering and waking those around me ... my Papa was a kind man.

Except when he was drinking, she remembered. Bobbin closed the journal. Her head throbbed, and she covered her eyes from the light. Her stomach began to churn, those blinding yellow, red, and blue zigzags would cross over her eyes again and again.

Gently, without bending over, she quietly slid the journal under her pillow. And if she would sit very still and put her hands over her eyes, she knew the blinding zigzags would go away, and peace would fill their place. The pain would slowly go away.

It took Bobbin a good while to reason that the words she wrote about her father's drunkenness gave her those terrible, wrenching aches behind her eyes.

She learned to be careful to write quickly and with as few words as she could, not wanting to disappoint Miss Neilson. After all, how could she tell the sweet Miss Neilson that the journal was making her spit up? No, that would not do. Though she felt the journal was sacred, there was another side

of Bobbin that troubled her deeply. For many times she wished
she could burn it.

* * *

The next morning's early light barely allowed Bobbin to
find her clothes. As was customary, she carefully reached
under her pillow to feel that her journal was still there. Pulling
off her nightgown, she briskly rubbed the flesh-bumps that
covered her skinny little body and grabbed her grey day frock.
Bringing it to her nose, she smelled it, and finding nothing
disgusting, hurriedly put it on.

No matter how hard she clenched her teeth, she could not
stop their chattering. She pulled on her long woollen stockings,
thinking how wonderfully warm they felt. Deftly slipping her
feet into her leather boots, she shivered, finding that they were
still wet from yesterday's rain.

Cold wind blew through the chinks in the walls, and even
though Mr Halliwell-Phillipps kindly gave her scraps of paper
from the rubbish bin to stuff into the bigger holes, it was not
near enough paper to seal every one. Bobbin, though, took it as
a blessing, for were it not for the wind she would not have
dressed so quickly, and since Miss Neilson always commented
about how good a girl she was for always being first down, she
remained not quite so critical of the wind.

Besides, she knew when she descended the steps into the
kitchen that it would feel as if she were wading into a warm
bath, but she wondered at such a thought, *Silly girl you are,
Bobbin ... you have never taken a real bath in your life.* All the
same, it was a miraculous thing, she thought, that the kitchen's
heat would be floating there, waiting there somehow, she
marvelled, just half-way up the stairs. She hurried along down
the steps into the kitchen where Mrs Moll was preparing
breakfast.

Cook was a happy, kind woman who found goodness in all
things. Bobbin overheard Miss Neilson, whose opinion she
revered above all others, comment about Mrs Moll's sweet,
grandmotherly nature and Bobbin wished she was her
granddaughter.

Sitting on the bottom step, Bobbin rubbed her eyes and
yawned.

"Well then, little miss," said Moll, "it is a cold one this morning. You go now and bring me some wood, then fill the bucket. But first wrap my shawl about your chest, child."

"Yes, ma'am." Hurrying from the steps, Bobbin lingered in front of the massive hearth to warm her legs and sneak a quick peek at herself in the old cracked-veined wall mirror. She smiled. *Will I ever be as be as beautiful Miss Neilson?*

Bobbin was maturing into a pretty girl, with large brown eyes, dark lustrous brown hair, and a complexion that was fair and smooth. Her teeth were naturally straight and white; her nose was often tweaked by the others because it was so small. She caught the cook watching her and yawned. "Oh, Mrs Moll, the fire feels so nice and warm."

"Aye, and the sooner you bring the wood and water the sooner you can poke it for me."

Bobbin hurried out into the cold morning air. She slipped a little in the muddy side-yard. One-by-one she carried large pieces of split, aged wood, heavier now for being wet, and dropped each awkward piece into the woodbin until full. That being done, Cook sent her off for water, though she could carry the bucket only half full.

"Thank you, Bobbin. Now be a good girl and tend the fire."

This was her favourite chore on such cold spring mornings as this. She stood poking the snapping flames, dreaming and hoping that the sun would soon break through and warm the house. She was to go back upstairs to ready the younger children for breakfast, such as it was: porridge, bread, and milk. "Oh, Mrs Moll, your bread smells good. Shall I ever learn to make bread as you do?"

She continued kneading the dough. "Yes, Bobbin, you will learn soon enough, but you already know a great deal, child, for I don't know how to read or write like you."

"Oh, but Mrs Moll, even though I can read and write I would surely starve, for I do not yet know how to even make bread."

Moll lifted her head and smiled. "Aye, child, I suppose you're right over that one." The rough, red-cheeked old woman, with one lazy eye, stood a little straighter at the child's respectful words. "Keep on a watching me bend and push this dough, child, and you'll catch on soon enough."

The kitchen door flew open and Millie, the milkmaid, came in juggling two huge oak buckets full of milk.

"Forevermore, all it does is rain every day of life. And the cow's teats a dragging in the mud." She set the buckets on the floor near the fire. Putting both hands on her hips, she tried catching her breath.

Bobbin leaned over the huge wooden milk pails and spied some floaters. When she reached in to remove them, Millie slapped her hand.

"Nay, Bobbin, I'm gonna pour it through the rags; just you tend the fire, girl. I'll tend the milk 'fore it clabbers."

Recoiling from the slap, Bobbin nodded. "Yes, ma'am." She watched as Millie and Moll lifted the bucket. Then one held the cloth steady as the other poured the dirty milk over it.

"The rag catches everything?"

"Not everything," said Millie, her voice straining as she held the bucket.

"Bobbin, 'bout time for the others to be gettin' dressed," said Moll.

Wiping her hands on her frock, Bobbin nodded. "Yes, ma'am." She climbed the back stairs to the attic room where the ice-cold air met her half-way up. "Ooh, it will not take me long to dress them this morning." When she reached the top of the stairs, she called to the children: "Wake up, wake up, time to wake. Hurry now, it's warm in the kitchen."

The early morning quietness was shattered as the children sprang from their beds helter-skelter, jumping from one foot to the other, shivering, crying for the cold, changing fast into their clothes.

There were coughs and runny noses, messy beds, chamber pots to empty, and just as Bobbin was helping one of the children put on her woollen stockings, the smell of raw urine stung her nose. "Who didn't use the pot again? Tell me now so I can hang the blankets to dry."

The children moaned and coughed, pointing to the littlest hovering in the corner, crying. "Me, Bobbin, I'm sorry. I dreamed I was sitting on the pot ... I was so cold, and the pee felt so warm."

The children giggled.

"Shush, now," said Bobbin, her breath floating in the frigid air. "Come now, it is too cold to stay here. Hurry with your clothes and go down."

Bobbin found the wet bed, and since there were four other girls sharing it, she had to take all their sleeping gowns and blankets and lay them out to dry. The children hated sleeping on a cold, wet bed, but until they learned to use the pot, that was their punishment—a wet mattress.

Usually the retribution from those who shared the bed brought a halt to lazy sleepers, and in this case, little Kitty was learning a hard lesson. Besides all that, the smell was dreadful. Bobbin was thankful spring was coming, and soon to follow, summer.

"Come now, hurry, all of you, hurry. Let's go down and get warm." Bobbin shooed the children down the stairs and into a room off the kitchen where they scrubbed their hands and faces. The older children made sure the younger ones were buttoned properly and had clean hands and faces, and their hair plaited in neat rows.

There was a commonality among the orphans, and when one would leave the orphanage, be it on her own or being adopted, it was a sorrowful time. However, most orphans, at a young age, already knew the common facts of life. And most often without prejudice, they understood what most people only realise at the end of their lives, the cold reality of coming into the world alone and leaving it alone.

Each morning as Bobbin and the children raised their heads after the daily prayers, Miss Neilson would sing her sweetest poem:

" 'I love these little people;' la la la. Oh, it is not a slight thing, when they, la la la, who are so fresh from God, love... me!' la la la." [7]

Everyone would laugh and sing along with her, thinking her the silliest lady in London. She sang while they ate. Bobbin would shake her head side-to-side being just as silly, but this morning she sensed sadness in Miss Neilson's demeanour, and she knew why.

Toby McComb stood abruptly, and the laughter and singing ceased. His face was dark. "Oh, yes," he said coldly, "you all can be happy, but today Merchant Jones comes to take me. Not from caring, but because of my size and strength."

Feeling a sick throb forming in her head, Bobbin closed her eyes. *I am just too puny for anyone's particular notice.*

The room vacated, Bobbin and Miss Neilson cleared the table.

"You know, my dear Bobbin, the most severe occasion that I dread more than anything in the world is when a wiser,

---

[7] Dickens, *The Old Curiosity Shop*, (1841).

more evil person should take one of our orphans and use him or her like a little slave, thinking the child to be devoid of feelings, hopes, and aspirations."

"I am sorry for Toby, Miss Neilson," said Bobbin blinking back tears, "but maybe he will find a happy place."

Miss Neilson put her arms around her. "I am so fortunate you have remained here with me."

She was sorely aware that there was just so much one could do to help the children, to get too involved. To love too deeply was at times excruciatingly painful, and she had taught herself wisely to let go of the children when it was time—and so, it was with Toby.

The mantle clock chimed eleven and Bobbin sighed. "Oh, Miss Neilson, I am sorry, but I must be on my way to the bookstore now, or I shall be late, and Professor Halliwell-Phillipps does not like tardies."

"Very well, child, I shall see you then for dinner."

* * *

Bobbin scurried down the back steps and ran up the alleyway to the street-side. Just as she turned the corner, she ran head-on into Maria Collier.

"Hold it, girl," cried Maria. "What in heaven's name are you up to that you nearly knocked me down?"

"Oh, excuse me, Miss Collier. I was on my way to the bookstore. Professor Halliwell-Phillipps does not like tardies."

She looked scornfully at the impish little girl. "Oh, he is just an old man. He certainly would not miss one of *your kind* for hours."

Bobbin lowered her head. "Yes, Miss Collier."

"Well, go then, but be mindful of those on the pavement."

"Yes, Miss Collier." Bobbin curtsied, hurried around her and ran up the bookstore steps.

Maria was envious of anyone who had a place to go and something to do. And now, imagine, an orphan girl of no consequence, hurrying past her with a place to go and something to do. A mean spirit moved her. *I shall follow her and see just what she does in that store.* Promptly she directed her governess. "I wish to return to the bookstore, Mrs North."

Entering the busy little shop, Maria took in the scent of cherry smoke from someone's pipe. She glanced around the entry room, but she did not spy the orphan right off. *Then I shall just wander about the store until I find her.*

And with that, she walked past the hearth that had gone cold. Turning up one aisle then down another she finally spied Bobbin. "Yes, I now see how you spend your day. Do I remember your name correctly? Is it Bobbin Derby?" Maria sniffed the air.

"Oh, yes, Miss Collier. You have a very good memory. Yes, it is Miss Derby."

"Tell me, Miss Bobbin Derby," her nostrils flared, "what sort of name is Bobbin? I was wondering."

"I cannot tell you, Miss Collier. I have never heard of it before either."

"You do not know? How can that be? So, you do not have a mother or father?"

"No, Miss Collier." Uncomfortable at her questions and impertinent air, Bobbin kept her head down and continued to dust the books.

Professor Halliwell-Phillipps noticed Maria and shuffled over. He was a tall man for the average Englishman, an Oxford professor long since retired, and his love of books kept him in good spirits. "Good day, Miss Collier. Is there something I may do for you?"

"No, there is not. I wish only to speak with Bobbin for a very little while. Do you mind, sir? She will recommend a book for me."

Though Maria spoke confidently, there was a decidedly nasty edge to her voice that Bobbin disliked very much. It seemed to her, somehow rude.

"Why, I do not mind one thing over it, Miss Collier. Miss Bobbin will do very well at recommending a book. She has read almost all of them here." He smiled, patted Bobbin on the head, turned and walked away. Passing a window, his silver locks shone in the late morning sunlight.

Maria watched the old man cross the wooden floor to the hearth, toss a log atop the red, glowing ashes and poke at them vigorously. She turned back to Bobbin and was just about to speak again when her governess came around the corner. Curling her lip, Maria walked briskly away, searching for a place to hide.

Maria hurried up one aisle then down another and finally came to the stairs that led to the loft. She hurriedly climbed them and quietly tiptoed to where she had full view of the store below and watched as Bobbin put the books away. When she got close enough, Maria softly called, "Pssst, Bobbin."

Bobbin lifted her head, and finding two eyes peering down at her from above, squealed at the silliness of Miss Collier. Imagine, hiding in the storage loft.

Mrs North, who was one aisle over, heard Bobbin's shriek and looked around the corner spying her standing alone. Suddenly, as if an eerie chill ran through her body, she dashed away. "That orphan is surely an off-spring of Old Harry." [8]

Maria giggled. "Pssst, Bobbin, come up," she whispered. "Hurry."

Bobbin hastily put the final armload of books away and joined her in the loft.

"Well then, Bobbin, you found me." Maria's eyes were shining from the joke.

"Oh, yes, miss. I see that you do not care one straw for your—ah, your—" Bobbin did not know who Mrs North was.

"She is my governess, Mrs North." Maria's nose wrinkled. "No, I do not care very much for her. She is much too old and not at all amusing."

Bobbin could not help but admire such a spirit of play, and felt giddy that Miss Collier singled her out with such attentions. "You seek amusement, miss?" responded Bobbin. "But you buy and read many books and ride in a beautiful carriage and wear beautiful clothes."

Giggling, Maria covered her mouth. "Those things are not *amusing*, child."

Bobbin frowned. "Miss Collier, please, I am not a child."

"So you are not." Maria knew she had offended the girl and offered somewhat of an apology. "Well, it is that you are a full head shorter than I, and that is why I called you a child."

That was the extent of the apology from Maria. However, it was simple enough of an explanation for Bobbin, and she smiled good-naturedly. "Well then, I will wear taller boots, maybe."

"Maybe, indeed and where would you find such boots being a penniless orphan?"

Bobbin's smile vanished. "I would not find any, Miss Collier."

---

[8] Old Harry: familiar name for the devil.

"No, I thought not, orphan, but here is a very good plan. Rummage through the rubbish bin and fold pieces of paper until they are very thick, then lay them in your boots. I am sure it will add inches to your height, and no one will then think you are but a child."

"Oh, that is a very good idea, miss, but I already take the paper to stuff in the chinks in our walls to keep the cold winds from blowing in. You see, I sleep in the attic with four other orphans, and it gets very cold at night. The very kind Professor Halliwell-Phillipps gives me all the scrap paper he can, but I thank you all the same, Miss Collier."

Glancing away from the sad-faced orphan, Maria felt a twinge of guilt touch her heart, but she quickly brushed the feeling aside and leaned over the loft bannister. From her vantage point, she could see Mrs North now moving up and down each aisle.

"She is searching for me again, Bobbin." Maria held an impish grin just as Mrs North stopped directly beneath her. Working up a glob of spittle, she leaned over the bannister to spit on the governess's hat. Bobbin, realising the terrible deed, raced from the loft and clambered down the steps.

Startled at the noise, Mrs North backed into a shelf, nearly toppling the books.

Aah, well done, thought Bobbin. *The glob missed her entirely.*

"There now, little girl," scolded the governess, "I dare say you took those steps as if you were running from the devil himself." She glared at Bobbin. "Tell me, you little imp, where is Miss Collier?"

Catching her breath, Bobbin pointed. "I believe she is in the Shakespeare Room, ma'am." She watched the governess walk away, and just as she reached down to wipe up the spittle, Maria took her arm.

"Nay, leave it."

"I cannot, Miss Collier. I will not." Bobbin frowned. "Such a nasty thing to do." She found no humour or fun with this insolent Miss Maria Collier.

Professor Halliwell-Phillipps overheard Bobbin's warm words. "What is the fuss here, pray tell?"

Maria coughed. "Nothing is the matter, sir. I merely cleared my throat, and that is all. Bobbin is cleaning it."

"Well then, that is no matter, I assure you. Bobbin, you will accommodate Miss Collier then?"

"Yes, sir."

Flittering about in a great huff, Mrs North came upon them. "Miss Collier, I have been searching and searching for you. You seemed to have vanished into thin air, again." With knitted brow, she glared at Bobbin, her eyes bulging. "She was *not* in the Shakespeare Room, little girl."

Maria stepped back in indignation. "Indeed I was not, Mrs North. I walked past *that* room when I found Bobbin. She is now finding me a book."

The beady-eyed governess once again turned her attentions back to Bobbin. "Hmm, and just what book might that be?"

Bobbin's faced coloured; she almost never told a lie and felt disgusted at now being in the middle of one. Turning to face the bookshelf, she felt her lip quiver and noticed within an inch of her nose: Charles Dickens. *Oh, I am safe, thank you God.* Without hesitation, she slipped *Hard Times* from the shelf and handed it to Maria. "There you are Miss Collier, *Hard Times.*" Her lip was no longer in a quiver.

"*Hard times?*" replied the governess. "*Hard times?*" she repeated with a question mark on her wrinkled frown.

"Yes, Mrs North, Hard *Times for These Times,*" squeaked Bobbin as she swallowed dry, crossing her fingers behind her back.

"Indeed, the very book I have wanted to read," said Maria. Holding it close to her heart, she moved along, perusing this and that, up and down each aisle, gazing nonchalantly; finally moving into the lobby where she found the fire growing dim. "I say, Professor, you are losing your fire again."

"Oh, dear me, so I am." The old gentleman scurried to the massive, open hearth and tossed in two logs and poked them with such alacrity that it surprised even him. "There now, capital warmth, capital. Please, Miss Collier, come and enjoy it."

"We are leaving now, sir." Still ignoring her governess and Bobbin, Maria instructed the professor, "Put it on my bill." She held the book to her chest and casually walked out of the shop.

"Well now Bobbin, tell me, what was all that gibberish about?" asked the professor. He wisely detected some displeasure from the usually happy Bobbin girl.

"Sir, I do not know right-off, only that I do not think Miss Collier is happy."

"And do you suppose *Hard Times* will cheer her?" he asked in bewildered amusement at Bobbin's insightful summation of the banker's spoiled daughter.

"Oh, I have read the book, sir, and it will be a good diversion for her mind."

The old professor laughed at the orphan girl. Shaking his head, he eyed her inquisitively. "Bobbin, you amaze me with your sophisticated ideas. Wherever did you find the idea that reading a book is a good diversion for the mind?"

"That is exactly why I read, sir." She smiled innocently into his eyes.

"Yes, I see, I see." He patted her head affectionately, feeling such pity for the orphan. Walking slowly away, he added, "Yes, I would say to escape in a book is quite safe."

Chapter 4 – A Proper School for Maria

An idle brain is the devil's workshop. [9]

As the Colliers left Liverpool for home, Mr Collier gazed out the window recollecting the conversation he had earlier with his friend, Oliver Trusswell. He decided now was the time to discuss his plans for Maria with his sons. However, his thoughts were momentarily derailed by the many grand and elegant ladies walking along the avenue. He stared after them from his carriage window, smiling.

"Father?" said his son Edward, "you had something important to discuss with us in private?"

His thoughts interrupted, Collier mumbled something and looked over at his son. "I have found just the school for your sister."

"Is that so, Father?" said Philip.

"What sort of school, Father?" said Edward.

"While conversing with Trusswell at the bank, I happened to mention that I was interested in a short-term boarding school for Maria." Collier discreetly leaned forward to catch a glimpse of an alluring female. He could feel his sons watching

---

[9] Quoted from *A Dictionary of Thoughts* by Tryon Edwards, (1908). There are several versions of this popular English proverb. Traces back to Chaucer, *Tale of Melibee*, (1386). "Dooth somme goode dedes that the devel, which is oure enemy, ne fynde yow nat unocupied." (Do some good deeds so that the devil will not find you unoccupied.)

him and quickly hemmed. "Trusswell's daughter attended a place called the Mary Arden Academy." [10]

"Oh, yes, Father, the very best," said Philip. "I know it well. You must remember James Halliwell-Phillipps, do you not?"

Collier's mind shifted and pondered—trying to place the man.

Edward nodded. "Oh, indeed, I remember him, Philip. Indeed, a very good chap. We went to school together, Father. Professor Halliwell-Phillipps, his father, owns the More Towns End Bookstore."

"Well, in any event, I should like to stop on our way home and look the place over." Collier was convinced that the Mary Arden Academy would suit Maria very well. However, to be absolutely sure, he arranged for a walk-about—he needed to see it for himself.

*   *   *

Their carriage broke from the dark wood into a lovely meadow called Arden Lea. The academy lay just ahead. Stepping from the coach, Philip and Edward immediately spied Professor Barnaby Zany walking toward them. Whispering to one another they discretely positioned themselves behind their father.

The portly Professor Zany's nose was rather large and bulbous, handy for his spectacles; he apparently mislaid his hairbrush, as a few wiry hairs jetted upward from his shiny balding scalp. He looked rather humorous, all in all, thought Collier as he waited for his approach.

"Yes, hello to you all, I am Professor Barnaby Zany, yes, that I am." He flapped his lapels and sniffed the air. "I was just reciting, haha, aloud to myself a silly bit of literature from one of my favourite fellow professors, Lear ... allow me to go on:

"How pleasant to know Mr Lear,

---

[10] Mary Arden, Shakespeare's mother, inherited 60 acres of land from her father, Robert Arden, c.1556, Wilmecote, the Mary Arden Academy is, however, fiction. Source: *Shakespeare's Complete Works*, Halliwell-Phillipps, 1925.

Who has written such volumes of stuff!
Some think him ill-tempered and queer,
But a few think him pleasant enough. [11]

There you have it, sir." He smiled looking out over the meadow.

Edward and Philip grinned at one another and remained half-hidden behind their father.

"Tell me, sir," inquired Professor Zany of Mr Collier, "are you here for any particular reason in this season?"

"Yes, my name is John Collier. My sons and I have come to look about the academy, sir. I have a daughter ..."

"Oh, please allow me to first introduce myself. I am Professor Barnaby Zany, and I am acting on behalf of the Schoolmaster, James Halliwell-Phillipps, he is away. Let me say, sir, that the academy is a quiet secret in England, Mr Collier."

Although the professor appeared dishevelled, Collier simply theorised these brainy scholars were all a little twisted. He was listening to the odd little fellow when Philip interrupted. "Excuse us, Father, will you? We should like to visit ... ah, visit ... the library."

Collier excused his sons, though he thought such a request an odd one. However, it was little time when he realised *why* his sons had abandoned him.

"This way, Mr Collier," said Professor Zany. "This academy is one of the finest boarding schools in all England, sir; one that is revered by all those who know of its very existence and purpose." His voice lowered to a whisper, "It is a secret one guards jealously."

"Hmm, indeed," said Collier glancing around for his sons.

"To be invited here is proof enough that one is worthy, rich or poor. It is an honour to walk the halls. William Shakespeare walked here, spoke here, and blessed the very walls. It is a sacred place, a place where one young woman, at graduation, shall be passed the Mary Arden Key, one that is worn proudly about one's neck. It is such a key that those familiar with its power will bow in respect to any lady on

---

[11] Professor Edward Lear (1812 – 1888) English poet laureate of the limerick. *Book of Nonsense*, (1846).

whose neck it hangs." His eyes lit up. "This Key opens many doors."

"Aah," said Mr Collier, walking alongside the professor, "indeed."

"As you can see this old Gothic-styled academy is situated on a lovely piece of ground, higher actually than all the other structures in the ancient town of Wilmecote-Asbies. Now it is simply called Wilmecote, or affectionately, *Wilms*." Zany swung his arm in such a fashion that Mr Collier was obliged to follow it, ducking now and again.

"From a distance, sir, perhaps as the road there breaks from the dark forest onto the pebbly granite roadway, but a thousand yards from the academy, one first notices the piercing church steeple as it forces one's eyes to the heavens, up, up, up and away from the old, blunt-chiselled, grey-stone, water-stained façade of the house of worship that sits near attached to the academy." He took a deep breath. "I mean, sir, near, attached by the covered balcony, open-sided, there held aloft without trouble by two stone pillars, square and rough. However, upon closer inspection, Mr Collier, one shall be enlightened to harbour one's eyes a bit longer there, on that particular covered balcony, the *trottoir*." Zany pointed.

Squinting, Collier nodded. "Hmm." Watching the peculiar professor from the corner of his eye he added, "Yes, yes, I see it now."

"Indeed. This particular walkway, the *trottoir*, which leads to the church from the academy, was indeed designed to be a painful walk; the sharp-stoned path was lined with the master's tailings from its marble etchings. A Frenchman whose name he knew would long be forgotten chiselled his legacy into the marble keystone atop the archways to and fro God's house. Fashioned there in marble, smoothed, brushed by his very breath, sir. Indeed, chiselled there in such perfect work his words 'Step lightly for one should always be reminded where one is going, and where one has been.' Ha ha ha, such a clever man, aye, Mr Collier?"

Twisting the tip of his moustache, Collier replied, "Indeed, Professor."

"The eye will now move to the academy, erected when architects of the day thought in terms of thousands, rather than hundreds of years in the life of a dwelling such as this."

Eying Mr Collier to see just how impressed he was of that fact, Zany continued, "The Mary Arden Academy, being built with the same stone as the house of God sitting to its right, holds a dignified grace of its own. Ah, yes, a soft, forgiving look much like that a gentle lady acquires from years of living with humility, graciousness, and humour. If one should be standing in the garden gazing upon the old place they might see the patina of its soul glistening in the sun."

The professor bowed his head.

Mr Collier bowed his head, searching the ground for clues as to why he was still there. "I wonder when my sons will return?"

"And on that very place left sitting on the earth for so many lifetimes spent, near back, in the churchyard, the eternal resting place. And there also the house of many mansions, for there is room enough on such a plot of ground, this "garden of souls," haha, if you will, I just made that up, sir."

"You simply must teach literature, professor," replied Mr Collier, looking smug.

"Thank you, sir. I do."

Casually meandering beneath the shadow of the lone church steeple, the professor paused to read something that he had jotted down on the palm of his hand. Uttering a few indistinguishable syllables, he began again, "The academy consists of three great stories with twenty very tall windows in the front prospect, there you can see for yourself, Mr Collier. Fifteen to each end, making them identical if one is counting, and thirty along the back that face our many gardens, fountains and shrubbery hedgerows. The lush green meadows and woods begin within squinting distance from the main alcove entrance and circles the old place, allowing but one road to disturb our vast grassy manger."

"Grassy manger?" said Collier. "Did I hear correctly?

Ignoring him, the professor continued, "The Mary Arden Academy is, as one would expect, ageing. The numerous oaks, poplar, and shrubbery were planted when they first named it Wilmecote-Asbies. Though the trees were intentioned for lending shade, the oaks proved a better fortress altogether, or so they fancied themselves, to temper the worst tempest's ire."

"Indeed, well, I really must be on my way." Collier shook his head glancing around for his sons.

"Oh, the mighty oaks equalled every bit the terror with their whipping, scratching and groaning. Aah, moans of their own particular choosing, and of the worst sort, Mr Collier. They rip the howling winds if not by wide-leafed assaults, then by winter's naked limb, stark and deliberate, reaching, pointing, jabbing, and no less brittle the clinging tendrils holding fast to trunk and limb alike. Oh, I am an honoured witness to the mighty oak, sentinels of the great old granite lady they surround, well done. Well done, indeed." The professor ran his fingers through his much thinning hair.

"Hmm, been teaching long, professor?" said Collier.

"It was a private donor who had it built and who chose the name. Some say it was William Shakespeare himself. After all, conjectured some, his mother's maiden name was Mary Arden, but then again there were others in her family who may have desired to memorialise her as well. Be that as it may, the donor wished to remain anonymous, and after nearly three hundred years of anonymity, one can only suppose who really was the wealthy provider, Mr Collier."

"I quite agree."

"Ideas and minds are changing, sir. Albeit slowly in this last half of the century, when issues regarding women's individualism are finally being cultivated. It was the hope passed on from its donor that a woman graduating from this school should be refined, cultured, educated, and in her own lovely, sweet way should mingle in the world becoming a seedbed for change.

"Mathematics, geography, literature, philosophy, and self-discipline, not to forget proper etiquette are taught here. The accommodations are austere to the very rich, and extremely luxurious to the poor. The library is second in sacredness only to the church—its book collection is the very finest in all of England. Might I add that professor Lear's *Book of Nonsense* is on the shelf?" He glanced at Mr Collier, his face a little twisted, smiling.

"You don't say," said Collier.

Zany nodded. "And sir, just what is it that you do?"

"I am a banker ..."

"Oh, well yes, well, sir, scholars, poets, professors, noted authors of the day from around the world can be found lounging in and about our many library fireplaces situated herein. It is quiet, serene, and dignified. It is not unusual to see Charles Dickens casually stroll through the hallways, in the courtyard, or near the quad fountain—in tolerable weather, that is. It seems the young ladies never know from one week to the next which prominent author, scientist, or poet laureate will be here."

"It is just the place for my daughter, Professor Zany, just the place. She would make a lovely seedbed for change."

"Very good, sir." He patted him on the back. "Now let me tell you a little something of the Schoolmaster, Mr James Halliwell-Phillipps, Oh, lest I forget his dog, Holly." And he pulled from his long black professor's robe a prepared text.

As the professor continued on, Collier turned toward the Library. "Good day, Professor Zany, I really must be going."

But the professor continued on walking and talking. "There are things that are not in my prepared text, Mr Collier, the human elements of the Schoolmaster. He was an only child, and the young man's voracious reading habits turned him intellectually superior. However, his weak eyes rendered him socially inferior. He wore thick spectacles, though he got on well with his peers, he was very shy and backward around girls. His father thought perhaps not having a nurturing, loving mother early-on set his son aback in the modus operandi of female allurements.

"And because he was so totally unprepared at deciphering the female code, he was often laughed at, though his motives were, and remain still, sincere and gentlemanly. He found the female species more than lovely; oft times he noticed their fragility and soft, delicate manners. It struck him odd when witnessing the birth of his hound Holly's pups that the female species could turn from such delicacy to ferocity within seconds ... and he thought about that too.

"The schoolmaster grew through those awful, frustrating adolescence years into a tall, dark-haired, rugged looking man. He was appointed to the prestigious Mary Arden Academy by a board of six trustees a few years back. He accepted the position at the academy with gratitude and honour and these past several years has devoted his life completely to it. Since he had acknowledged to himself that his love life was not apt to improve on any grand scale, he put aside personal, inner desires and kept busy. He has matured into a self-assured intellectual who stands as open as Shakespeare's inkwell. To those women not as gifted to dip their quills, he seems remote and unconquerable—not so, Mr Collier.

"But, alas, even with such a devoted heart, the Schoolmaster still roams the campus halls without a lady on his arm, Mr Collier." Zany stopped and looked around, scratching his head. "Ah, Mr Collier, sir, where the dickens have you gone off too?"

Chapter 5 – Mr Collier Returns Home

Thinking: the talking of the soul with itself. [12]

Maria Collier took to her room. It was a dismal, rainy day; had it not been for the book she was engrossed in, she would have pouted the entire week for being abandoned by her family. Oddly enough, though, she was enjoying the book, *Hard Times*. Regarding the book, she wondered how a father should teach his children nothing but facts, as the story goes. Moreover, how should a lowly orphan, such a Bobbin Derby, read such a book, and most of all, understand it? Maria scoffed. *But of course, she has not read this Dickens book, the little liar. When next I see her I shall scold her for it.*

Still reading about Mr Thomas Gradgrind and his experimental school, Maria's ears perked up at the familiar sounds of an approaching carriage. She dashed to the window. *So they are finally home.* However, instead of greeting her family at the door as she usually did, she remained in her room, sitting by the fire, reading her book. There came a knock. She ignored it. Then another knock and she ignored it as well. Soon she heard footsteps move away. She tiptoed to the door and quietly opened it, slightly. Peering down the hallway, she caught sight of her brother Edward descending the stairs.

Let them all wonder if I died while they were away on their stupid business trip without me. Maria returned to her chair and picked up her book. The warmth of the fire soon put

---

[12] Plato (427 – 347 BC) Greek philosopher.

her to sleep and when she awoke her father was standing over her, holding the book.

"Well, my dear, Charles Dickens I see. What should provoke one into reading such a story?"

"It was recommended, Papa." She yawned, not rejoicing at seeing him, still pouting at his notice.

"I see, and who should recommend such a book, Maria?"

"An orphan girl, much my own age, she works at More Towns End Bookstore, Papa. And I rather like the book, actually." She watched the flames flicker and twist, hiss and pop.

"An orphan? And how would you know her personal business, Maria?"

"Earlier this week while Mrs North and I were going to the bookstore, I stumbled over a book lying in my path. The orphan made herself known to me, claiming the book was hers. They are such thieves you know, Papa, those little urchins of the street. That is when the girl said she worked at the bookstore for Professor Halliwell-Phillipps. She lived down the alleyway at the Newpark Orphanage. Mrs North was with me."

"Hmm, well then?"

"Well, then, sir, Saturday, Mrs North and I returned to the store, and I found the orphan girl. Her name is a strange one indeed, Papa. Imagine, Bobbin, if you will. Haha."

"She may have an odd name, Maria. However, if she recommended such a book, she must not be illiterate. I have read it myself. It appeared weekly in *Household Words*. It is very sophisticated for such a young mind."

"Oh," replied Maria, not very surprised at her father's repertoire of reading materials, "but Papa," she continued, "I do not believe the orphan is illiterate, since she assured me she read the book. And I will soon know if she has. I intend on finishing it by this evening then visiting the bookstore by week's end. Surely if one recommends a book, one would have read it first."

"I do not know if that will be possible, Maria. That is—" he hesitated, "to visit the bookstore next week. I have a plan in mind, one which I will explain after dinner this evening. Your brothers will be present." He bent over and kissed her forehead. "So nice to see you, my dear."

When he left the room, she did not bid him well, but sat staring aimlessly into the fire. *I should wonder at the plan they have for me.* Tears welled in her eyes. *Oh, Mama, I wish you were here.*

* * *

After dinner that evening everyone gathered in the music room to exhibit at the piano. Philip sat down and began playing while Edward brought out a package and sat it on the mantle ledge. It was wrapped in brown paper, tied neatly with string.

Eyeing his still pouting sister, he took a seat next to her. "Come now, Maria, let us not have any more of your ill temper, I have brought you a gift."

She glanced at the package on the mantle and managed a wee smile.

Philip lifted his fingers from the keys and turned on the piano stool to face her. "Do not tell me she smiles? I thought perhaps she forgot the whole business of being a lady." He smirked.

"I have not forgotten how to smile, Philip. It is a lady's prerogative to show displeasure when she has been wronged."

Edward handed her the package. "Very well, then."

She studied the neatly wrapped package for a moment and then carefully untied the string and removed the brown paper wrapper and stared at it. "Oh, it is a book." She thumbed through a few pages and looked up. "But, Edward, the pages are blank."

"Oh, silly girl, it is a journal." He smiled feeling very smart. "I thought you would like to keep notes on your travels and boarding school experiences."

Mr Collier interrupted. "Ah, Edward ..."

"What do you mean Edward, keep notes? What boarding school?" Glancing at her father, she sensed her world would soon change.

"Maria, my dear, I was trying to find just the right moment in which to tell you of the most proper boarding school where I have enrolled you. Many young ladies of your age attend there. It is called the Mary Arden Academy. It is not so very far. Your brothers and I can visit upon occasion."

Reading the unsettling look on her face, Philip put his hand on her shoulder. "There now Maria, it sounds the best of plans. You remember Louisa Mounten? Yes, I am sure of it.

She attended there for a year, and what a miraculous difference. I assure you, sister, you shall adore it."

Edward agreed. "Yes, Maria, you shall. Philip and I will visit you often."

Staring in disbelief at her two brothers, she turned to her father. "Papa, when am I to go then?"

"Next week begins your first session, my dear."

The room grew quieter. Both Edward and Philip were disturbed at the thought of leaving their sister at the academy. Though they teased her incessantly, neither wanted her to leave. They loved her, but they knew beyond a doubt that she was ready for the Mary Arden Academy.

"Come now, missy," Philip tweaked her nose, "you shan't cry now, will you?"

She bristled. "Of course not, Philip, least not while in *your* company. And please stop pulling my nose; it shall grow long if you do not stop."

"Ha, ha, there you have it." He laughed. "You see, you are much more the grown-up sister after all and are growing quite tired of my affections already. All the while Philip knew how devastating the news must have been to her. Wondering how she should remain at a boarding school taking orders and sharing with other young ladies. He concluded under his breath, "I should doubt she stays a week." He shook his head at the inevitable conclusion.

"What do you mean by such a look, Philip? Do you think me so immature that I cannot remain from home so very long without crying like a child?"

"No, no, sister, not at all. I believe you have the spirit to do anything you set your mind to. It is finding that thing that motivates you. I shall only remain half-convinced, however, at your steadfastness, that is all, Maria."

"Well," added Edward, "I think she is quite steadfast already." He put his arm around her shoulder. "However, a little polish will make you glisten all the more." He smiled, happy at finding just the right words.

"Glisten?" Maria's upper lip curled.

"Yes, my dear," said her father, "Edward is quite right. I must agree." He shifted the conversation to his son. "Let us then convince Philip to play a little longer at the piano, what say you, Maria?"

Folding her arms, she shot an acid glance his way. "Hmm, yes, please Philip, do continue on."

He resumed playing, though feeling his sister's pain very much. Edward took her hand. Her father remained by the fire, wisely choosing to watch Philip rather than Maria.

Chapter 6 – Bobbin Comes of Age

The good are heaven's particular care. [13]

Saint Anthony's baptismal records indicated that Bobbin had been, at birth, Christened in the month of July, 1855. It was now 1869, and she would turn ten and four within days. It was the established rule at the Newpark Institution that when an orphan comes of age, she must begin a life of her own and sent out.

It was her ever mindful teacher, Miss Neilson, who, years before, had introduced Bobbin to Professor Halliwell-Phillipps. And it was she who had helped secure Bobbin's current position at the bookshop, and now, it was she who hinted to the professor that Bobbin have a room tucked in somewhere at the bookshop.

To have such a dear young girl lodging in the city alone and unprotected would not do, certainly not. Miss Neilson would not have such a thing. And so they both, the grandfatherly professor and the motherly Miss Neilson, formed an alliance of protection for the girl—until she found her feet.

And now, glancing down at her feet, Bobbin nodded. "So, you are now ten and four," holding a small bundle of all her earthly possessions, she sighed deeply, "and it is time to leave." Glancing fondly about the attic room—the oft-scrubbed near-white wood floor, the neatly made beds, and the remaining

---

[13] Ovid (43 BC-18 AD) Roman poet.

candle nubbin yet burning on the sill, she snuffed it. Picking at a bit of hardened wax from the floor, she recollected her first night in this little space, near five years hence. With a smile, she recalled cuddling with three other little girls; how safe she felt sleeping in the middle.

She exhaled softly and felt the finality of leaving; it was a finality that orphans never seemed to question. It was not a sudden, shocking dilemma for them; and to her, it was simply her turn to move on. Life seemed to fit in little pieces she reasoned, and thanked God daily for the good things that came to her. She looked for them, welcomed them, and named them as her own. God was always good to her, she felt. Now and again she would question the misery and misfortune of others, but He chose to remain silent on that score. Bobbin eventually came to realise that His silence had meaning, too.

Closing the door of the little attic room behind her, she descended the steps, running her hand along the well-worn mahogany handrail. It had been loose when first she came there, and it was loose still. Bobbin was glad that Miss Neilson waited for her at the bottom of the steps—she found her sweet smile a fitting benediction.

Together they silently left the orphanage. Walking up the alleyway to the bookstore the cook called out from the kitchen, waving and weeping. "Good-bye, good-bye."

Bobbin blew her a kiss. "I shall come to visit soon, Mrs Moll."

The two continued up the alleyway and around the corner. Carrying her little bundle, Bobbin felt the firm, square corners of her journal poke through the flimsy roll of clothes.

As they approached the bookstore, Professor Halliwell-Phillipps stood just inside, peering through the display window. Smiling broadly, he opened the door. "Welcome. Come, come in." He bolted the door, turned the open sign to closed and cheerfully hugged Bobbin. "Come now and see your little place, Bobbin. It is on this floor, in the back. I have worked near all night making it a fit and proper place for a lady."

He stood as proud and erect as his poor old body would allow. Bobbin, touched by his sweetness, sighed. "Oh, sir, I could not be happier, I assure you."

"Right this way then you two." He shuffled along the dark squeaky hallway and stopped. Standing aside, he opened a door. "Here you are, then, Bobbin."

"La," she marvelled looking about the room. "Such a beautiful wood-slat bed, Professor, neatly covered with such a thick wool blanket and," her eyes widened, "a fluffy pillow?"

Her pillow at Newpark had been a ball of rags, but she had been content even with that. Opposite her bed stood a lovely oak pedestal toilet-table, holding a water pitcher and washbasin. Very near that was a spacious hearth with a delightful fire, a cloth-covered chair next to it.

"A cloth-covered chair?" Bobbin sat on it with reverence carefully running her hands over the red velvet fabric, feeling its softness. She spied two oil lamps and many wax candles sitting on the windowsill. "Oh, sir, there shall be much light for reading" Twirling in awe, she added, "A lovely window by day, lamps and candles by night." She closed her eyes, "Oh, and warmth. Thank you, sir, thank you." She took up his hand and kissed it. "I shall work very hard for you, Professor Halliwell-Phillipps."

"You are indeed fortunate, Bobbin." Miss Neilson kissed her forehead. "I must be getting back now, dear. Come often to visit me." She left before they could see her tears.

Bobbin made haste hanging her few things on the wall-pegs and slid her journal safely under her pillow. She poked the few remaining coals in her fire, and just before reverently closing the door behind her, she glanced back at its loveliness and smiled.

Heading up the hall, she smelled the sweet wood burning from the Great Room's fire and knew the book-room would be warm. Eager to show her thankfulness, Bobbin began sweeping the floors humming Miss Neilson's sweetest song, 'I love these little people'..." [14]

Professor Halliwell-Phillipps was working the fire, poking and shovelling, feeling very happy, for he was lonely when Bobbin was not around; her humming filled a void in the quiet solitude of his days.

Betimes, half-open books lying about would sidetrack her. They were like open doors, and she often peeked, within seconds she was enveloped by the story. She knew many of the authors by name, for many frequented the store.

She was particularly fond of Jane Austen's *Emma*; though Miss Austen had died years earlier, Bobbin revered her stories.

---

[14] Dickens, *The Old Curiosity Shop*, (1841).

She loved Charlotte Bronte's *Jane Eyre*, but had never met her either. *David Copperfield*, by Dickens, was certainly a novel she favoured. She respected Mr Dickens immensely.

Professor Halliwell-Phillipps once told her he had overheard Mr Dickens say Copperfield was his favourite. "Mr Dickens writes what he knows," said the professor patting her on the head.

She nodded as her head began to ache just a little when she thought of her journal and what she knew.

During one autumn morning, when she was filling the woodbin, Professor Halliwell-Phillipps sat rocking in his favourite chair near the fire. "Bobbin, you are very quiet today."

"I was just thinking, sir," she said while pausing before the warm fire, "your friends who have written so many of these books come and go, but their stories will remain eternal, I should think. There is nothing new under the sun [15] and yet there are so many books, and many more will be written. How can that possibly be?"

"Aye, young lady, many more, many more. Think upon it, Bobbin, it is not what is written, but *how* it is written. There is always a different slant in which one may look at any particular situation in life. In our minds, we harbour a unique perspective of everything that surrounds us. And only very particular words will do to explain exactly our interpretation of it." He smiled. "Words are powerful instruments, my dear." He nodded. "Those with wisdom choose them *very* carefully."

"Indeed, sir." She thought deeply about *his* words. "I had not thought about being so discriminate, sir." Her head began to feel achy for thinking.

"Well, child, do not be too serious over the matter. I assure you, you do very well for one so young."

"Thank you, sir."

"So there, my little philosopher, our lesson for the day." The professor sat for a little while eyeing Bobbin as she worked about the bookstore, and he knew his "plan for Bobbin's education" was finally at its fruition. Today was as good as any day to approach Miss Neilson.

"Bobbin, do you mind, my dear, delivering a package to Mrs Clarke, just around the corner? I know very well how you

---

15 Ecclesiastes 1:4-11.

enjoy her company. Do stay and chat, for I must also leave, but I should not be gone so very long."

* * *

As the professor walked the little distance to the orphanage, he recalled the many stories his customers shared with him regarding the widow, Mrs Peter Newpark and the lavish balls held there in the once stately, fashionable old mansion. He climbed the few steps to the door and read close up the sign: Newpark Institution – Charity School. He knocked lightly.

A young boy opened the door. "Yes, sir?"

"I am calling on a Miss Neilson, young man." He handed him his card. "Take this to her."

The young boy nodded as he looked him up and down. Taking the professor's card, he smelled it. "Are you here to take one of us?"

"Oh, I hardly think so, young man. Now, go about delivering my card. I am in a great hurry."

The professor was shown into the drawing room, once grand and well furnished, now a room converted into a study, he supposed.

"Sit there, if you please," gestured the young boy. "I'll fetch Miss Neilson." He stood staring at him.

Removing his hat, the Professor eyed the young boy. "Be about your business, young man. Rest assured, I am not here to take any one of you."

The boy nodded, "Yes, sir." He closed the door behind with a thud. As the professor stood holding his hat, the door re-opened, and Miss Neilson bustled in with a few children clinging to her skirt.

"Professor Halliwell-Phillipps, good-day to you, sir." Smiling, she held out her hand.

He bowed slightly over it. "Yes, good-day, Miss Neilson." He glanced down at the children. "Ah, I was wondering if I could speak to you for just a moment, in private."

"Oh, please, sir, sit by the fire, sir. I would offer you a cup of tea, but ... "

"Oh, no, miss, now don't trouble yourself over the matter. I know you are terribly busy."

She instructed the children to go into the refectory and stand by the hearth. "Practice your numbers, and I will call for you soon." One by one they straggled away eyeing the professor before finally quitting the room.

"Miss Neilson, I have come to ask your permission that I may become patron for Bobbin Derby's education. I had in mind a school for higher learning."

Her brows arched, her mouth dropped. "An education, sir?" Overwhelmed by his generosity, she stammered, "Oh, oh, my, y-yes, professor, yes, certainly. Bobbin will be most pleased, most honoured at being singled out. Her mind is one of the finest I have ever taught."

Pacing excitedly about the room, she added, "The young girl is only ten and four and already knows almost as much as I. She reads constantly, but of course, sir, you know that."

"My son is Schoolmaster at Mary Arden Academy, Wilmecote." He glanced at Miss Neilson, but she seemed not to recognise the school. "I wrote to him last month. I was eager to share my enthusiasm over such a child as Bobbin Derby. He is equally joyous in her coming. My son, Miss Neilson, is a scholar who delights in serious-minded students, bright, serious-minded students."

"Well, then, sir, he will be well pleased with Bobbin." A frown gathered on her brow.

"Yes, what is it?"

She exhaled sadly. "Oh, sir, it is her clothes, she owns only two frocks. How will she fit in?"

"Oh, there now, miss," he replied kindly, "I will own that the class of young ladies who attend the Mary Arden Academy are usually from the wealthiest of families," he gestured with his pointing finger, "but not always. All the young ladies wear simple pinafores, all being the same. However, if you would be so kind as to take her to the merchants nearby and buy her other needs, I will be happy over it."

"I see, sir, simple that." Smiling, she took his hand and shook it. "Oh, sir, you are more than generous and very kind." She wiped her eyes. "Thank you."

"Oh, I think you are the kind one, Miss Neilson. I have noticed how well you get on with the children. You are not from a poor family, though, I think."

"No, sir, actually my mother and father are from the middling class. My father owns a small chandler's shop in Bath. He caters to the wealthy, selling soaps, fragrances, oils, and such. Mama helps him. Indeed, I was raised very comfortably, sir." She smiled. "Though we were not rich, we were a very happy family and comfortable. I have always loved to teach and help orphans. To be abandoned is a desperate sort of cruelty, but then the death of one's parents must be the worst."

"I should think," he replied nodding sympathetically.

"Well, then, sir, I will be very pleased to buy her the necessary things. God knows she has nothing."

"I have heard my son remark betimes at how the seemingly poorer children sometimes make the ideal students." Walking slowly to the window and pulling aside the heavy, drab curtain, the elderly gentleman gazed out, absentmindedly picking at his long, greying eyebrows. "Bobbin's manners are exemplary, no schooling needed there. However, her clothes Miss Neilson ..." twisting his eyebrows he continued, "her clothes, dear me, are dreadful. Dress her well, dress her well for her arrival. For right off she should look the little lady that she will become. Though not born a lady makes it all the more important that she is set off on the right foot, I should think." He turned away from the window and in his usual polite posture stood quietly, listening from behind his eyes.

"Sir, I know very well how stinging tongues can dampen an eager heart. Bobbin has heard every conceivable insult, and still she smiles." She sighed. "Such a forgiving heart, I must say. Where she finds the inspiration and strength, I do not know."

"What of her mother and father, do you know of them?" He inquired, turning again to the window.

"Long ago Bobbin came to the orphanage. It was on Christmas morning, at first light actually; I remember it well. She was near naked, wishing only to stand by the fire. She explained that her father had been drinking. He was lying next to her in front of the hearth, on the floor, apparently, when the place caught fire.

"The poor dear cannot remember her mother, thinking only that her name was Mary. Bobbin used to speak of her father when she was a wee thing, and would say only very nice things about him. But," Miss Neilson's head dropped, "but, I later gathered from the newspaper that every living thing perished in that terrible fire that night. The next morning Bobbin came to the orphanage. No doubt, it was arson, sir.

"Bobbin's few words on the subject were that there was a fire. Rumour on the street was that her mother ran away with a local band of gipsies, for another she drowned. Her name indeed was Mary.

"After realising Bobbin escaped from such an inferno, I did not think it necessary to contact the newspaper explaining that she alone survived. Who would care? Certainly not her mother, she ran away. Nay, it was the child's providence to have come here, Professor. I have not told her more regarding the fire and her family. I believe in time she will remember.

"I cannot forget when I bathed her that morning there were bruises and burn marks all over her body." Miss Neilson covered her face. "It is difficult and painful for the child to remember. We do not discuss so very much of the experience. Though I encouraged her to write her feelings in a journal I gave her, thinking perhaps it might relieve her mind."

"Oh, now, I understand, miss." The old man bowed his head. "Please, miss, do what is necessary for the young lady. And do come by the store, if you will, now and again?"

Wiping her eyes, Miss Neilson moved toward the door; she was anxious for him to take leave. Just thinking about how mistreated Bobbin had been was a memory of such proportion that it drained her by times. She quickly regained her good humour though, and assured the professor with a smile. "Yes, sir, depend upon it. I will often come to visit, thank you."

"Dear me," he replied as he pulled something from his vest pocket, "I near forgot. Here, take my card and buy what you need for her. Simply tell the merchants to put it on my bill. Just tell them. They will know."

"I will, sir, I will."

"Well, I must be going." Suddenly he stopped, as if being turned around by an idea of great magnitude. "Miss Neilson, would you like to accompany Bobbin to the academy? Perhaps you would do me the honour of riding in my carriage. I would show you both around the academy with my son, James."

She cocked her head in her familiar, natural way, one in which pure delighted pleasure radiated from her soul. "Why, sir, that would be most excellent, most excellent, indeed. I am certain she will be more than pleased. Going to a new school will be worrisome enough. Now to have two friends accompanying her, well, it will soothe her nerves immensely."

"Then it is all settled, Miss Neilson, my carriage will call for you both at first light, Wednesday next, April 7."

Leaving the orphanage, he felt an extraordinary goodness swirl about his heart. However, there was an uneasiness that gnawed beneath the wiry, white hair on the gentleman's head. He, at one time, supported the 1834 New Poor Law, which stated: 'to pauperise the recipient is to make them weak.' [16] But now a disquieting feeling haunted him, and it was from the revered Dickens' book *Oliver Twist*.

"Oh, I should not want to make little Bobbin weak for such a gift from me," he fretted. Then thinking upon it a little longer, he lamented, "Surely to send her to a school would not weaken her?"

In deep thought over the words 'pauperise the recipient,' the old gentleman walked directly past his bookstore and directly past all the faithful who had been waiting patiently for him to reopen his shop. As he passed them by without notice, they realised that once again oblivion was his closest neighbour, so they resumed their weary idleness until the kind wordsmith should eventually find his way back. Amongst one another they commented, good-naturedly, about how thankful they were that it is was not a rainy day.

Professor Halliwell-Phillipps hated anything that should lodge itself in his brain like this Dickens flap of a thing, this controversy over pauperising. That such an ill seed should suddenly find its way into his conscience was, at the very least, extremely troublesome to him. "I agree with my good friend Dickens," said he to his own ears. "Moreover," he countered, "what sort of persons should think that charity was counterproductive, degrading, bah. They must all be rich to favour such stingy, mean-spirited ideas." And he continued to admonish himself, "How could I have ever thought such a thing?"

As he wandered along the pavement, he recollected precisely the words that Dickens had so courageously written to that most selfish society, and he became even more puffed up. Readjusting his tall black hat to sit properly atop his head, he assumed the familiar mannerism of *Professor* Halliwell-

---

[16] Pauperise the recipient—Those in favour of the New Poor Law of 1834 (which Dickens had attacked in *Oliver Twist*, pub. 1837-1839) maintained that charity was counterproductive, since it degraded those people whom it was designed to help. Note from Chapter 1, *Hard Times*, pub. 1854.

Phillipps, so very long ago when he wore a younger man's vestments.

The professor stood tall, and as if addressing a crowded lecture hall at his beloved Oxford, he instinctively outstretched his left hand into the cool morning air and gestured into it mightily with much swinging, pointing, and flapping.

Though deeming such a man's speech worthy of forestalling the impatient lugubrious gathering, Mother Nature held off the approaching storm for a little while longer, for no harm done.

Thus the Oxford man continued talking aloud the great author Dickens' opinion, 'It will generally be found that those who sneer habitually at human nature, and affect to despise it, are among its worst and least pleasant samples.'

"Oh, but the orphan will never be weak, never." He exhaled the very air that had puffed him up, and he tipped his hat to the rainless sky.

As he stood at the curb, holding fast to his lapels, he teetered a few steps backwards. He became bewildered over the unfamiliar faces staring at him. And as he made his return to more familiar terrain, he wondered just where the great author's words had carried him. And at the notice of the many amused beggars who knew the man never to pass them by without tossing a stipend for their ills, well, yes, they smiled, the Oxford man had been carried away again.

They watched protectively as the old gentleman headed back up the street, passing the grateful beggars once more, but they held their hands over their cups, honouring the generous man's first gift just moments earlier and knowing that he would absentmindedly toss them another. They had their own code of ethics—these paupers.

The old man's spirits lifted after witnessing such integrity, and in an affirmation of his own convictions said to himself, *I will not think one thing more over the matter of charity weakening such a soul as Bobbin Derby's.*

When the professor finally found his way back to the bookstore, everyone sitting on his steps suddenly stood.

"Oh, I do hope you haven't been waiting long?"

Chapter 7 – April 7 – Bobbin Leaves for Mary Arden

How sweet, how passing sweet, is solitude! But grant me still a friend in my retreat, whom I may whisper, solitude is sweet. [17]

It was a breezy cool morning with just a slight mist in the air. Miss Neilson held softly to Bobbin's warm little hand. Her calloused palm and fingers would soon be soft again, no work in holding a book. "I shall miss you dearest, write to me very often." She kissed little Bobbin's hands and face and helped her into the professor's carriage.

Miss Neilson was disappointed that she could not go along as planned—the institution could not spare her. She stood in front of the bookstore and waved.

"Good-bye professor, good-bye Bobbin." She watched the black, mud-splattered carriage move in and about the other coaches, chaises, and carriages along the boulevard. As it turned onto Water Street, she could still see Bobbin's sweet little head. Faintly, she spotted her little white handkerchief fluttering at the window. *God bless you, Child.*

* * *

---

[17] William Cowper (1731 – 1800) English poet. Quoted from S. Austin Allibone, *Poetical Quotations from Chaucer to Tennyson*, 1878.

"She is a very good woman, Miss Neilson." Professor Halliwell-Phillipps spoke over the city's early morning clatter.

"Aye, sir, I love her very much," said Bobbin. Though she was disappointed that her dear Miss Neilson was not with her, she understood full well the press of her teacher's duties. Within the hour, she had regained her natural disposition and settled in for the long ride to Wilmecote-Asbies.

Sitting on the soft cushion the professor had provided, Bobbin could now see out the window. She sighed as it began to rain again, but it was a warm spring rain. Soft breezes swayed the verdant, tall meadow grass to and fro, to and fro in such beautiful unison. The natural ebb and flow of everything, the beauty of nature's rhythm never ceased to amaze her eye. Passing many villages, she counted the cattle and horses grazing contentedly; now and again she spotted a voyaging dog chasing a fox.

"It will be a very long ride, my dear," he said, interrupting her reverie.

"Oh, I do not mind, sir." Adjusting her bonnet, she sighed. "This is only my second carriage ride in my life." She marvelled that people could all sit together comfortably in a wooden box, pulled by horses. Amazed that anyone would develop such an idea, she questioned the professor about it.

"Indeed," he smiled, "many years ago Mr Farquhar suggested: 'Necessity is the mother of invention.' " [18]

"Hmm." She glanced at him with a nod. "Is Mr Farquhar a friend of yours?"

He laughed. "Oh, dear me, Bobbin, no, no, the gentleman has been long gone, by well over a hundred years, I would suppose."

"I have often wanted to invent something, sir." She paused examining her beautiful, new gloves. "However, such thinking leaves me feeling stupid. There is plenty of need, but I cannot seem to fashion one new thing in which I could claim as an invention."

The elderly professor nodded sleepily.

Inhaling the close, warm smell of the leather interior, Bobbin took in his breath; that familiar sour breath that old people have for dozing too frequently. Talking refreshes the breath. I must try to think of something to engage him. But his

---

[18] Plato (428 – 348 BC) Greek philosopher. *The Republic*, Book II, 369C, (360 BC)

droopy eyelids dashed her plans, and she turned her attention to the passing carriages and marvelled at the different shapes and sizes.

Some were very big, pulled by four horses, others by two; however, her favourite was the one-horse chaise. And that thought put in mind her friend, Morocco, the gentle spotted grey, Roman-nosed, old nag that pulled the supply wagon to the orphanage. Occasionally Moll would give her a carrot for him, and while the giant beast stood half asleep in the orphanage's side yard, she would stroke his forelock and fondly kiss the softest part of his muzzle, promising to never ever forget him.

Awakening quietly from his nap, Professor Halliwell-Phillipps was met with Bobbin's sweet profile as she gazed innocently out the window.

Finding him now awake, she was happy for the company and immediately filled the quiet air. "Sir, I memorised something from Cowper these last few days."

"Is that so?" He yawned and stretched. "Well then, I must hear it."

"How sweet, how passing sweet, is solitude!
But grant me still a friend in my retreat,
Whom I may whisper, solitude is sweet." [19]

His heart was touched. "The orphanage must have been a lonely place for you, Bobbin. Did you not find young girls your own age?"

"Nay, sir, those my own age did not stay long."

"Perhaps you shall find a good friend at the school."

"Oh, Professor that is a wish I hope comes true. I want a friend more than anything."

Pausing for a moment, she reflected out the window. "They are all rich, are they not?"

"Are you speaking of the academy, Bobbin?"

"Yes, sir."

"I do not believe so, Bobbin. Most of them are, though. However, all the girls will be dressed in simple frocks, blue stockings. One is not dressed over the other. Actually, all the frocks are the same, so I have been told by my son."

"I wonder at that, sir." She looked at him questioningly.

---

[19] Cowper, *Poetical Quotations from Chaucer to Tennyson*, 1878.

"I would suppose, Bobbin, that the professors do not want unnecessary diversions to the study."

"Diversions?"

"I have been told that the school day begins very early, dear. And one does not have the luxury of time to dress as one would when in leisure time, as the wealthy young ladies do at home. They shall have a rude awakening, eh, Bobbin? No one to wait on them hand and foot."

"Oh, yes, sir," she nodded. "I know exactly what you mean. It must take many servants to dress each lady properly. I have seen them walking in the park looking so proper and beautiful in their fine clothes and sturdy walking shoes."

"Aye, vanity, my child," he sighed, "but quite a normal thing for ladies and gentlemen. I read a delightful piece the other day that made me laugh. '... every one at the bottom of his heart cherishes vanity: even the toad, he says, thinks himself goodlooking; rather tawny, perhaps, but look at his eye!' " [20]

She smiled broadly, envisioning the toad. "Haha. Indeed, sir. I have witnessed such proud looks, so I have." She giggled.

"You will do well in life, Bobbin, you will do well."

He leaned his head against the leather bannister and within a few minutes fell asleep again, snoring loudly. Bobbin put her fingers in her ears. Frowning, she leaned closer to him, studying inside his mouth and up his hairy nose. I wonder why the two must make such a racket?

Alas, she gave up, and concentrated on the noises the carriage wheels made whirling along at such a pace over the hard-packed roadway. When the lumbering, squeaky carriage would slow for the muddy sections, she could feel the mud slap at the bottoms of her feet as it splattered hard against the undercarriage. Indeed, mud, I know it well.

Eventually, boredom claimed Bobbin too, and just as she dropped off to sleep, the professor drew in a huge gasp of air and bugled off a thunderous snort that startled her awake. Wide-eyed, she found his face so contorted from his own noise that she began to giggle. He even woke himself.

"What? What was that?" He jolted awake. Hastily wiping his mouth, he found her giggling. "Eh? Well, well then I must

---

[20] John Wilson (1785 – 1854) Scottish writer, professor of philosophy at Edinburgh University. Quoted from *The Parterre*, Vol. 4, (1836).

have dozed, Bobbin." Trying to compose his bearings, he glanced out the window. "Oh, it is raining again, is it?"

"It started miles back, sir, and has not stopped, but it is a lovely rain all the same."

"Lovely?" he said frowning. "Humph, I think it not so lovely, for I would like to see a bit of sun now and again."

"Oh, yes, sir, a goodly bit of sun."

"A goodly bit of sun?" He nodded. "Aye, child, an entire day at least."

The carriage rambled along the rutted road, bouncing through huge puddles, deeper ruts and squishy mud holes. More often than not, the professor had to tap the ceiling of the carriage to stifle the cursing coachman. "Hear, hear, Oliver, we have a young lady aboard. Now mind your tongue."

Bobbin would strain at the driver's curses, trying to hear them all; however, the professor seemed to sense their coming and would tap the ceiling, drowning out the remaining half-curse as it hung blue in the air.

"I remember some of them, sir," she blurted, covering her mouth in shame.

"Remember? Remember what, Bobbin?" he inquired.

Her face turned pink. "Ah ... those naughty words, my papa spoke them too, sir."

"Yes, yes, but then that was not your doing, was it, child? No, not your doing at all. Soon enough you shall learn better words that will erase those bad ones."

She retied the bow under her chin. "Yes, sir."

It was but another hour's ride when they finally pulled under the stone carriage-porch of the Mary Arden Academy. Professor Halliwell-Phillipps took Bobbin's arm. "Come, my dear. Let us walk just a little way along the pavement here in front, my legs you know. Then we shall go directly to my son's office, where," he winked, "we shall make ourselves at home and find a bite to eat." He bent over, whispering, "And I know exactly where he hides apples."

Her eyes widened. "Apples?" Taking his hand, Bobbin kissed it. Her heart was full, feeling as if it would burst. Taking a deep breath, she felt that no more excellent good fortune could possibly find her, but then, looking at the beautiful grounds, she realised she was wrong. "Cool air to breathe, Mr Halliwell-Phillipps. Clean lawns, fresh shaven and well trimmed. Trees, hundreds of trees, shrubbery, flowers ... ." She sighed as she squeezed his hand.

"Different than London, eh, Bobbin?"

Chapter 8 – April 7 – Maria Leaves for Mary Arden

> The rays of happiness, like those of light, are
> colorless when unbroken. [21]

Setting her hat carefully upon her hair, Maria leaned into the mirror to examine her red, swollen nose and puffy eyes, patting them one by one. *So what of it? I do not care one thing if I look sick for crying the whole night long.* She turned and glanced once more at her room before going downstairs to join her father and brothers for the long ride to the Mary Arden Academy. She felt betrayed by her family. If not for her proud and stubborn determination, she would have locked herself in her room forever.

*   *   *

"Well, well, my dear, you have not left much time for breakfast. Come now and have a bite before we leave." Mr Collier spoke without a hint of pity in his voice. He knew his daughter was absolutely against going away, but he wisely ignored her swollen face. "It is a long drive, my dear Maria. Will you now come for breakfast?"

---

[21] Henry Wadsworth Longfellow, (1807 – 1882) American poet. Quoted from *Treasury of Thought* by Maturin Ballou, (1884).

"No, thank you, Papa, I am not hungry, really I am not," she replied without looking at him.

"As you please, my dear."

Leaning sideways, Edward glanced around his paper." Good morning, sister. I have decided to come along for the ride after all. Do you mind?"

"Of course not, Edward," she replied dryly.

"Philip will join us as well, imagine that, will you. I would not have thought he would come. However, at the last moment, he changed his plans in order to tour the academy. He is very good friends with the Schoolmaster, Halliwell-Phillipps, you know."

"Mr Halliwell-Phillipps? Really? And who might that be? I know only one such person, an old man at More Towns End Bookstore." She dabbed her nose. "A man of no consequence, surely."

Edward smirked. "That so-called man of no consequence is the Schoolmaster's father … owner of your favourite bookshop, Professor Halliwell-Phillipps."

"Really Edward," she replied haughtily, "I do not care one way or the other regarding the professor or his son."

"Well, the schoolmaster is a disciplinarian. You had better care," warned Philip.

Arching her brows, she sniffed. "I shall certainly make my own way, I am ten and four you know. If he is too harsh, I shall simply board a coach and come directly home."

Holding his coffee cup in mid-air, Edward shook his head.

Mr Collier eyed his chilly-voiced daughter.

"Well, sister," replied Edward, "I do not think it is as easy as that."

"That will do, Edward," said Mr Collier. "That will do."

"Yes, sir." He raised the *Daily News* to his face and resumed reading.

Maria strolled into the vestibule. Pulling aside the white lace curtain, she watched the servants stack her cases neatly, one upon the other. Her bandboxes, glove boxes, umbrella cases and portmanteau. She thought it simply dreadful that the academy made all the students wear the very same frocks, stockings, and hats.

All the same, she insisted upon bringing a small portion of her vast wardrobe. *One needs to travel roundabout to and fro looking presentable. I cannot think of what horrid creature I shall look exactly like—for all of us being dressed the very same.*

Maria felt her father's hand rest on her shoulder. "Yes, Papa, I suppose I am ready." She exhaled heavily, all the while staring out the window. "I have just a bit of a swollen nose this morning, but really the long ride should do me good."

"You are very right, Maria," said Edward as he pulled her hair. "A long ride in the fresh morning chill runs my nose like anything."

Mr Collier shook his head in mild disgust. "Will you ever stop teasing your sister, Edward?"

"She loves it, Father." He laughed. "Come now, Maria, let me see that shiny face."

When she turned and exposed her pale skin, red and swollen eyes and drippy nose, he felt a tinge of guilt, though he hid it well. "Here then, use my handkerchief." He tenderly lifted her chin and wiped her eyes. "Maria, calm yourself, I promise to come and visit you at every opportunity."

"No need, brother." She pulled away from his grip. "I shall be fine. Perhaps at Christmas, though, would be thoughtful."

The butler half-bowed. "The carriage is ready, sir."

* * *

Leaning forward to catch a better look at the surrounding countryside, Edward nodded. "Aah, yes, Wilmecote-Asbies. The academy looks very much the same when last I was here."

"You have been here, then?" Maria looked a little astonished.

"Yes, though, it has been a few years, Maria." He leaned back. "Well, except when we accompanied Father just last ..."

Edward laughed. "Philip, remember when James Halliwell-Phillipps lost his spectacles and stumbled over the podium during graduation exercises? Poor fellow, Oh, how we laughed, felt quite sorry for him actually, but look at him now. Indeed, schoolmaster of such an academy."

"Well, yes, now that you brought back that episode," said Philip. "It was quite an exhibition; however, he has done exceedingly well for himself. Though I daresay, he will never be wealthy—oh, prestige and authorships aplenty, but no, never really very wealthy."

Maria frowned. "Well, then, that does not speak so very highly of him, does it? Not rich? Why would you associate with such a man?" Her eyes had long since cleared, her nose was not as swollen; she dabbed at her mouth. "Are you two going to rekindle his friendship to perhaps embarrass me?"

"Rekindle?" said Philip, bristling. "I have not extinguished it in the first place. Indeed not, he's a fine man if there ever was one." Eyeing his snippy sister, he shook his head. "Maria, you have an edge about you that needs grinding. Indeed, you have a lot to learn."

"That is quite enough, Philip," said Mr Collier.

"Yes, sir." Philip leaned forward in his seat and glanced out the window.

"Maria," said Edward, fearing a tantrum rising from his sister, "I have a most excellent plan. That is if Father agrees. Philip and I shall remain in the carriage until Father tucks you safely away, and then we shall make our presence known to the schoolmaster, saving you any embarrassment. What say you?"

"As you wish, Edward, as you wish. Though, I assure you, I shall mask my embarrassment very well. Moreover, I shall find my place just like all the others." Exhaling heavily, she closed her eyes and folded her arms. "I'm finding this conversation very annoying. I hope, Father, you put an end to it."

Mr Collier sighed deeply.

* * *

The carriage turned onto the academy's well-kept granite drive and stopped beneath the massive stone carriage-porch. The ancient grey stone academy was streaked black with centuries-old soot and green moss; the pavement was slick and dark from rain.

Maria shuddered at its bleak and dreary appearance. Late afternoon fog swirled about its many turrets. Rubbing her arms briskly, she anticipated the damp bone-chill room, no doubt, where she would be lodged this very night. Choosing to remain in the carriage until her father and brothers got out she glanced out the opposite window, perusing the stone archway. She was startled to recognise a familiar face. *Could it be Professor Halliwell-Phillipps from More Towns End Bookstore? It is, but he is strolling alongside that little orphan, Bobbin. Cocking her head in disbelief, Maria cleared her eyes again. I know it is she, but what is she doing here?*

"Come Maria, come now, it is time." Mr Collier leaned into the carriage and took his daughter's hand.

* * *

Holly, the schoolmaster's hound, lounged wherever she wished at the Mary Arden Academy, and this afternoon, she chose to lie in the vestibule. The faculty, being quite used to their mascot's lounging preferences, simply walked over, around, or by her as she slept remaining oblivious to the inconvenience she caused.

When the Colliers were escorted in, Holly did not move; she did not even open her eyes. The servants merely offered up simple apologies for the animal's behaviour and nothing more.

Making a wide path around the hound, Maria positioned herself behind her father, recollecting something about letting sleeping dogs lie. Her brothers and father merely laughed at the sight. Edward stopped to stroke her shiny head. Her tail thumped once as she exhaled a groan, but remained asleep.

The Collier family was then led into the great reception room. The walls were covered with books from ceiling to floor. At one end was a roaring, well-tended fire hissing, spitting snaps of red-hot sparks which flew dangerously close to the pitch-black cat curled in the circle of his tail, asleep on the hearthrug.

Above the huge, ornately carved mahogany fireplace was etched: *'Those who school others, oft should School themselves.'* [22]

Moving away from the hot blazing fire, Maria stared up at the words. Feeling a tug on her hem, she glanced down. "What on earth?" She instinctively drew her hands to her face and backed away. She did not take to animals, never being around them since Mrs North detested all things furry.

"Well, hello girl," cried Edward. "Come now Maria, she only wants you to pet her. What is the harm in it, I ask? Look there at her wagging tail. She is seeking you out."

---

22 William Shakespeare (1564 – 1616) English poet and dramatist. Quoted from *The Handbook of Oratory* by Ferd Kaiser, (1901).

"I have no desire to have such a beast seek me out, Edward." She turned her head. "What have we come to here? Dogs, cats? Is this also a breeding farm?"

"I bet your pardon, miss," replied a servant, "they are harmless creatures, I assure you, but all the same, I shall put them out, immediately. Come Holly, come Foss, come along now."

At his command, the dog and cat obliged, obediently. Just before leaving, Holly stopped and looked questioningly at Maria, then left quietly.

Glancing back up at the sayings etched above the mantle, Maria continued to contemplate the words.

Philip took her hand. "It is not so difficult to understand, Maria." He squeezed her hand.

Stepping back, she looked deeply into his eyes. "Understand?" She respected Philip, looked up to him; she adored him. He was so much like her father, but he, like her father, didn't *understand* her. All the while she suffered intolerable yearnings to be free and challenged. Her desires to explore and learn were often misread or repressed, and her frustrations were interpreted as willfulness. Yet there was an iron streak of reasoning that worked in her brain, and she grew increasingly aware that something was missing in her life. There was a different world out there, and she was deliberately being kept from it.

Her brothers and father lived in that world, perhaps even the orphan, Bobbin. And she wanted to explore it; however, the fear of death haunted her. Had her mother the same yearning to break away from the suffocating little world of idleness women found themselves? Was that what wore her mother's strength and allowed the typhoid to claim her?

"Indeed, Philip," she glanced once more to the etchings above the hearth. "Then why is it so difficult for my family to understand me?" she abruptly withdrew her hand from his.

A voice came from behind them, a gentle and kind voice. Glancing up at the words, the man said, "I believe Mary Arden's son meant that we, as teachers, should never be above learning ourselves. We should practice exactly what we teach by learning from our students as they learn from us." He smiled down into Maria's face. "Hello, there, I am Schoolmaster James Halliwell-Phillipps."

"Well, well, James," cried Philip, as Edward and Mr Collier moved in, closing the circle, "so very good to see you again. You have met my father, Mr John Collier. I know you have, but it has been near five years."

"Yes, sir, Mr Collier, a few years ago, I am so very pleased to see you again, sir." He half-bowed.

"Indeed, Schoolmaster, good to see you. You have not met my daughter." Mr Collier turned and found Maria standing at a distant window. "Maria, dear, do come back."

Rejoining her family, she held a stiff smile. "Good day, Schoolmaster."

"I am pleased to meet you, Miss Collier."

"Say there, James," said Edward, "you are looking very well indeed. Have you a wife yet?"

"I have not had the time, Edward. The academy keeps me very short on idleness." Holding his smile, he turned to Collier. "Sir, by your letter of introduction you requested a tour of the library. If you permit me first to have Miss Collier attended, I shall rejoin you. We have much to reminisce."

Collier nodded his approval. "But of course, sir. We shall remain here by the hearth."

Maria's face held steady a half-smile. Inside she was frozen with fear, yet spoke without a hint of alarm. "Goodbye Papa, goodbye Philip, goodbye Edward." Turning slightly, she awaited direction from the schoolmaster. *I will not weaken.*

Edward smiled at her tenderly. "Sister, let me look into your eyes. I must be satisfied that you will be happy. We shall visit, and I promise to answer promptly every letter you write to me."

She glared at him.

"Well now ... ah, I am quite satisfied you shall prevail."

She lifted her chin. "Oh, I shall do very well here. I can feel it in my bones."

Philip took her hand. "Well done, my brave little sparrow, well done. I shall write, I promise. I shall miss you even though I know you do not believe me."

She frowned slightly. "Philip, why would you say such a thing in front of the schoolmaster; he would think I do not esteem my brother." She turned her frosty attentions to her father. "Goodbye, Papa." She did not make an attempt to go to him but held her ground, painfully disappointed and disillusioned over the myth of fatherly devotion and other such rot. Her lower lip quivered.

He tenderly kissed her cheek. There was a masked pain in his heart and had not his stout English breeding held him in check, he would have wept. He loved his children dearly and knew his daughter was suffering terribly. However, he was wise enough to know the school could offer her far more than what she was receiving at home.

He spoke firmly, "Dearest, I shall miss you. Write often. Goodbye, Maria." He turned and nodded to Halliwell-Phillipps to take his beloved little girl.

"Right this way, miss." The schoolmaster bowed slightly, motioning with a sweep of his arm the way in which she was to proceed. Hesitating briefly, she moved ahead, quickly regaining her stubborn determination not to cry.

In silence, the Colliers watched the schoolmaster and Maria traverse the well-worn parquet flooring, move directly across the black-and-white chickened vestibule floor and eventually disappear down a dimly lit hallway.

Maria never looked back. There were no echoing voices to allay the inquisitiveness of the Colliers as they stood quietly on the hearthrug. John Collier surmised correctly that his daughter had chosen to ignore James Halliwell-Phillipps entirely.

Chapter 9 – An Open Window

Poor is the friendless master of a world:
A world in purchase of a friend is gain. [23]

Holly, sensing the schoolmaster's movement throughout the academy halls, pined to be inside with him. Scurrying along each entryway, she hoped to find someone entering or leaving who would allow her a way in, but this afternoon, oddly enough, no one made way for her. Spying an open window, she stood on her hind legs and looked in. She had jumped in many windows at the academy before, but not through *this* particular window.

Bobbin was shown to her quarters by a student volunteer.

"This small space is your study room, Miss Derby. You will share it with your roommate."

Bobbin noticed two desks sitting side by side. "Oh, how very nice, then."

The other two rooms are your bedchambers. "You must remain here until the headmistress comes." She smiled. "And since you are here first, you may choose which bedchamber you prefer."

Bobbin looked confused.

"Come, I will show you." The escort took Bobbin's hand and opened the door to her left. "I would choose this one, Miss Derby. Of the two, this is the warmest."

---

[23] Edward Young (1683-1765) English poet, on Friendship. Quoted from Wellins Calcott, *A Collection of Thoughts*, 1766.

"Oh, this is lovely," said Bobbin looking around in awe. "Thank you for choosing it."

"You are very welcome. I must go now. Your roommate should be along shortly. Good-day, Miss Derby."

Bobbin followed her back out into the small study room and laid her empty draw-string purse atop one of two desks. Suddenly there came a light tap to the door, and when she opened it, a manservant stood holding her portmanteau.

"Miss Collier or Miss Derby?" he asked.

"Ah, I am Miss Derby."

"Right or left?

"Ah ..."

He glanced at the open door. "Very good, miss, you've chosen the one on the left." He situated her things on the floor with a smile. "It's the warmer of the two."

Bobbin smiled. "Thank you, sir."

Now left alone, she was taken by her room's beauty. Lustrous wood floors and a magnificent four-poster bed, pillows piled everywhere. And then, wonder upon wonder, another fire was burning brightly. Sitting atop a shiny mahogany table was a vase stuffed full with huge bunches of flowering lavender. Their scent, mixed with the burning fire, near took her breath.

Walking around the room, she thought the academy a part of heaven. The warmth from the fire felt wonderful. While examining the beautiful hearthrug, she was astonished to see that it was without even one scorch mark, for there was a fine little brass fire screen in place. Toiletries of one sort or the other sat on the first shelf of a small closet to her left.

The white lace curtains were billowing slightly. Thinking it might rain, she thought it wise to close the window. However, when she moved the curtain aside, she gasped. A huge black dog was trying to climb in. "Oh, dear me, what are you doing? You cannot come in here. Shoo now, go away."

But Holly would not go away. Puzzled at the rude reception, she dropped back down atop the flowers, but not to be put off by a fresh-faced newcomer, she leapt up again and this time wedged her rather large rump onto the sill and slid in. Shaking off, she wiggled up to Bobbin—her tail wagging as she licked her face.

She's a very friendly dog by all accounts, thought Bobbin as she stroked her head and giggled. "Happy dog, happy dog. Well then, girl, your resolve won you in, but now I must find a way to put you out. Yes, indeed, I would surely be sent away if someone found you in my room."

Searching for a rope to lead the dog away, she heard voices in the study room just outside her door. In a frantic pitch, she pushed the big dog into her wardrobe closet, latched it and gulped. Wide-eyed with fear that they would find her with the dog, her heart thumped madly. Leaving her room, she quickly closed the door behind her.

"Good afternoon, Miss Derby," smiled the schoolmaster.

"Oh, good afternoon, sir." Bobbin smiled politely. "Thank you, sir, for the apple Professor Halliwell-Phillipps gave me earlier ... he found it in your office, sir."

"Oh, indeed, Father has a nose for that sort of thing." Smiling he turned to the gentlelady standing next to him. "Miss Derby this is our headmistress, Mrs Aesop."

Bobbin curtsied, not sure exactly what a headmistress was. "Oh, Madam Headmistress Aesop I am so happy to greet you. Oh, I mean meet you." Bobbin's face turned pink.

The schoolmaster and Mrs Aesop smiled at one another. Just then Maria Collier entered the room explaining to the escort that she was entirely capable of finding her own room and was promptly excused.

Schoolmaster Halliwell-Phillipps smiled. "Well, Miss Collier you have arrived at the best possible moment."

"Sir, I was bored silly in the reception room and wanted only to find quiet and solitude."

"Indeed, well then, let me introduce you to the Headmistress here, Mrs Aesop."

Maria slowly took in Mrs Aesop's slightly tattered hem up to the drab day cap on the top of her head. Not the least bit impressed, she nodded. "Mrs Aesop."

"And your roommate, Miss Bobbin Derby."

Swallowing hard, Bobbin curtsied. "A very good day to you Miss Collier." She thought she heard the dog whine and her hands began to perspire.

Maria sneered. "We have already met in London, not so very long ago."

Mrs Aesop smiled. "Well, then you are very blessed that you shall share quarters with an acquaintance. Most young ladies here are not as fortunate in that regard, Miss Collier."

"Well, Mrs Aesop, I would not consider it fortunate to be roomed with an orphan." Maria glanced around the room, weighing no consequence at how such a rude remark would affect Bobbin.

Mrs Aesop, used to the ways of the wealthy and the poor, glanced at the schoolmaster. They ignored the comment. Miss Derby seemed to be a sturdy young girl, and since she did not colour at the insult, they felt the two would meld, eventually.

"The rule at Mary Arden Academy is: two paired remain paired." The schoolmaster smiled politely. "Mrs Aesop is available at all times if you are in need of anything. She is headmistress at the academy and manages all the students here. I manage the curriculum. Tea is served at four; I will see you both then. Good afternoon." He bowed slightly and left the room.

Mrs Aesop hemmed, "This desk is yours, Miss Derby. I see your purse resting on it. That desk, Miss Collier, is yours." She gestured about the room. "Miss Derby, that door there leads into your bedchamber."

Bobbin's eyes widened. Fearful she would find the dog, she curtsied again. "Oh, thank you, ma'am, thank you. I already found it very beautiful."

"Very well, then. Miss Collier, I shall show you your room." The headmistress opened the door across the vestibule and stood aside.

"Is there anything more, Mrs Aesop?" asked Maria walking into her room.

"No, Miss Collier, that is all."

"Very well, have my things sent up, immediately." She entered and closed the door behind her.

Bobbin's eyes widened at the insolent Miss Collier. She glanced at Mrs Aesop who remained emotionless.

"Well then, Miss Derby, is there anything you need?"

"No, ma'am, it is just that I shall be very happy here, I promise. I shall be very happy here." Her fingers twitched nervously.

"I know you will Miss Derby, I know you will. I only ask one thing of your old soul."

"Yes, Mrs Aesop?" She wondered why she was called an old soul.

"It is only that Miss Collier is a very lonely young lady and needs a friend very much. Will you be her friend, Miss Derby?"

"Yes, ma'am." Bobbin knew exactly what she meant since she had helped Miss Neilson with the orphans at Newpark. "I will, Mrs Aesop."

"Thank you, Miss Derby." At that, the headmistress hugged her. "Bless you, little angel." Before leaving she added, "Do not forget, tea at four."

"No, ma'am, I will not."

* * *

There came a knock at their door. It was the student messenger, Emma Shelley, scurrying down the hall. "Tea time, hurry along. Tea time, hurry along. One must not be late to tea."

Hearing the clamour in the hall, Maria stuck her head out the door. "Oh, it is only that ugly freckled thing supposing to be important announcing this announcing that."

Bobbin suddenly felt the freckles on her nose swell and multiply. She exhaled heavily. "I have heard we are all to be messengers here, each in our turn."

"Not I," Maria tossed her head defiantly. "I assure you, I shall never wait upon anyone."

"Hmm, yes, that just might be a possibility, Miss Collier."

"Might be?"

"I will gladly take your turn. I cannot see enough of this grand, beautiful academy. I want to walk and walk and walk the halls." Bobbin exhaled dreamily.

Maria shook her head. "You are an odd girl, Bobbin Derby, no doubt because you are an orphan. Walk the halls, indeed. Well, then, come along, Dormouse, we must not be late."

Together, in silence, they walked down the grand staircase and followed the others into the tearoom.

"Tell me Bobbin," said Maria, "do you wish to step step step all the stairs in the academy as well?"

Bobbin coloured. "You find my faults very easily, Miss Collier."

Scanning the room, Bobbin spied the schoolmaster. He stood next to his high-backed, over-stuffed chair by an enormous fire. He was wearing a long, billowy black robe with a black satin collar that lay flat around his neck, draping down his back in a 'v' shape. His scholar's hat was of the same soft black material, rounded about in four corners with red satin piping along each seam.

Looking around in awe, Bobbin seemed enthralled. "So, Miss Collier, this is the Victoria Tea Room."

Sniffing the air, Maria nodded. "Just a tea room, like all tea rooms, I would suppose."

Slowly moving over a strip of carpet, Bobbin noticed early on that everyone stayed on it. *It must be the shiny floors that they do not want to be marked.* Gawking about the beautiful room, she teetered a bit and steadied herself by taking Maria's arm. "Oh, miss, I must be careful not to wander from this rug."

Maria frowned. "Pray tell, now what is it?"

"One must stay on the carpet, Miss Collier and not scuff the floors."

"Humph, I shall walk where I please." She smartly stepped off the carpet and twirled on the shiny wood floor, not once, but twice.

Bobbin's jaw dropped. "You are very brave, Miss Collier."

"Brave?" She rolled her eyes. "No, no, that was not an act of bravery. To step off the carpet was an act of ..." she thought for a moment and sighed. "Bobbin, you must not always follow someone else's rules. You must make a few rules of your own." She whispered in her ear, "You may even break a few, if you wish."

Bobbin drew back, dismayed. "I would not want to do such a thing, Miss Collier. I would be scared of reprimands."

Maria exhaled with a smirk. "And do you see anyone chasing me with a broom? Do you hear anyone scolding me for twirling on this floor?"

"But if you jumped on those sofas." Bobbin gestured toward them with a nod.

Maria thought for a moment and giggled. "So, there is impishness beneath that innocent façade of yours. No, sofas are a different matter entirely. Come, now, let us find a seat before they are all gobbled up. We simply must sit in the front."

Bobbin smiled. "It is a beautiful room, a long, spacious room." She counted ten sofas situated here and there, with as many easy chairs in between. "Oh, I think there are chairs and sofas enough for all to sit in front."

Along one wall were tall windows festooned with plush, green velvet drapes, gathered by silver filigree tiebacks. The hazy late afternoon sun lit the entire room making it appear the colour of soft gold.

They came to a huge white marble fireplace where Bobbin abruptly stopped. Gazing up at a portrait hanging above the mantle, she stared at it in awe. "Oh, but she is lovely. I have never before seen a *real* painting."

"Hmm," uttered Maria looking up at it, "indeed, it is Her Majesty, Queen Victoria and Prince Albert with their children."

"Oh, she is very beautiful, Miss Collier," said Bobbin in awe. "This painting would please Her Majesty very much, I should think."

Maria shrugged. "There are hundreds of such paintings, Dormouse."

"But I have never seen a real one."

"Of course you have not."

Servants moved about pouring tea and offering sweet cakes to the milling crowd of anxious students. There were a few adults there, and Bobbin assumed they were teachers. Suddenly there came the tinkle of a bell. Mrs Aesop announced that tea was now over and everyone must take a seat. Bobbin hurried nearest the schoolmaster. Maria sat next to her.

Halliwell-Phillipps nodded to Bobbin and Maria. "Good afternoon, ladies. And how are you doing?"

Maria chose to ignore him, first studying her fingernails and then her shoes.

"Good afternoon, sir," gushed Bobbin. "Oh, sir, I am very comfortable in my room. My bed is so soft, and all my things are hanging neatly on their hooks. My boots are cleaned and lined up correctly just underneath my frocks, I have two pairs, you know, sir."

"I am very happy to hear of it, Miss Derby." He smiled tenderly. His heart was always deeply touched by the poorer children the academy accommodated. Just as he began studying his notes, he overheard Maria admonish Bobbin.

"Really now, Bobbin, it was not necessary to explain to the schoolmaster about your wardrobe hanging on hooks or that your boots were sitting in order." She rolled her eyes. "You really must begin to understand a few rudimentary examples of polite conversation." She exhaled heavily and continued, "I suppose I must explain a few, but not now."

Bobbin folded her hands in her lap and nodded to her politely. "Indeed."

Maria's voice lowered so the schoolmaster could not hear the rest of the conversation. He smiled at Bobbin, and she acknowledged his understanding kindness with a nod.

The schoolmaster stood and glanced around the room while removing his notes from his vest pocket. Taking the lectern, he adjusted his spectacles. Suddenly, a fluffy black cat wrapped its tail around his legs. He picked her up, fondly cradled her in his arms and then gently sat her on the lectern. The fluffy feline, acting every bit the pharaoh's guardian, peered from its elliptical yellow-green eyes at the giggling students.

"A very good afternoon ladies, as you know, I am Mr James Halliwell-Phillipps, Schoolmaster of Mary Arden Academy here in the ancient town of Wilmecote-Asbies. You have been chosen to come here, ladies. 'Chosen' is a very special word. I look upon your presence here as an honoured one." He paused to scan the anxious faces. "Thus far in my life, I can count on one hand the number of honours that have been bestowed upon me, one of which is the honour of being chosen—

"Your learning experience here will be one of hard work and much personal gratification. I must tell you I have never been disappointed with any student, with one exception, in all my years here."

At the mention of 'one exception,' a deeper hush settled over the already silent audience. It was as if all breathing stopped.

Bobbin sat up straight. *'Except one'? God in heaven, what had she done? What wicked evil thing could she have done?* Suddenly she remembered the big black dog she hid in her closet. Her breathing became shallow. She closed her eyes praying with a fervour that somehow, someway the hound had broken out and jumped back out the window. *But I closed it! Oh, mercy, mercy, I shall certainly be the second disappointment to the schoolmaster. I shall be expelled before I sleep here one night.*

"However, I do not believe," the schoolmaster continued, "anyone here to be so grievous in nature as to earn my disapproval—I do not."

With that, he smiled at Mary Aesop, who sat a few chairs away. "Mrs Aesop is headmistress. She will share a word with you, and then we shall enjoy more tea." The cat sprang from the lectern, evoking a polite laugh from the girls.

Mrs Aesop was not an early bloom, perhaps thirty and five summers, but certainly no more. It was obvious that a forgiving nature stood guard over her years afoot, for she held very good command of it. Her curly, thick strands of hair were not lighter than at birth, still black. There beneath the chin and cheek, not surrounded by puff and wax, no, but taut, firm skin. Her eyes mostly clear; now and again brooding as if remembering a broken dream.

That aside, Mrs Aesop had laugh lines around her mouth and eyes. *A very good sign*, thought Maria Collier as she sized her up. *Easy enough to ploy. Perhaps not as easy as Mrs North, but easy enough all the same.*

The headmistress held the gaze of each young girl sitting before her. She paused to read their smiling, expectant, fresh faces. A few were timid and proper. A few were arrogant and defiant. *Ah, a fair sample.* And then she came to Miss Derby. Bobbin's eyes were closed, her little face screwed up, intent and serious (she was still praying about the dog) and Mrs Aesop's heart was warmed; she could not help but love the child. She covered her mouth quickly with a handkerchief, stifling a laugh, without success.

Maria followed Mrs Aesop's eyes to Bobbin, whose eyes were closed. She nudged her. "You cannot be sleeping, girl," she scolded in a whisper.

"No, miss, I was praying."

"Ladies," said Mrs Aesop, "I want to say a few words about the academy." She petted the pitch coloured cat pawing at the hem of her billowy black day frock. "First, cat's name is Foss. She is adored and catered to here at the academy. Foss belongs to Professor Zany. She is our mouse trap, ladies."

A murmur of disdain rumbled through the audience. A few girls lifted their feet from the floor.

"I shall oversee your marks, morals and manners ... and all of your personal needs. Mr Hermann is the caretaker regarding things outside. All other business is done by polite inquiry at my office. Tomorrow I will escort you and your roommate about the academy. I will explain in more detail our expectations of each student at that time. I look forward to meeting you."

She smiled, deepening the creases in her face. "Professor Sharpe," and she nodded his direction, "will explain the daily academic curriculum."

He stood and approached the lectern. "Ladies, welcome to Mary Arden Academy, welcome ..." his crooked, twisted teeth, sprayed spittle with each word.

Gagging, Bobbin covered her mouth.

Maria leaned into her. "What is the trouble, girl? Are you not well?"

"I, I need a sip of water ..."

Maria shot a harried look at Mrs Aesop and without permission, grabbed Bobbin's hand and hurriedly led her into the hallway. "What is it, Bobbin? Are you choking?"

"Oh, no, miss," she said, wiping her mouth. "Mr Sharpe's spit was spraying on us."

Maria giggled just as Mrs Aesop came around the corner.

"Why are you laughing, Miss Collier? What is the humour in someone choking, pray tell?" Frown creases deepened on her face as she examined Miss Derby.

Maria instantly froze. "Oh, dear me, that wasn't a giggle ... I find no humour at all, Mrs Aesop. Miss Derby was in need of water."

"Hmm, very well then," she said, eyeing Maria with suspicion. "I shall be but a moment."

Bobbin shook her head and whispered, "Miss Collier, how well you recovered in front of Mrs Aesop. However did you do it?"

"It takes very much practice, Dormouse. And since you are my roommate, I shall teach you the art of masking. All ladies do it. And by the way, you may address me as Miss Maria."

"Thank you, Miss Maria."

Within seconds Mrs Aesop was back with a pitcher of water and a small teacup. "Here you are, Miss Derby, drink a little."

Fearful that she would snap such a delicate little handle on the porcelain cup, Bobbin tried desperately to steady her shaking hands.

"Come now, Bobbin," Maria urged, "sip it down."

Foss, rounding the corner to investigate the commotion, hopped atop Bobbin's lap. Sniffing about her mouth and hands, she suddenly purred loudly and lay down.

"Well, then," said Mrs Aesop, smiling, "Foss knows you are out of danger. Come then, you both will stand with me. I have only a few words more."

Quietly the three reentered the room as Mr Sharpe concluded his speech.

Mrs Aesop took the lectern. "We shall all retire to the music room and enjoy our tea. If anyone plays the harp or piano, she may exhibit, being mindful to take turns. I might add that the schoolmaster adores Mozart."

Feeling very clever, Maria grabbed Bobbin's hand and led her into the music room. Situating herself and Bobbin a safe distance from the others, she began to enlighten the dormouse on the art of facial disguises—masking.

"Bobbin, regarding masking one's expressions, well, it is very handy betimes." Trying to find a suitable situation such an orphan might understand, she added, "In anger, have not you wanted to stick your tongue out at someone?"

"Uh." Bobbin searched for such an occasion and recalled one in which Miss Collier was rude to Professor Halliwell-Phillipps. "Aye, miss, I have."

"And you could not stick out your tongue because adults were there?"

"Aye, miss." Bobbin stifled a giggle.

"Well, upon such occasions one must ever so carefully suck in the inside of one's cheeks thusly." Maria gestured with her fingers. "Keeping the tongue lodged securely."

"Say again, Miss Maria, the reason for all this?"

"Well, it is really very simple, girl," she exhaled deeply. "You are actually sticking your tongue out at the person, but they do not see it."

"I should think one would bite her tongue rather than hold it in check."

"You have no imagination, Dormouse." Maria sighed. "It is tomfoolery, Bobbin, tomfoolery. It relieved me from my governess's stupid reprimands. And I have read that it is quite natural to trifle with others—if it should make one's self suffer less."

"Miss Maria, one may mask an impertinent gesture, but not the spoken word. For once uttered, it cannot be taken back. One without the other should not make one suffer less, I should think."

Maria was stymied at Bobbin's thinking. However, never to be outdone, replied, "All the same, Bobbin, orphans need to know these things, depend upon it."

"And, Miss Maria, are there more stratagems that I should be aware of, perhaps?"

Maria puffed up at Bobbin's obvious naiveté. "Oh, yes, little orphan mouse, there are many." Maria felt her self-esteem well up inside her chest. She felt dutiful and superior, sisterly in a good way, and in a remote section of her heart, motherly. She stood and took Bobbin's hand. "Come along, then. I shall take care of you, orphan. No one shall harm you. For I am very wealthy, and you have not one farthing to your name."

"Thank you, Miss Maria, but I am not a beggar. One day I shall repay you, handsomely."

"No need, Bobbin girl. Money is not so very important, I assure you."

"Indeed, miss," smiled Bobbin, "I was not speaking of money."

Hesitating for a brief second at the girl's remark, Maria felt the memory of her mother's lips tenderly kiss her brow.

* * *

It was near three in the morning as Bobbin lay in deep wonderland sleep on a very soft, warm bed. The early, windy morning air outside did not disturb her slumber; she was well used to the noisy blustery winds, but Maria's urgent, tearful cries awakened her in a start.

"Wake-up, Bobbin!" Her hands were like ice, her voice quivering as she shook her. "There is a monster in the room. Oh, God in heaven, wake up, will you."

Bobbin sat up abruptly as Maria jumped into her bed, dug under the covers and held tight to her warm little body. Rubbing her eyes awake, Bobbin pulled the covers away. "What is the matter, Miss Maria?"

"Oh, there is a monster loose about the room." Trembling, she pulled the blankets back over her head, crying. "You must hide."

"Tell me, what kind of monster. Where did you see it?"

"I heard it, Bobbin. I heard it moan." She dug deeper under the covers.

Bobbin listened intently. "Oh, no, I forgot about the dog!" She nudged Maria. "Do not be afraid, it is not a monster after all, but only a dog."

Maria sat up, hiding under a quilt. She looked very much like a ghost herself. "A dog?"

"She is hiding in my closet."

Maria pulled the blanket from her head. "Hiding in your closet?"

"Wait here, Silly Goose. I will show you she is not a monster at all."

Bobbin jumped from the bed, giggling as her bare feet hit the cold hardwood floor scrambling harum-scarum to the wardrobe. Just as she opened it, Holly leapt out landing atop the bed next to Maria.

Bobbin was laughing so hard she barely made it back into bed. Wrapping the covers around her icy little feet, she watched the dog lick Maria's face in happy gratitude at being set free. Maria, startled at first, didn't know what to make of the hound, but when Holly's tongue tickled her nose, she giggled.

Joining in the fray, Bobbin stuck her frozen toes on Maria's backside and laughed uproariously.

Maria, now giggling hysterically as the dog nudged her with a cold, runny nose, grabbed one of the pillows and threw it at Bobbin. "Put your feet on this, girl!"

Holly playfully seised the pillow in mid-air, and the fracas began.

When Mrs Aesop and the Schoolmaster arrived at the scene, white feathers were floating softly about the room. In the middle of the bed sat two shadowy figures—three shadowy figures.

"So this is where you have been hiding all the day long, Holly," said the Schoolmaster holding up his lamp. "Come, girl."

Holly ran to him, wagging her tail in grand excitement. Feathers still floated gently in the air as her rump wiggled wildly side-to-side, in absolute delight at seeing him. Squirming around Mrs Aesop's legs, Holly licked his hand. While the Schoolmaster quietly backed out of the room with Holly in tow, his face held a wry, twisted sort of grin. He pulled the door closed.

Mrs Aesop remained, and the two girls could not interpret exactly, the expression on her face.

Chapter 10 – A Blustery Autumn Day

Friendship is the shadow of the evening,
which strengthens with the setting sun of life. [24]

Many months had passed since that pillow fight, and Bobbin and Maria delighted in many more pillow frays. It released something in each girl, perhaps a long-repressed emotion just to be silly little girls, and with each encounter they grew closer. Together, their childish pranks bridged them as sisters.

It was a cool, fall day as Maria sat at her study desk, reading. Foss was swatting at a ribbon dangling from her hair.

There came a knock at the door. "Come," said Bobbin.

It was a student messenger, Anne Spencer. "A letter for you, Miss Derby."

"Do come in, Miss Spencer."

"Good morning, Miss Derby. Good morning, Miss Collier."

Maria glanced up and down at her. "Lovely frock, Miss Spencer."

"What?" she replied, "but it is the same as yours."

"Oh, miss," Bobbin half-laughed taking the letter, "Miss Collier has become quite the tease."

"Indeed, she has." Miss Spencer smiled sweetly, looking Maria up and down. "Too bad they didn't have one in your

---

[24] Jean de La Fontaine (1621 – 1695) French fabulist and poet. Quote is from John Hayward, *Book of Notions*, 1850, p 236.

size." Leaving the room, she glanced back at Bobbin, "Good day, ladies."

"Impish little thing," Maria called out as Miss Spencer closed the door. Turning to Bobbin, she gasped, "Dare you laugh, Bobbin."

"Well, you must admit she is a clever little imp, Maria. Come now, you must laugh at her while you laugh at yourself. It becomes you."

Pouting, she sighed heavily. "I find little humour in myself."

"Look deeper, Maria, it is there. Granted you are of a serious nature, but I have noticed your genius for pinpointing exactly another's pomposities. I marvel at your sarcastic banter, for rarely are you wrong."

"Really? I had not noticed." She casually took Bobbin's letter and fanned herself.

"Just do the same to yourself, Maria. Pamper your sweetness and temper your razor's edge. Dilute the nasty with light-hearted humour."

"Yes, yes, now you must read your letter … or shall I?" She teasingly waved it above Bobbin's head.

"Oh, I cannot imagine who should write to me, except Miss Neilson, of course."

"Well then, Bobbin, open it."

"Let us read it together."

Maria nodded agreeably as Foss meowed. "Very well then, you spoiled thing." She gently lifted Foss to her lap.

Bobbin broke the seal and began reading aloud:

*"10 Nov Thursday Morn Newpark Orphanage, London
My Dearest Little Friend Bobbin,*
       I love you and miss you very much – everyone here misses you. The cook tells me often that no one gathers wood and stacks it as neat nor even as you. Never do they carry the milk buckets for the milkmaid, Nell, without spilling most of it. I have very good news, my little friend. You shall come to pay us a visit over Christmas. Professor Halliwell-Phillipps will send his carriage. He misses you, also, very, very much and sends his best wishes to you. If he can manage he will come along to visit you when he visits with his son. He has enclosed a small envelope with mine. I have not the

faintest idea what is in it. I must go now, the children are crying. I look forward to kissing your sweet face for such a Christmas present. Your friend forever, affectionately Miss Susanna Neilson"

Bobbin felt hot tears slip from her eyes and roll down her face, dripping freely on the envelope in her lap.

Maria put her arm around her. "There, now, Bobbin, do not cry. When I cry, I cannot see. Do you not want to see what is in the other envelope?"

She looked up at Maria's serious face and giggled. "Oh, silly me, Maria." She wiped her eyes, kissed the top of Foss's head and tore open the envelope. There inside was slender cloth pouch, neatly sewn on all sides.

Maria squirmed in anticipation. "Open it, Bobbin.

"I have never received anything before. What could it be?"

"Silly girl, open it. Do you want that I should open it for you?"

Bobbin smiled and with nimble fingers, carefully separated the stitches. Both girls gasped in delighted wonder.

"It is a miniature painting of you, Bobbin!"

"Of me?" She was all astonishment. "Maria, it *is* me. How should my likeness be copied?" She was dumbfounded at such a thing. "What is its purpose? Surely I cannot wear it. One does not wear one's own likeness. One would think me vain or something."

"Oh, no, silly girl, you must save it and give it to your lover," said Maria, as if well versed in such matters of the heart.

Bobbin's eyes grew wide. "Lover?"

"Your fiancé, Bobbin. Then when you wed, he may keep it close to his heart all the day long."

"All the day long?"

Maria laughed, affectionately tweaking her nose. "Now I am envious of you, Bobbin, for I do not have one of myself, but I do have one of my mother."

She jumped up, hung Foss on her shoulder and ran to her room. Shortly she returned with a purple velvet pouch from which she removed a large pink cameo. "Here she is Bobbin, my mother. Her likeness was engraved on a seashell. Father had it carved in Italy."

Bobbin reverently fondled the beautiful pink engraving. "Oh, she is lovely, Maria." It felt cool to her touch. "I am sorry she died, Maria."

"Yes, I suppose you are. Everyone says that—that they are sorry." A dark cloud crossed over her eyes; a troubled look settled on her face.

"I do not remember mine, Maria. Though I seem to recollect her name was Mary."

"She died, too?" Maria brought the cameo to her lips.

"I do not know exactly, but I think she ran away with gipsies."

Maria looked at her in disbelief. "You must not say that out loud, Bobbin. Some things you must keep to yourself. If you are not sure of such a disgraceful thing, then you must not speak of it, ever."

Bobbin shrugged. "I should like someday to go search for her. Would you like to come along, Maria?"

"Come along?" Her mind raced with wonder. "What do you mean, Bobbin? Search London? Why, it is raw as anything, and if the gipsies did not have your mother and they found you snooping, they would certainly boil you in scalding water in one of those huge black pots. Have you never seen the steam that comes from seep holes on the city streets in cold weather? They are down there, Bobbin, beneath the streets, boiling water."

Bobbin's face crinkled. "Maria, who told you that?" It was obvious she was not worried one thing over her scary words.

"My brother, Edward."

"I know that cannot be true, Maria. My mother would only run away with gipsies that ride fast horses, free as the wind, and she certainly would not ride beneath a city."   "Fast horses?" Maria shook her head. "Oh, I doubt that."

There came a knock at the door. It was the messenger scurrying down the hall calling out: 'Classes are resuming. To resume immediately. Classes ...'

The two quickly put their things away and obediently followed everyone downstairs, past the SILENCE IN THE HALL sign.

Maria whispered, "There is a guest lecturer today."

"I know, and I cannot wait to see who it is."

"A very important writer, Bobbin," Maria teased, "however, I am not a liberty of divulging just who it is."

"Oh, I suppose I must wait then."

"Oh, very well, it is Mr Dickens."

"Oh, my friend, Mr Dickens from More Towns End Bookstore," said Bobbin gleefully.

"Your friend?" Maria laughed. "Bobbin, you amaze me."

Chapter 11 – Christmas Eve

All who joy would win
Must share it, —happiness was born a twin. [25]

Bobbin stood in the vestibule peering out at the light snow that was falling, splotches of brown-green winter grass were still visible here and there. She was waiting for Maria to put her coat on, since her carriage had just arrived.

Touching her nose to the windowpane, Bobbin frosted it with her breath. Suddenly one of the footmen cried out, "Happy Christmas." The voice immediately put to mind the poor-box thief in the church the night she escaped from the burning inferno.

I near forgot ... I near forgot. Oh, dear me. I near forgot that Christmas. I have never prayed for him, the beggar who carried me to the orphanage, he saved my very life.

"I do wish you would come home with me, Bobbin," said Maria, coming up behind her. "Certainly my family would welcome you." Fumbling with her scarf, she added, "And you must not even consider your clothes not worthy enough to wear around them. No one will care one straw what you choose to wear from one day to the other."

"That is the problem, Maria. I have only one frock to wear from one day to the other."

"I shall have Papa buy you seven, then."

---

[25] Lord Byron (1788 – 1824) English poet. Canto II, Stanza 172 in *Don Juan*, (1819).

"Thank you, Maria, but I could not accept such gifts."

"No, I thought not. So then come and stay one day."

Bobbin laughed. "Oh, my friend, we shall be apart but seven days and that is not such a long time. You will have so many fine parties to attend and places to go that your mind will be quite content without me."

"All the same, I shall miss you, Bobbin." Maria hugged her affectionately and kissed her cheek.

"I shall miss you, Maria. You are more than welcome to visit the orphanage, we have very few visitors who come to call on Christmas day—the parson comes with the poor box offering and the grocer with a goose. Do come, Maria. Everyone would welcome you and your family."

"We shall see, Bobbin," Maria hugged her again. Climbing into her waiting carriage, she waved good-bye.

It was little time when Professor Halliwell-Phillipps's carriage arrived for Bobbin. Tightening her scanty cloak around her shoulders, she was ready to brave the snowy weather when she heard someone call. It was Mrs Aesop.

"Miss Bobbin, have a delightful time in London, my child. Have a happy Christmas."

"Thank you, Mrs Aesop, I shall. I am so looking forward to seeing everyone again. It has been a long time, you know."

"Yes, I should say it has." She came closer. "Miss Bobbin, I was wondering if you would do me a kind favour before you leave."

"Yes, ma'am, I will be happy to."

"You know, of course, my happiest moments come when sitting in front of the fire, when I am sewing."

"Yes, ma'am, I have seen your beautiful needlework."

"Then, please, take this." She wrapped a beautiful, deep-purple, heavy wool-knit cape around Bobbin's shivering little body. Smiling, she pulled the hood up over her head and took a few steps back. "There now, miss, I must say, it fits perfectly."

Bobbin felt the warmth envelope her shoulders and her chest—its length covered her legs exactly. She looked down and admired its beauty. "Oh, it is the warmest and most beautiful cape I have ever seen, Mrs Aesop."

"Miss Bobbin, would you be so kind as to accept it from me?"

"Oh, Mrs Aesop, I would be very pleased to accept it. Thank you very much, ma'am. May I ask what I have done to deserve such a gift?"

"It is a small token of your goodness, my dear. Do not think that what you do for others here goes unnoticed." She kissed her forehead. "Go now, child, before the snow gets deeper. I shall see you next week, happy Christmas."

"Thank you." Bobbin wrapped her arms around Mrs Aesop's neck and kissed her. "Happy Christmas, Mrs Aesop."

Walking to the carriage, Bobbin did not feel the biting, bitter cold wind cut her through her chest and neck. She climbed in and sat, feeling the most perfect warmth all around her. Smiling, she felt proud to wear such a garment.

Snuggling in the cape, she thought it the most beautiful thing she had ever seen. While feeling the material, she happened to notice on the inside lining Mrs Aesop had embroidered the initials *SBD*.

How could she have made such a mistake? She would never mention it for the headmistress was much too kind, and she fancied the initial 'S' to mean special or sweet or smart, perhaps. For a few miles, she played the word game trying to think of words beginning with an 'S', and it dawned on her that it meant sampler. *But of course, that is often the case, that one who embroiders expertly shows her skill.*

And with that, she was quite satisfied. A few miles farther down the road, when the stark bareness of the winter trees and the frozen white meadows offered little to feed her imagination, her eyes waxed heavy, and she fell off to sleep. Suddenly a clear, familiar voice of a woman called to her, "Stella."

Bobbin opened her eyes. "Yes, I am Stella."

The voice went away and did not answer her. Thinking it a dream, she closed her eyes. Snuggling deeper into her new warm cape, she smelled the familiar scent of Mrs Aesop lingering yet in the wool, and she thought of the kind woman who had always been so very pleasant to her at the academy. She felt a deep sadness in her heart for the headmistress since she would be spending Christmas alone.

Chapter 12 – Early Spring at Mary Arden Academy

A proverb is the wisdom of many and the wit of one. [26]

Schoolmaster Halliwell-Phillipps quietly entered the Shakespeare Room amid the giddy chatter of students. His presence immediately settled the young ladies, who obediently took their seats. He looked wonderfully handsome this morning, thought Bobbin, but then she always thought him handsome.

"Each spring we set aside one day as Visitors' Day. Next month we have set aside 10 April for that special occasion. You have all been very hard at work with your studies, and Mrs Aesop has assured me everyone is doing marvellously well."

He brought the spectacles resting on his head down, and glanced about the proud, smiling faces. "On Visitors' Day, we present a program for your parents and friends, affording you the opportunity to exhibit your talents. With that in mind, this year I would like something extraordinary from each of you. I want you to exhibit a bit of something you have acquired from these sacred halls."

He looked about the room. "Some of you play the pianoforte very well." A polite murmur from a few of the

---

[26] Lord John Russell (1792 – 1878) English statesman, UK Prime Minister. Remark to James Mackintosh on October 6, 1830, reported in his posthumous memoir, *Memoirs of the Life of the Right Honourable Sir James Mackintosh*, Vol. 2 (1836), p. 472.

musically inclined students could be heard. "Oh, yes, I have heard you play. Some play the harp exquisitely. A few of you have exceptional abilities at memorisation and could perhaps repeat a poem, a sonnet or a limerick. Act out a bit part of a play perhaps. Well, the choice is yours. I only ask that you exhibit for a few minutes only since there are many of you here and we have many things on the schedule for that day."

"What is a limerick?" whispered Maria to Bobbin.

She shrugged. "I do not know exactly."

"Miss Collier, it is a rhyme scheme of sorts, similar to a sonnet only shorter and nonsensical," replied Professor Barnaby Zany, overhearing her inquiry.

"Oh, I see." She turned to him. "Then that should suit me very well indeed, Professor Zany, thank you."

"There is a *Book of Nonsense* in the library, Miss Collier," he added with a wink-ish smile.

"Oh, indeed, sir, thank you, sir." She again smiled politely as she nudged Bobbin.

Foss hopped up on Professor Zany's lap, turned and sniffed Maria. It then twirled within its long tail and curled into a little ball, purring loudly.

"Our guest this morning is Mrs Charlotte Bronte Nicholls," crowed the schoolmaster proudly as he relinquished the lectern to his friend, the much-admired authoress.

* * *

Rising early, Schoolmaster Halliwell-Phillipps noticed a break in the dark churning clouds; it had stopped raining, at least for the moment, offering a welcomed opportunity for a walk with Holly.

"Come then, girl," he called, "this way."

The early morning air was cool and crisp; the tall wet grass lay trodden, laden with rain. "Stay off the wet grass, Holly."

He followed behind his silly, lop-eared hound as she bounded up a narrow bridle path, wagging her long thick tail, skimming the fresh earthen sod with her nose. Her easy manner assured James that all was normal; all was well in the world. Amused, he sighed, "Ah, safe again. No evil abounds in the woods this morn."

In her fresh exuberance, Holly gained a good distance up the hill. James, near out of breath, called out, "Wait there, girl."

She obediently stopped by the old tree-fall and waited.

"Aye, Holly, good girl." He stood for a moment catching his breath. The beauty of the morn was in his heart. "Well, now, look at that prospect. Ay, 'Spring hangs her infant blossoms on the trees, Rocked in the cradle of the western breeze.' " [27]

Holly whined and moved a little distance to squat. "There now, girl, Cowper does not please you, I see?"

Ruffling the thick black hair on her head, he thought how easy and uncomplicated the life of a dog. "Hmm, to be one for a day; to run free and chase birds; to lie in a cool stream, sipping water ..."

Holly interrupted him, whining.

"What is it, girl?" Her floppy ears perked, she stood atop the hill looking down and whined again.

"What is it, girl?" He followed her gaze. "I only see a carriage moving." He squinted. "I cannot tell, right off, who it is, but apparently you can."

Dancing about excitedly, she pawed the fresh, wet grass, and still, he did not recognise the carriage as his father's. He watched it amble along toward the academy, the very one carrying his future bride.

Holly nudged his leg.

"What brought that on? Do you have a premonition? Tell me, Holly is something good coming my way today?"

Holly scurried down the path.

"Well then, I suppose I must go now and prepare for the event." Laughing, he called out, "You are a treasure, you know." And he watched her disappear into the shrubbery. "Indeed, run, you wild little beast."

Leisurely walking the narrow path toward the academy, James felt the wind suddenly pick up and close the measly break in the foul weather; it began to drizzle. He glanced up into the heavens. "A little sunshine perhaps? After all, it is Visitor's Day." He hurried in and found Holly standing by the vestibule door. "What is it, girl?" She whined scratching at the door. "You are expecting someone then?" He opened the door,

---

[27] William Cowper (1731 – 1800) English poet. Quoted from *Poems*, Volume 2, by Cowper (1819).

and she hurried out. Later he found her sitting patiently staring out the large window in the vestibule.

* * *

As Holly remained at the window, Maria Collier stared out her window as well. Twisting a loose curl, she wondered if her father and brothers would actually come to Visitor's Day. *Well, if they do not come, I shall not be surprised at all. Only Papa has written me, and a sorry few letters at that.*

Bobbin sat in her chair rehearsing her verse for the Visitors' Day presentation. "What are you going to recite, Maria?"

Still at the window, she sighed. "Oh, I have memorised a limerick from Professor Edward Lear's book."

"Oh, most excellent, Maria, your father will be well pleased. Is it lengthy? You have such an excellent memory."

"No, not so very long, and what are you going to recite?"

Bobbin let out a sigh. "Oh, the very same, except mine is a ditty from Queen Elizabeth. I don't know what else to do. I can't play the piano like you." She gazed up at her in admiration. "You are so clever, Maria."

"Oh, I am not so admirable, Bobbin." Maria exhaled a glimmer of self-truth. "However, I do want to pay my respects to Papa for boarding me here—*if* he should come."

"Indeed." Bobbin nodded, smiling, "I do hope your brothers come, too."

Maria smiled. "That would be too much to hope for." She gazed down at the yardmen and gardeners as they trimmed and chopped, swept and toiled, making the grounds and fountains just right for the guests.

"Come, Bobbin. I am very tired of this room. The rain has finally stopped, and it is lovely out. Not a cloud in the sky, come, let us take a turn in the garden."

"Very well." She took Maria's hand and noticed her nails. "Maria, you really must stop biting them."

"I know, Dormouse, I know."

Sprightly descending the long, grand staircase, they stepped onto the black and white chequered vestibule floor and met the schoolmaster, Holly was at his side. "Good morning, ladies."

Besotted with him, Bobbin's face coloured as she managed a sweet reply.

Eyeing them over his spectacles, he inquired, "Out for a walk?"

"Yes, sir, it has quit raining." Maria took Bobbin's hand giggling. "Come along, Dormouse." She looked back over her shoulder at the schoolmaster, "Good morning, sir."

The girls hurried out into the warm sunshine and straight away to the hedgerow maze.

"Come Bobbin, let us try and get lost." They skipped through the wet, freshly shaved grass and entered the maze.

Rubbing her arms briskly, Bobbin shuddered. "It is cooler in here without the sun on us, Maria."

"Just walk faster, and you shall warm up soon enough."

Venturing one way, then another, they came to a small gardener's window in the old, foot-thick hedge. Maria could see the gravel road approaching the academy and spied a carriage approaching; however, it was not her father's. "Well, Dormouse, a carriage approaches, some guests are arriving early—I would suppose." Her voice was subdued.

"Oh, let me see." Maria lifted her so that she could see for herself. "It is Miss Neilson and the Professor! Make haste, Maria. Make haste. We must hurry to greet them."

"Go on, go on. I shall be there soon enough." A forlorn Maria could not force herself to witness the happy reunion, knowing full well her father's carriage would never come.

Bobbin cried with joy as she broke from the hedge, "Oh, Miss Neilson, Miss Neilson!"

Running as fast as she could, Bobbin's hat flew off, and Holly, fast approaching the frolicking child, knew full well this was a game she was invited to play. With great enthusiasm she nabbed the hat in mid-air—buttons and bows, lace and trim, now ripped to shreds.

Miss Neilson's smile faded at the sight of the monster dog chewing and mangling her dear friend's bonnet. Suddenly the hound lunged at Bobbin, and Miss Neilson gasped in horror. From out of the academy, a black-robed blur rushed past her shouting for Holly to sit.

Bobbin stopped and turned toward the shouts. She was laughing as the dog licked her face. Their jovial congeniality stymied Miss Neilson. *What about that ruffian hound? Is it not to be scolded? Subdued, tied?*

She watched in awed wonder as the gentleman picked up the pieces of Bobbin's hat, and while laughing, petted the dog. He then embraced Professor Halliwell-Phillipps warmly. Her face relaxed. *Why, he must be the Schoolmaster's son, James.*

"Dear Miss Neilson!" cried Bobbin, "I love you. Oh, how I have missed you." She wrapped her arms around her dearest friend, lovingly kissing her face.

"Bobbin," she said, "I was frantic when that huge dog chased after you." She eyed Holly with dismay. "Just look at your lovely bonnet, it is but a rag."

"Oh, that," she said, dismissing such antics. "I am quite used to Holly's playfulness. It is a naughty thing she does, but schoolmaster always buys me another.

"Oh, well, now, I see," she said, wondering at such a place for wild, beastly animals to run free. "You are well, Bobbin?" She turned her around in circles. "I find no bite marks on your hands or arms. No rips or tears in your frock nor gouges in your cheeks," she hugged her, "well, then, they are mine for kissing."

The schoolmaster overheard Miss Neilson's appealing manner, loving Miss Derby as she did with teasing words. He was quite taken with the informality and playfulness from the lady, and he remained in the background with his father.

Bobbin proudly pulled Miss Neilson along as she joyfully greeted the professor by taking his hand and kissing it. "Oh, sir, how very good it is to see you. I am very happy here, sir."

"Indeed, child, I can see for myself that you are very contented." He patted her head. "My son has written to me at how well you are doing."

Bobbin cocked her head in wonder at such a thing. *I have done nothing so important to warrant such a letter.* When she turned to the schoolmaster, he was standing in his best long black robe, her favourite, the one with the wide collar with red satin piping, and as usual, it was lying askew, and as often as not, his spectacles were sitting atop his head. He could not see one myopic foot in front of the other. And dutifully taking his hand, she whispered, "Schoolmaster, your spectacles are atop your head again, sir."

"Thank you, Miss Derby," he whispered.

She straightened his collar.

As he had done a thousand times before, he then straightened and brought his glasses to his nose, adroitly fixing the stems around each ear. He glanced out across the fountain to assure himself that they were on correctly. "Indeed, very good, Miss Derby."

Miss Neilson looked on, smiling at the two.

The professor hemmed. "Miss Neilson, I do not believe you have met my son."

"Sir." She smiled at James, gazing into his soft green eyes. Her mouth parted ever so slightly. She was at a loss for words. Her mind was travelling at great speed, searching, wondering and wishing. The old saying 'the eyes are a window to the soul' moved warmly through her mind. She thought him very much part of the earth, the sky, and the moon. His soft wavy light brown hair framed his ruggedly handsome face. She could hear the faintest chime of distant bells.

James smiled. "So, it is very nice to finally meet you, Miss Neilson." His voice was strong and self-assured; he stood straighter, and for once he did not feel his feet heavy on the ground. His thoughts were crystal clear and calm. Her face was unbelievably beautiful; he knew her to be a kind soul, one he would revere eternally. Holly whined and wiggled at his side.

The schoolmaster's voice seemed far away. Anxious to hear his every syllable, Miss Neilson moved closer. He responded, leaning closer to her. He reached for her hand.

Bobbin stood motionless, bewildered as she watched the two. She glanced at the professor as he offered his arm to her.

"Shall we go in, my dear? The recital will begin soon."

She glanced back at the two. "Is Miss Neilson becoming amazed, professor?"

"Very," he replied, smiling.

* * *

The nervous, but smiling students, escorted their family and guests into the assembly room. Bobbin led Professor Halliwell-Philips to the centre of the room where she had Maria save three seats. She gestured for him to take a seat. "Sir," she whispered, "the seat next to you is saved for Miss Neilson. The other two are for Maria me."

"Very, well, my dear," he nodded with a whisper.

Just as the professor sat, Miss Neilson arrived, and he stood. "This seat next to me is for you, my dear."

"Indeed, Miss Neilson," smiled Bobbin. "Oh, I am very happy you came."

Miss Neilson's face was pink, her smile dreamy.

"Miss Neilson, I do hope you will stay a very long time after the sweet cakes and teas have been served." Chattering in a whisper, Bobbin went on, "I would love to show you my papers."

"Oh, that will be splendid, my dear." She glanced through the program. "Oh, my, you and Miss Collier are due to recite very soon.

There was a commotion at the back of the room.

Everyone turned to find the interruption. It was the wealthy Collier family, Mr John Collier and his sons, Philip and Edward. Looking very distinguished, they took their seats.

Maria's face coloured; her heart pounded.

Bobbin pinched her thumb. "You see, Maria, you worried for nought. I told you all along they would not miss your very first Visitors' Day."

"Well, all the same, I am very sure they are happy that I am out of their hair."

Schoolmaster Halliwell-Phillipps stood and applauded as Miss Herman pounded out a few bars of a Tchaikovsky's concerto. He smiled handsomely; everyone clapped politely. The young student's mother fanned herself modestly; her father clapped loudest. When the clapping eased, the proud schoolmaster invited Miss Derby to the lectern.

Bobbin's sweet face shone as she smiled, first at Miss Neilson, then the professor, then at the schoolmaster. "From the Oxford Book of English Verse, Her Majesty Queen Elizabeth I, composed a limerick, of sorts." She glanced at Maria who stood a few feet from her. "My very good friend and I shall recite limericks, and mine begins thus:

'The daughter of debate
Who discord aye doth sow,
Hath reaped no gain
Where former reign
Hath taught still peace to grow.' " [28]

---

[28] Queen Elizabeth I (1533 – 1603). Quoted from *The Wordsworth Book of Limericks* by Linda Marsh (1997).

Bobbin curtsied and smiled at Maria, it was her turn. The audience clapped, nodding in polite appreciation for such a nice, brief limerick. Professor Barnaby Zany lifted his cat Foss to his lap and clapped but little.

Maria walked to the lectern. She could see her father sitting in the audience. He was handsomely dressed, as usual. *Well, we are a wealthy family after all.* And her eyes moved along to her brothers. Edward smirked. Philip looked stoic and important. *Always trying to mimic Papa.*

She curtsied.

" 'There was a fat lady of Bryde
Whose shoelaces once came untied;
She didn't dare stoop
For fear she would poop,
So she cried and she cried and she cried.' " [29]

There was not a sound in the hall except the soft patter Foss made when her paws hit the floor. Professor Zany leapt to his feet clapping, laughing, and shouting, "Bravo! Bravo!"

Mr Collier's face was white, his lips pursed. Philip strained in his seat. Edward busted out laughing and clapped along with Professor Zany. Miss Neilson's face drew crimson. Bobbin stared up at the ceiling, her fingers twittering behind her back.

Schoolmaster Halliwell-Phillipps remarked something to the effect that the recital was now at a close. He briefly thanked all the students for their very good works, and invited everyone for tea. "Please, the students will escort you to the Mary Arden Garden."

Everyone stood and stared at the laughing Professor Zany, who was still engaged in riotous, raucous conversation with Mr Edward Collier, son of the very wealthy John Collier, Governor of the Bank of England, personal friend, and sound financial advisor to Her Majesty Queen Victoria.

"Papa," said Maria, smiling, "so very good of you to come."

---

[29] This less proper version of limerick by Professor Edward Lear, (1812-1888), Book of Nonsense, (1846,) reworked by anonymous, *The Lure of The Limerick*, (1967).

"Well, dear, it was near impossible that I could be here today... " he caught himself, realising it was a ruse of his clever daughter to exasperate him further. "However, I see it was worthwhile, after all. Indeed, I find your literary pursuits to be in tune with your age." There was a slight smile on his lips.

"Papa," she said incredulously, "you are amused?"

Edward kissed her cheek. "My dearest sister, that was very entertaining. Why, do you know, Professor Zany jumped in glee as you spoke?"

"Indeed," she smiled, "I do, Edward. It was he who suggested it. Would you care to hear the rest of it?"

Philip nudged his way in and kissed her cheek. "Later perhaps, little sparrow, later."

Tears glistened in her eyes. "Really, I am happy to see you all."

Collier took his daughter's hand and kissed it tenderly. "I must say that was sporting of you, in front of everyone, to recite such a limerick, my dear. Am I to say next that I am very proud of you, Maria? And might I add, please, do not dare stoop?"

A huge smiled spread across her face as she tried to read him. "Ah-ha," as she searched his stern countenance, she noticed there, there at the very corners of his mouth. Could it be the beginning of a smile? Giggling, she took his hand. "Papa, you are amused after all."

"I would not admit it in public, Maria," he replied dryly, screwing his mouth up to mask a smile. He felt very self-assured that he had chosen the perfect school for his daughter; she had changed. *Can it be that she is finally beginning to understand me?*

Proud to escort her family to the Tea Garden, Maria took his arm smugly. "Come Papa." She smiled into his glistening eyes. *Can it be that he is finally beginning to understand me?*

* * *

The Garden was in early bloom, though many flowers were not full out, their tender buds and lovely green leaves added a charming backdrop to the secluded garden area. The white wrought iron tables and chairs were situated just off the many paths that curved in and around the shrubbery bushes, hedgerows, and trees. Everywhere one should chance to gander, stone pedestals sat about with quotes etched from the likes of Shakespeare, Voltaire, Plato, Dickens ...

"Bobbin, Bobbin," cried Maria, waving, "over here."

Proudly holding Miss Neilson's hand, Bobbin led her under the ornate copper rose trellis and into the garden. Excited and proud of Miss Neilson, she approached the Collier table.

"Sit with us, Bobbin, please do. There is room enough for twenty." Maria's eyes shone in great warmth as she turned to her father. "Papa, please meet my dearest friend in the world, Miss Derby, and her very good teacher, Miss Neilson."

Mr Collier and his sons stood.

"Miss Neilson, Miss Derby, I am very pleased to make your acquaintance," said Mr Collier. He turned to his sons. "My sons, Philip and Edward."

The brothers bowed politely and bid their extreme good fortune at their meeting.

Mr Collier added, "Please, will you do us the honour of joining our party, Miss Neilson and Miss Derby?"

"Thank you, Mr Collier," Miss Neilson smiled, "however, I really must find Professor Halliwell-Phillipps. I would not want to slight the gentleman. I promised to hold a table. His son, the schoolmaster, wishes to have tea with us as well." Smiling politely, she nodded. "If you will excuse me then?"

"Certainly, Miss Neilson, but as my daughter said, there is room enough for everyone. That is, if it pleases you. Surely the gentlemen shall find you. If you wish, I shall have the servants bring them to our table."

Not knowing the proper etiquette of the very wealthy, Miss Neilson became flustered, she did not want to leave Bobbin nor did she want to slight Mr Collier or the professor. And above all else, she wanted very much to see his son again. Her head swirled with indecision when she heard a familiar voice.

"There you are, my dear," said the kind old professor. "So, I have found you."

Mr Collier, who had remained standing, gestured to him. "Sir, please join us." He pulled out a chair.

Bobbin's little face glowed. She was so proud of her very special friends.

Edward Collier was immediately taken with the lovely Miss Derby's obvious naiveté, her sweetness. He remarked over it in jest, "There now, Miss Derby, it looks as if a Chinese lantern is glowing behind your eyes."

Bobbin's face froze; her smile left. She did not know right off what a Chinese lantern was and felt she had, perhaps, embarrassed Maria in front of her family. "Oh, dear me, sir, I am very sorry for it."

Laughing, Maria took her hand, whispering to her. Suddenly Bobbin's face turned pink, and she sighed in relief.

"Pay him no mind, Bobbin, my brothers tease me the very same way."

Bobbin could see that Edward was flustered, and to ease his embarrassment, she smiled at him. "I have never seen a Chinese lantern anyway, sir."

"You see, Papa, why I love her?" Maria laughed.

Edward's face coloured as he became even more besotted with the dear Miss Derby. She did not guess at his affection. However, everyone else at the table noticed.

Maria nudged Edward. "I think now, my dear brother, you shall be writing and coming to visit me very often?"

The schoolmaster was making his rounds to each table, and at his side, Miss Neilson noticed, was a very handsome lady, an older, dignified looking woman.

"That is Mrs Aesop," said Bobbin. "Our headmistress, she is a widow."

Edward joked, "Aesop? Tell me sister, is she a ..."

Good afternoon, everyone," said the schoolmaster. "Please meet Mrs Aesop, the headmistress at Mary Arden."

Having overheard Edward's jesting remark, Mrs Aesop smiled at him. "No, sir, I am not a fable. [30] Though, I have been known to drop a morsel from my teeth now and again."

Standing immediately, John Collier brought his napkin to his mouth, laughing. Everyone good-naturedly joined in the guffaw. Edward was not at all amused, but remained very much the gentleman for being the butt of his own joke.

There were polite nods and words of introductions around the table as Mr Collier, still smiling over the widow Aesop's witty repartee, became instantly intrigued with her. He invited them to join the table. "James, please do sit with us. Miss Neilson was kind enough to save you all a place."

---

[30] Referring to Aesop (Greek, 6th Century B.C.) Aesop fable: The Dog and the Shadow, Treasury of World Literature, 1956, D. Runes.

James's eyes swept over the very lovely Miss Neilson, again.

In awe at the chemistry between the two, Maria thought them a very good match. She noticed, etched in the stone archway's half-circle: *Love Reasons Without Reason - Shakespeare*. She sighed. "Well, then, that explains it."

"Explains what?" said Bobbin.

Edward stood. "Excuse me, everyone, I have sat long enough. I would like to take the air. Would my dear sister care to join me?"

"Certainly, Edward." Maria stood. "Come along with us, Bobbin. We shall show him our maze."

Bobbin turned to Miss Neilson. "Do you mind? I should not be very long."

"Go, my dear. I am enjoying the air where I sit."

Taking Edward's arm, Bobbin excused herself. Maria took his other arm.

Watching the three casually stroll through the archway and disappear into the lush flower gardens beyond, Mr Collier broke the silence. "My daughter retains her wit, and her heart is come back. I did not expect such a miraculous recovery in so little time." He gazed out over the spring green meadows as they softly touched the early afternoon sky.

The schoolmaster set his cup down quietly. "Sir, if you would allow me to comment?"

"Why, certainly, James."

"Miss Derby has the uncanny ability to bring out the goodness of all those who seek her company. Her innocence and goodwill, her constancy and high expectations of those around her, make it near impossible to act otherwise. I do not believe one would want to disappoint her good appraisal of us."

"How well put, schoolmaster, that you speak of my dearest little friend in such a kind way." Miss Neilson smiled warmly into his eyes. Her heart was touched, indeed, and touched deeply.

Eyeing his son with pride, the professor nodded. "He has always been a philosopher, even as a young boy. Indeed, 'Each one sees what he carries in his heart.' " [31]

---

[31] Johann Wolfgang von Goethe (1749 – 1832) German poet, dramatist, and philosopher. Quoted from *Faust: A Dramatic Poem*, by Goethe, (1860).

"I see very clearly now that you passed along the gift of speech to him, sir," said Philip."

"Thank you, Mr Collier. However, I am quite sure it was his mother from whom he inherited his gift of speech. Often she would quote Fontenelle: 'A well cultivated mind is, so to speak, made up of all the minds of preceding ages; it is only one single mind which has been educated during all this time.' " [32]

"Indeed, Father," said James, reflecting back, "I remember seeing that written amongst Mother's things, I had almost forgotten."

Miss Neilson, shielding her eyes from the sun, looked curious. "Professor, has your wife been gone long?"

His sad eyes scanned the horizon as he pictured his wife's sallow face cradled on the white lace pillow, her stiff hard body pressed dead against the white satin-lined coffin. Now and again a whiff of wild lavender would bring back her dead face, and he hated the flower. "It seems as if she left but yesterday."

Reading the misery in the old gentleman's eyes, John Collier said softly, "Aye, 'What springs from earth dissolves to earth again, and heaven-born things fly to their native seat.' " [33] He slowly shook his head for thinking of his own dear wife. "Oh, then let us move on; we have become too melancholy."

Philip Collier had never before heard his father recite poetry. Ever since his mother's death, it was as if his passion to love again had wilted, curled and dried, decaying to dust within him. He spoke of her but rarely these past few years. And being a virile, handsome man, surely he desired the companionship of a woman.

However, this side of his father was a private one. Never had he witnessed him showing disrespect for her memory, even after the years of grief wore thin the layers of his devotion. *Perhaps he shall never recover from her.*

Miss Neilson closed her eyes, taking in the warm sunshine. She set loose, in a private tone: "I do not want to

---

[32] Bernard Le Bovier de Fontenelle (1657-1757) French author. Quoted from *The New Dictionary of Thought* by Tyron Edwards, (1908).

[33] Marcus Aurelius Antonius (121 – 180) Roman Emperor and philosopher. Quoted from *A Dictionary of Thought* by Tyron Edwards, (1908).

leave this garden, this place. Oh, I could die this very second and not feel the easy slip into eternity. Aah, yes, I am very sure of it."

"I cannot blame you, miss," said the quiet, unassuming Mrs Aesop, who took a chair next to her. "I come here often for the very same reason."

"Excuse me, Mrs Aesop," she quietly apologised. "I did not mean to speak so loudly."

"Oh, nothing to alarm oneself over, not at all, Miss Neilson, this garden is so very lovely, magical at times, so I have found it."

"Indeed it is." She glanced around slowly. "Magical, yes, I would agree."

Not losing notice of the quiet, reflective Miss Neilson, James concluded his conversation at the table. "It is time that I, and Mrs Aesop, escort our good company about the academy. Through a most generous donation, we have acquired the most extensive and well-stocked library in the entire country. Beyond a doubt it is." He stood smiling. "The library is only one of many fine buildings here, although, I think, next to the chapel, it is the most sacred."

Mrs Aesop added, "Mr Mason, the librarian, chooses to sleep there, in a room off to the side. He keeps the fires burning, you see, insisting so to keep the books from damp rot."

"Well, then," replied Mr Collier, "let us go and see this grand library and meet this Mr Mason. Perhaps along the way, we shall find our stray lambs." And, at the notice of everyone, he offered Mrs Aesop his arm.

Miss Neilson smiled agreeably as the schoolmaster offered his to her. "I cannot wait to see such a fine library," she smiled. "And, sir, perhaps afterwards I may visit with Miss Derby, she was eager to show me her school papers. I am anxious to read her works."

"And so you shall," said James. "Her work is superior. You have every right to be anxious to read them."

Feeling proud, Miss Neilson regarded the schoolmaster's high praise for Bobbin. *What a perceptive, intelligent man he is.* Gazing into his eyes, she could feel her face flush, and wondered at what power he had over her. After a few reflective moments walking along the narrow path, taking in the great beauty of the academy grounds, she experienced a sense of near over-whelming gratitude to his father, the wise old professor. Turning to him, she gushed, "And to think, Professor, you made all of this possible. Why, you can see for yourself how Miss Derby is flourishing, and all this in little over one year. Her effect on Mr Collier's daughter, according to his praises, is immense. All of this is such good news to my ears—at the orphanage, there is little hope for most of them."

"Yes, yes, my dear Miss Neilson, I must agree," he said, patting her hand affectionately. "My son has been sending good reports regarding her studies."

James nodded as the three continued walking toward the library, Mr Collier, Mrs Aesop and Phillip following close behind.

"She has a good mind," added the professor. "The only troubling thought is the damaging early years with her drunkard father. And who really knows what has happened to her mother. I believe there is yet more to come from such a bad history. It could possibly be ruinous for her. I cannot think what more to do for the dear girl."

Miss Neilson's heart sank at his words. She had also reflected on the same consequences for the orphan if such a mother should resurface and claim the girl as her own, particularly if she should marry well. She suddenly felt the beauty of the moment slip away; the beauty of the day, this place, the fine institution, a place where her dear friend could, hopefully, break away from such a dismal, horrid past. "Oh, such a mother of Miss Derby, such an anchor! How is one to dismiss such a wretched, dreadful woman wherever she may be? Oh, let us hope she is ..."

Mr Collier hemmed. "Miss Neilson, I thought Miss Derby was an orphan. Is there trouble in our midst? He glanced at Mrs Aesop.

"Apparently, sir, there *could* be trouble," said the schoolmaster in a sombre tone.

"Miss Derby, the young lady that shares a room with my sister? asked Phillip. "What trouble could that innocent young woman possibly bring to anyone? If there was a false bone in her body, believe me, Maria would have found it."

"Oh, not for a moment do I think Miss Neilson means to imply the trouble lies with Miss Derby," said the schoolmaster coming to Bobbin's defence.

"Of course the trouble does not lie with the young lady," interjected Mrs Aesop suddenly. "It is just that she is an orphan with a questionable lineage: one of drunkenness, foul behaviour, imbecility and weaknesses of all sorts. Her father beat her mother often, and at the end, he set a terrible fire ... or so the story goes. Her mother ran away with some gipsies, or perhaps she is dead."

Listening intently, John Collier turned toward her; his naked wrist touching hers. He felt her pulse beating rapidly; her breathing was shallow, her body stiffened. "Ah, yes, 'As is the mother, so is her daughter', Ezekiel, is it? Well, 'The devil can cite Scripture for his purpose. An evil soul, producing holy witness, is like a villain with a smiling cheek.' " [34]

" 'A goodly apple rotten at the heart,' sir," said Mrs Aesop smiling respectfully, wiping an imperceptible tear. "I would not have imagined a banker being so well versed in Shakespeare."

"And that I am not, Mrs Aesop, for I was only repeating what is written here in this very garden. And standing at the foot of a plaque, he regarded the Bard's own words. Gesturing with his foot, he glanced down. "See for yourself, madam." Securing her arm closer to his heart, he inquired, "Mrs Aesop, tell me, have you ever seen the intimate workings of a bank?"

"Never, sir, but for having so little money of my own, I deposit my savings in a shoe."

"Do you?" he said, smiling down onto her face.

"And Mrs Aesop, did you wear the shoe out?" said Philip in a joking manner, thankful the conversation had turned polite.

"Indeed, sir, and the shoe is worn out—not worth a shilling, I assure you."

Also relieved to change such a melancholy subject, they continued on with their light-hearted banter.

"There they are, sir," said Mrs Aesop as she waved at Collier's children, but they soon disappeared again.

"My daughter is extremely fond of this Derby girl, Mrs Aesop. I should think nothing would ever dampen the orphan's spirit."

"Aye, Mr Collier," she replied. "Miss Derby is strong. However, society is stronger. You yourself must know that, sir. Perhaps her only real happiness in life would be in teaching. What honourable, decent family would ever consider their son to wed such a history as Miss Derby's? No, I have thought long and hard over these particular types of young ladies who come here. I try and mould them to be the best sort of lady. Ah, best

---

[34] Shakespeare, *The Merchant of Venice*, Act 1, Scene 3.

sort of woman, with expectations not too high, you see." She nodded. "High enough to please polite society, and nothing more."

Collier grew silent; his stomach felt queasy as he mulled over her exact words *'expectations high enough to please polite society'?* He looked over at the brooding face of the schoolmaster and then to Mrs Aesop. "Surely you cannot be serious. I cannot imagine what a lady schooled in this fine academy would wish to aspire to, but I cannot fathom my daughter being a mere "genteel-ion" for anyone's simple, polite conversation, Mrs Aesop, and Miss Derby's spirit is too strong. Why, already she demands respect and equality."

"As should women everywhere, sir," she returned in a gentle tone. "No, sir, poor Miss Derby does not have the money, prestige, or family connections to command such a streak of individualism, Mr Collier. Why, the very same streak, if not kept in check, would certainly destroy her. Yes, perhaps the learned scholars of Mary Arden Academy are more right than wrong; the young lady should be persuaded to remain here, shrouded, I am sorry to say."

Reading the sadness in Mrs Aesop's eyes, he light-heartedly scoffed, "What is all this doom? Come now, I have much to see and very little time before I must mingle among the money changers in London." He glanced around impatiently for his daughter and son. "Edward and Maria should have returned by now."

It was as if they heard his words. The three came around the hedgerow almost bumping into the professor and Miss Neilson. There was an exclamation of delight at the run-in. "Oh, we got lost in the hedgerow maze."

Maria suddenly noticed how close Mrs Aesop was standing to her father. *Papa is smiling. Hmm, odd that.* It occurred to her that she had never seen him with a woman before, except her mother, and never so near as he was to Mrs Aesop. *He is touching her.* Maria smiled kindly at Mrs Aesop. *Her arm is nestled so close to Papa's heart.*

Suddenly her childish desire to keep him all to herself gave way to a deeper wish to see him happy once more, to see him smile again. At that moment she felt her mother's presence; felt her cool silvery lips kiss her forehead. She touched the very spot with her fingertips. "I love you, Mama."

Collier took her hand. "Maria?"

"Yes, Papa?"

"Well, I was wondering ... you looked so far away."

She squeezed his hand. "Come Papa and Mrs Aesop, let us walk a little."

Edward and Miss Derby, still side by side, followed. Edward could not help but notice his sister's face. "And now the Chinese lantern swings behind your eyes, Maria."

Chapter 13 – The Missing Journal

Each present joy or sorrow seems the chief. [35]

Standing with her hands on her hips, Bobbin looked perplexed. "Dear me, Maria, I cannot find my journal. I left it under my pillow. Every day of life I have put it there. And now, this morning, it is gone."

"I cannot imagine that someone would have taken it." She walked around Bobbin's bed and looked under it and around it. "Think now, when was it that you last wrote in it?"

"I tucked it under my pillow, just before I snuffed the candle last night. I then said my prayers."

They sat on the bed, thinking. Taking another turn about the room, Maria rubbed her chin in thought. "Who should be so interested in your journal?" She stopped. "Come, let us see if mine is missing, as well."

Bobbin followed Maria's quick steps into her room. "I hide mine under my mattress."

Bobbin leaned over her shoulder and watched as she picked up the mattress—it was there.

"Well now, mine is safe. Perhaps Mrs Aesop or one of the maids took it by mistake, thinking perhaps it was a book belonging in the library. After all, it was Visitors' Day yesterday."

"Yes, but I wrote in it last night."

---

[35] Shakespeare. Quoted from "Miscellaneous Poems of Shakespeare," in *Aphorisms from Shakespeare*, by George and Barker Bury, (1812).

Maria shrugged. "Oh, let us go to dinner, maybe when we return it will reappear." Maria took her hand. "Come on then, we shall eat and search for it later."

Descending the stairway, Bobbin sighed. "I hope I find it, Maria. Who should want to read what I have written?"

"Are you very upset, Bobbin? We could walk in the garden rather than eat if you wish, or search the library shelves."

"Oh, no Maria, it is no bother," she hesitated, "but, I ... I had written so much about my feelings. Miss Neilson gave me the journal a long time ago—when I was an orphan." Laughing, she corrected herself, "Well, I am still an orphan—but she wanted me to write about my father. I was, you see, always telling her about him. I was so little then, and I do not know how I should remember back that far again without it, Maria. The journal has been with me many years. Oft times I would sleep with it next to my heart ... as you do with your mama's cameo."

Maria nodded in sincere solemnity. "I understand."

Bobbin felt a wave of good cheer move through her heart. "Oh, let us not fret, Maria. I know someday it shall be returned."

* * *

He sat in front of his massive open hearth as the fire blazed. Sipping the last of his brandy, he sighed heavily, reached for the journal and opened it.

August 10, 1851, my journal, Bobbin Derby, My father, William Derby, London, born in the month of March and died in December, 1850. I cannot remember exactly my mother's name, maybe it was Mary, nor can I remember her face. My name is Bobbin Derby and I was born in July, 1841. I do not have any other family, but I wish I had a dear sister or brother to love. My teacher, Miss Neilson, told me to write every day in this journal the very words I have spoken to her about my other life, a life I want to remember, but somehow cannot. This then is my journal.

> *11 Jan It was a kind face, I remember. He had*
> *brown eyes and brown hair and a very long beard—my*
> *Papa.*

The gentleman noted there were sporadic entries in her journal, by times weeks, months apart, and he found some pages had been ripped out, some scorch marks. Months missing, but he continued reading:

> *I cannot but cry when I try to remember more of*
> *him. With bad dreams when I do, and so for relief from*
> *my head, my eyes hurt and I put this away...*
> *30 January It is raining this morning. There is very*
> *little light and it is cold, very cold. I put my fingers in my*
> *mouth to keep my teeth from chattering and waking*
> *those around me. Papa was a kind man.*
> *20 February I do not like to see it when people fall*
> *and hurt themselves, while others laugh, I cry. It puts to*
> *mind something mean.*
> *27 February I do not like the darkness. Miss Neilson*
> *gives me candles which she can spare so I can burn them.*
> *The darkness hides devils that roam around at night in*
> *my room. I can smell them even during the day.*
> *1 March I can hear a baby and children screaming*
> *when I sleep, and so I try to stay awake to find out where*
> *they are, but it is so cold I close my eyes and cover my*
> *ears for the noise. I see my dog Hester huddling with the*
> *others... but I cannot remember who they are.*
> *I must write a happy thing so I can see better... I*
> *thought a happy thought, being spring is very near; I*
> *can smell it in the air when I gather the wood for the*
> *cook.*
> *10 March I remember a lady across the room,*
> *sunshine bright upon the mass of curls, dark black curls*
> *and then the vision disappears as quickly. Who is this*
> *lady, I will wonder.*
> *13 March It is a rainy day again. Miss Neilson was*
> *crying since Willie McCombs had to go. A farmer came*
> *to get him and he was rough. She tells me often that it*
> *had to be a good family that should take me. I love her. I*
> *did not have bad dreams for a little while.*

10 April The devils are back, but I do not want to write about them, they are very clever and can read. I tell Miss Neilson about how their breath is so foul and she holds me since my head aches.

15 April Plain things about the kitchen bring back to my mind ideas and familiar dishes scattered about a table. The fire-poker, the sweep-broom, my papa's chair, the roller.

June – I hate to put my head down anymore, so I read and read, so I can dream happy things. At light, during the day there are pleasant things to see and remember. I have told Miss Neilson that I have become a young lady now.

6 July This month I am ten and four years of age. My body is growing out in certain places and Miss Neilson has fitted me like a lady should be. I have met a girl named Maria. She is very spoiled and rich, but her heart is good. She wears very beautiful clothes.

30 July Last night I smelled a sweet touch of rain … and suddenly I saw before me two children playing … and then the vision disappeared as fast as a summer rain shower. The children were pleasant enough and seemed somewhat familiar.

10 August I have made good friends with Professor Halliwell-Phillipps because he owns the bookstore, and now I will work there and he lets me read anything I wish. He is a very good gentleman and we talk long hours about the stories in the books.

1 September Professor Halliwell-Phillipps gave me a book to read, David Copperfield, by the very pleasant Mr Dickens, who betimes, brings his family in to visit. He told me he was once very poor too. I get along very well with them. But I have never met Mrs Dickens.

19 March I have finished the book and feel sorry for David C. I know very well his feeling and I asked the professor to say so to Mr Dickens. I told Miss Neilson how thankful I was to have her for such a kind teacher– and no mean stepfather like in Mr Dickens book. But … what of my mother? When I try to remember her there come betimes a flashing vision that I have of her, crying, I think, crying and running away. Oh, I hope she found a happy place. I have not thought of Hester in such a long time … my friend.

1 April Miss Susanna Neilson told me tonight that I was invited to go to Mary Arden Academy to study for a long year and some. I was chosen by Professor Halliwell-Phillipps at the bookstore, I will get new travelling clothes and shoes! New, I cannot believe it all.

1 May I love this academy – I do, I have the most beautiful bed and room. My clothes are beautiful and warm and I have new shoes that fit. I have a hairbrush for my very own, and for once in my life, I comb my hair every night and every morning. We all take frequent baths. And I have a tub to myself with warm water. I did not know about lavender soap and how heavenly one should smell. To put my feet into clean stockings every day is the best thing ... to sleep at night in such luxurious quietness and warmth and cleanliness... oh such good fortune.

29 May Last night Maria was crying for her family. I went to her and held her and she told me I would be the perfect sister. I realised then that loneliness visits the wealthy as well as the poor... And I finally have a friend! Miss Maria Collier. We are roommates. She is very wealthy, and her heart is very good and she does not mean to be nasty. I tell her in private that she will grow up very well despite her spoiled ways. She despises that I say those things, but since our happiest time the very first night of our stay at the academy when Holly, the Schoolmaster's dog, jumped into my bed and Maria and I had a pillow fight, we have been getting on very well. She seems to be growing used to every person, rich or poor. I told her those very words and how I knew about loneliness with the little children at the orphanage and how I would help them and love them, and how they loved me too. Though I could tell by the look on her face that she did not always believe me when I would tell her some of our misfortunes there. I invited her some time to come and stay with me at the orphanage to see for herself, but 'perhaps' was all she would say.

There were some pages ripped from the journal he noticed, and continued reading,

*9 April Visitors' day tomorrow, but for one of
Maria's bad dreams I thought how I have not had any
nightmares in a while, and what should have prevented
them I do not know, but by the grace of God I am very
thankful. And I told Maria about them and now they are
no more. She remembers her Mama and misses her so. I
think missing her is the cause, especially when the
bleeding comes, I have noticed that monthly time and
told her of the coincidence. And I told her to tell God of
the sorrow in her heart, I assured her He would lessen it.
He was very good at things like that... easy things for
such a God to do. That made her laugh... easy things for
a God to do. Ask for little things... one must not be too
greedy, I told her. And one day I will ask God to help me
find my mama.*

The gentleman closed the journal for there was nothing
more written; only a few blank pages remained.

The End, he thought, slowly shaking his head. Even God
cannot change the past. [36] He stood by the fire, thinking of a
plan and when the solution came to his mind, he smiled.

---

[36] Agathon (448 – 400 BC) Greek poet. From *Aristotle, Nicomachean
Ethics*, Book VI, sect. 2, 1139b. (350 BC).

Chapter 14 – The Search Begins for Bobbin's Mother

A shallow brain behind a serious mask,
An oracle within an empty cask,
The solemn fop [37]

Detective Brown closed his office door and locked it. Adjusting his hat, he descended the outside stairs and hurriedly stumbled off the last step. He did not notice the dead seagull lying at his feet and stepped on its head, cracking its decaying skull and smearing the foamy red cranial matter into the tiny crevices of his shoe, but he didn't hear a thing, he was in a hurry. The private detective had an appointment this morning. A very important client, a new one, and he meant to be there on time.

* * *

"Yes, sir," replied Brown. Shall I write what I find weekly or do you wish that I report to you in person?"

"I prefer, Mr Brown, that you report to me in person, weekly."

"Very good, sir." And the private detective left the serious looking man to his thoughts. Rambling about the busy London

---

[37] William Cowper (1731 – 1800) English poet. Quoted from *Modern Authors* by Gething, (1838).

streets, his old gig veered helter-skelter down the narrowest of allies, over curbs, porches and cats; never mindful of the angry shouts. Brown's rickety old gig finally pulled up at Tottenham Court Cemetery. Looking puffed up, and in such a serious tone, he threatened all those within earshot, "Mr Thomas Brown, I am, private detective. Make way, make way."

Beggars scurried as he stepped onto the walk. He perused the filthy street and shook his head. Thinking the air close, he wiped his nose for the stench. Brown pushed his way confidently through the heavy black wrought iron cemetery gate, highly annoyed that muddy water was seeping into his boots. He continued to walk about the soft, squishy grass, tramping over the sacred ground as he searched the grey moss-stained gravestones, one after the other.

Finally, he spied what he had come for. "Ah-ha, exactly what I thought." He removed his card, jotted the facing on the tomb and headed back to the cemetery office. Once inside the dingy, dark and dank place, he patted in and around the inner pocket of his vest searching for his identification papers. A satisfied look crossed his face as he pulled out the proper material.

Without making eye contact with the weird figure of a man standing behind the counter, he hemmed. "These are my papers, sir. I am investigating the disappearance of a certain Mrs Derby of Tottenham Court Parish, 'long time ago. I have discovered, there buried in the pauper's lot, four Derbys. I found a William Derby and three children. What do you know of such matters concerning that particular family?"

The rotund, self-imposing detective leaned on the counter, now eye-to-eye with the graveyard sexton who looked every bit the evil part of someone who should know about cadavers, death, and bribes. However, such a man, living alone in the allotted cemetery abode, was not in the least intimidated by the detective's roll of papers lying before him, and the old gravedigger, Mr Fossor, leaned into the face of detective Thomas Brown and replied with foul, sour breath, "Fire." While he fumbled with the detective's papers, pretending he could read, he grunted and broke wind.

"God in heaven, man!" Detective Brown moved back toward the door. "A fire killed 'em, you say?"

The small office quickly filled with odorous stink. "Damn you, foul specimen," grumbled the detective. He opened the door wide and took a deep breath. "Come this way, you," commanded the detective, "and hold your buttons."

"See here," replied the cemetery ghoul, "I'm an old man, I aren't used to someone shoutin' orders. Besides that," he pointed to the floor, "look at the mud on me floor you tramped in."

"Talk about the Derbys and make it hasty." Brown stood at the open door, one eye on the man's rotten teeth, the other on his own muddy boots.

"A fire burned 'em all up." Fossor scratched his cruddy head. "Years ago, now. Landlady, Old Mrs Waller, found drunken Bill Derby on the floor with a burnin' stick, the kids somewhere a lyin' in a closet where's they found 'em, charred—just bones is all. Waller went a runnin' for help, and when the constable came back, the place had burned up, and that's the end of it."

"What happened to the mother, Mrs Derby?" said Brown, breathing through his mouth.

"Don't know that one, but ol' drunken Derby struck her regular as a clock." And the filthy old gravedigger laughed at the pun.

"Ten shilling to shut your mouth," snapped Brown.

"Aye, ten shilling, then. I heard the missus left after hearin' all her children burned up crisp. Them workin' the streets say she puked, screamed and staggered toward the river pullin' at her hair. Me thinks she jumped in ... that is what I knowed—all I knowed."

"Ten shilling more," squeezed the detective.

"Nay, a hundred shilling more, there ain't no more." And the old man hacked up an oyster, spit and watched it disappear through the stinking haze of tobacco smoke.

The keen-nosed detective shook his head. "If you remember anything more, Fossor, come see me." And he dropped ten shillings on the counter and left. Just as he was about to board his gig, he remembered the old man's comment about beggars saying they saw Mrs Derby heading toward the river.

He looked up and down the street and, noticing the Thames just up the alley, he decided to walk it. Turning onto Oxford Street, he found an old hag sheltering herself in a tavern doorway. "You live around here long?"

"I were born here, sir."

"Know of a certain Mrs Derby, Tottenham?"

"Aye, went mad ove' kids being burned up, but dint jump in the river like everybody say. I knowed for a good reason she found a convent—Sisters of Charity set her mind to right."

"St. Patrick's?"

"Maybe." Picking her nose, she looked away.

Brown gave her a shilling.

"St. Pat's," nodded the snaggletoothed old hag.

"What's your name? He asked.

"My name's Waller." She scratched at a flea. "Call me *The Landlady*."

Handing her his card, Brown nodded. "See me if you remember anything." He headed back up the street. Passing many alehouses and taverns, he thought how good a tankard of ale would feel to his dry, parched throat. However, he continued on, and when he found his gig, he aimed it toward St. Patrick's Church.

★ ★ ★

"That was long ago, sir," said the housekeeper as she stood in the doorway of St. Patrick's Convent-House. "The only nun still here from them days is Sister Theresa, but she is very old."

"What do you do here?"

"Sir, I cook and clean and help the fathers and the sisters."

"I'd like to speak with anyone who's been around here longer than five years." Irritated that the housekeeper held the door open only slightly, he asked curtly, "What's your name?"

"Mrs Webster, sir."

"Well then, I should like to interrogate someone. Show me in then, madam."

"No one is home, sir." Her eye darted nervously.

"I thought this was a place where nuns lived?"

"That it is, sir," she replied with a lisp. He noticed her front teeth were missing.

"Where'd they go, then? Ain't no priests about either?"

"They are all in prayer. Perhaps four or five of the clock, until then, they mustn't be disturbed. I am not allowed ..."

"Ever hear of a Mrs Derby? Would have been here around maybe five year ago?" He tapped his hat. "Maybe a little mad in the head. Her children and husband burned to death in a bad fire. I heard she came here."

She shook her head. "I ain't allowed to talk about visitors, sir." Sniffing the air, she added, "I must go now for cookin' dinner. You come back some other time." Quietly she closed the door in his face.

Staring blankly at the ancient oak for a few seconds, Brown decided to try his luck at the church. Squinting through the thick bubble-glass windows, he could see candles burning. Following the stone path alongside the holy house, he found an unlocked door and entered the dark, quiet sanctuary whereupon he found five nuns kneeling at a statue of Mary. They were tending to at least twenty burning candles.

A priest crossed himself as he moved about fiddling with some silver bowls. Brown took a seat in one of the ornately carved pews and watched curiously as the holy people did their holy work.

"Sir," came soft-spoken words at his back, "Mrs Webster said you wanted to speak with a priest?" An old man wearing a black robe and a white collar whispered reverently, "Come this way." His thick solid head of white hair was a stark contrast to his black garb. Bits of old hair and dander lay about his shoulders. "I am Father Macy."

The bent-backed old priest shuffled out of the church, Brown followed. They traversed through a small vegetable garden on the sunny side of the church courtyard. Shortly they came to a heavy oak door studded with black iron clasps. The priest unlatched the well-worn iron handle and the door swung in easily. He stood back. "After you, sir."

The detective found a good, strong fire burning. Evidently the old man had just been there, for one did not have such a fire and expect to leave it for very long. It smelled like recent tobacco and ginger spice inside the small quarters. On the rough-honed table lay an open book, a religious book, an old one, at that, for stains and ripped pages. On the counter many wine bottles were lined up neatly, some full—most empty. Clean pewter bowls and cups were stacked alongside. There was a fresh white tablecloth yet folded on the sideboard. The detective noted it all; it was his job.

"Come, sir, sit by the fire." The hunched-back old priest gestured toward an empty chair. "Please, sit down. A glass of wine?"

Not waiting for an answer, the priest poured. "You have come here interested in Mrs Derby?" Smiling, he turned and set the glass on the table in front of Thomas Brown, smiling.

He then poured himself a drink and took a chair opposite the detective.

"Thank you," Brown hesitated at addressing him as Father and said, "sir." The detective reached into his waistcoat and took out one of his cards. "I'm a private detective. I have been hired to locate Mrs Derby, if she is still alive. A Mrs Waller at Oxford Street said some nuns here took her in years ago, said she didn't jump in the river over the death of her family."

Brown took a large gulp of wine, set the half-empty glass down rudely and wiped his mouth with the back of his hand.

The priest pretended not to notice the detective's disrespect for such a fine wine and slowly brought his glass to his lips, sniffed it as if it was such a vintage and reverently sipped at the edges—savouring every little bit before setting the glass down, gently.

His crinkled eyes smiled at the detective. "Yes, Mrs Derby was here for a little while. She lost all her children and her husband in the terrible fire. She was a Catholic, Mr Brown. She came here often, confused and terrified. Her husband, Mr Derby, threatened the vicar of their church for helping his ... his wife 'the Catholic dog' as he often called her.

"It seems Mr Derby beat her severely one night. She was with child, and she came here, bleeding. The sisters delivered a death-born baby. That very night while she lay in that bed there," he motioned with his head to the exact one, "we heard shouts, whistles, and the frantic cries of the town's people as they all ran in the direction of her house.

"When Sister Theresa ran to give aid, she returned within the hour praying fervently. She then pulled me aside. Mrs Derby suddenly sat up, her skin grey and wet, her eyes dark as pitch. Sensing that something terrible happened, she got up from the bed and walked over to us, crying, 'Father, what has happened?'

"I told her the fire was at her house, and they found the remains of her children and husband, Mr Derby. She staggered out the door, walked to her house and viewed the charred remains. Sister and I walked with her. While she stood there in her bloodstained skirt, ripped blouse, and tangled hair, vomit suddenly spewed from her innards; she sobbed and choked. We went to her, but she pushed us away and staggered back to this very room and lay down on that very bed.

"We heard the following morning that the drunken Derby set the place ablaze. Must have fallen and couldn't get up ... died right there; his children hiding in the woodbin.

"Several weeks later she left us, and we have never heard from her again. I have my suspicions that she is the very one who sends money for the poor, because every Christmas morn, money arrives here at the church."

"Did you happen to save the envelope that the money came in?" asked the detective.

"No, sir, it comes by private courier."

"Hmm." Brown removed his hat and scratched his head. "When did the fire happen?"

"24 December, sir, years ago."

"How old was Mrs Derby?"

"I would say twenty and five and no more."

"I see. Tell me, what was her name?"

"Mary Posea Derby."

The detective looked impressed. "You remember her maiden name then?"

"Oh, yes, Posea was her maiden name. Now, the Posea's were a good Catholic family, but Mr Derby hated Catholics, and she was beaten for that too—forced to be an Anglican." He pursed his lips.

"Posea, eh?"

"Hmm," he nodded, "she pronounced her name like the flower 'posy', detective."

"What sort of name might that be?"

"French, however, everyone on her side is dead now too—and long gone. No Derby's left, either."

"I see. Well, sir, you have my card. When the time nears for that private courier to come, you must contact me in a hurry. I want to speak with him."

"Yes, certainly you would, detective." And the old priest remained sitting, worn out from the little effort of conversation. His fragile head drooped as he ritualistically reached for his wine. Slowly raising the glass, swirling it as a connoisseur would, sniffing it with favour, then delicately tipping it to his watery, parting lips, the dark-purple fruit-of-the-vine slowly coated the old priest's throat. His thin, rheumy eyes closed in anticipated relief. "Ah, bless you."

Detective Brown gulped the remainder of his and stood. "Can find my own way, Macy."

* * *

The detective sorted through his papers, wrote a few additional notes, and then carefully slipped everything into his leather satchel. He didn't want to keep the gentleman banker waiting and so ordered his gig to be readied within the half of the hour. When he finally arrived at the Bank of England, he stood before the doorman. "See here, my good man, do I look presentable? He turned around. "You know, dirt, dust, dung ..."

"Aye, sir, nothing out of the ordinary."

"Very well." He tipped his hat, forgetting to tip the doorman. He entered the massive grey-stone *Old Lady*. [38] Promptly a young, stern-faced bank clerk, who, after examining Brown's papers, nodded. "Right this way, sir."

Brown followed the skinny, nervous young man through a glass door; etched in its centre was an ornately designed letter that he thought could possibly resemble a "*C.*" He was led up a flight of carpeted steps patterned with red and gold swirled flowers. The ascent was a quiet, subdued one, the only noise being the annoying squeak of the lad's right shoe.

Once reaching the top, the clerk turned to his left. After only a few steps past a potted palm, Brown stood in front of a door. It had a highly polished brass filigree door-knob that looked like a ferocious lion roaring for ...

"This way, sir."

The lad held the door as Brown moved quietly by him and into a long, wide hallway. He found young men hunched over their desks, their scorched lamps burning as wavy black fumes dissolved into the smudged ceiling. Their white shirt sleeves exposed a few thread-worn cuffs, their fingers ink-stained. Wadded balls of paper were tossed near and about the rubbish bins that sat very near the anxious, waning fire smouldering in the oft-used, once milk-white marble hearth that sat black-bellied on the opposite wall. The place smelled like a tallow factory.

Brown moved through their space without one head lifting in curiosity, though the seasoned detective knew every man there was fully aware of his presence. It was only the

---

[38] The Old Lady was the nickname for the Bank of England, 1797, The City of London, 1964.

scrape, itch, and squirt of their pens that was intelligible before he was finally ushered into an inner office and politely requested to take a seat ... and wait.

Brown sat, positioning his thin, shiny-butted trousers onto the cold leather chair. When he glanced to his right, he was startled to see an austere looking clerk sitting stiff and proper at a desk next to him.

How could I have missed him?

Acknowledging Detective Brown with a nod, the clerk peered at his hatless head to his rather well-worn oxfords. Brown knew the look and pulled his less than spotless shoes beneath him. Hoping to move the clerk's critical eye away from himself, he perused the oil paintings on the wall. They were of the English countryside, and after expelling a bit of phlegm into the rubbish bin, he commented aloud to the clerk about one of the scenes. He was promptly ignored. The hook-beaked clerk remained silent for what seemed an hour more, and when the chimes rang two o' clock, the clerk stood. "Sir."

Detective Brown obediently stood.

"This way."

* * *

"Gruesome details, sir. Gruesome," said Brown, "one of the worst cases I have ever been involved in." The detective remained sitting as the banker stood before the hearth, hands behind his back, facing the fire.

Brown went on, "Yes, sir, the three Derby children were found huddled in the closet, just charred remains, and the drunken father lying on the floor, crisp. Landlady says he started it, but must have fallen and couldn't find his way out. Mrs Derby was away, secreted. He gave her a beating the night before, apparently. She was with child, but delivered a death-born at a convent up the street. She was hiding from the very devil himself. And on the very night of the fire, they, ah, at St. Patrick's, the Sisters of Charity, took her in even though she wasn't allowed to be a Catholic any more."

Looking pale and sickened, the banker nodded. "Did you get the names of the children, Mr Brown?"

"Yes, sir. The oldest was a girl, Stella Babette, the second was William Percy, and the youngest was a girl, Jane Mary."

"They *all* perished, Mr Brown?"

"Yes, sir. They found the charred remains all stuck together in the woodbin. Three heaps, so they told me."

"And what of the dog, Hester, Mr Brown? What happened to the dog?"

"Ah, what dog, sir?"

Chapter 15 – The Mary Arden Key

I have here only made a nosegay of culled flowers, and have brought nothing of my own but the thread that ties them together. [39]

The debate over which student was to receive the coveted Mary Arden Key was held in the schoolmaster's office. Passing the Key was a long, proud tradition, and the stern-faced, sober professors took their job seriously. When they filed into the office they found a nice fire quietly warming the room; servants scurried about.

Directly in the middle of the massive, highly polished black oval shaped hardwood table lay Foss, legs tucked beneath her, tail wrapped securely at her side; she minded not one thing that she was surrounded by the schoolmaster, Mrs Aesop, and ten professors.

It had now been near twelve months since Bobbin Derby and Maria Collier first stepped into the halls of the academy, and now graduation ceremonies were nearing. The faculty had to decide soon who would receive the award. Five candidates had been singled out.

Bringing the table to order, Halliwell-Phillipps shuffled his papers. "I shall read the names again. They are, alphabetically: Miss Collier, Miss Collins, Miss Derby, Miss

---

[39] Michel de Montaigne (1533 – 1592) French essayist. Quoted from *The Works of Montaigne*, by Hazlitt (1845).

Mansfield, and Miss Tillyard. I shall begin with Professor Zany; your comments please."

"I cast my vote in favour of Miss Collier. In my opinion, she has grown the most in all areas of study. She now hesitates before speaking, obviously thinking about the chosen word—as proper young ladies should. Her diversity in subject matter intrigues me. She, being different from all the rest, snoops."

There came murmurs from around the table, but he spoke over them, "She snoops into fields of study far different from the others. She enjoys mathematics and the sciences and can calculate figures in her head as if she were a machine. She is simply brilliant. When I put a problem out, she has the answer almost simultaneously."

"I quite agree," remarked Professor Smithe. "With one exception, Edward, he smirked. "She did adore your required reading of that ... that ridiculous *Book of Nonsense*, such silly limericks, to be sure. And for that, I believe, you found her brilliant—but certainly not worthy of the Mary Arden Key. I am leaning toward Miss Tillyard, certainly—only finding one fault in that she simply excels in one area only, literature."

Professor Brown tapped the table with his index finger. "Oh, certainly she can quote Shakespeare, but she does not always *feel* the words, Professor Smithe."

"What then of Miss Collins? I tell you she is the most pleasant and beautiful young lady here. Her lustrous red hair ... she acts the type very much to wear the Key. She is pleasant and knowledgeable, perhaps not brilliant, no, but so worthy." Professor Hughes went on, "She grasps the concepts of thoughts and ideas very quickly ..."

Professor Winston chimed in, "Yes, yes, but she cannot always put them in order, professor. No, I believe she is too gooey."

"Gooey?" The professors mumbled, frowned, and slowly shook their heads. "Precisely, professors, beauty is only skin-deep, as the old saying goes. We need more than beauty. You must know that she is merely gooey and will always and forever remain gooey."

Mrs Aesop spoke up, "What about Miss Derby? Are we to ignore the brightest ornament in the school? She is by far the most talented and charming of the mix. Perhaps not as accomplished as Miss Collier in figures; however, she has a memory that far exceeds anything I have ever witnessed. She has the uncanny ability to put one at ease. We have all been witness to that, what with her more than pleasant ways and exemplary humble manners."

"But, Mrs Aesop, she is an orphan. We have never given the Key to an orphan," said Professor Waller. All the others nodded in agreement.

"All the more reason," said the headmistress. "She is worthy. Cannot we, such learned individuals from such an institution of free thought, break from the old mould of worthless notions because a human being, through no fault of his or her own, is motherless and fatherless? We must."

"That is the worry, Mrs Aesop," replied the schoolmaster as the professors turned their ear to him. "We do not know of her mother. Is she dead or alive?"

Everyone nodded in agreement. The schoolmaster continued, "If we pass the Key to Miss Derby and her mother suddenly calls to claim her, what then Mrs Aesop?"

"Sir, I do not think that will happen. Why, she has been gone these many years. How should such a woman ever hear of such an honour bestowed upon her daughter? I am very sure, if she is still alive, that she travels in low company," she continued, "ignorant of such esteem and importance."

The schoolmaster shook his head slowly. "Very well, then. Shall we sleep on this discussion and then cast our votes first thing tomorrow morning, here in my office?"

Everyone nodded.

"Very well, if no one has anything more to say then you are all excused."

Compiling his papers, Schoolmaster Halliwell-Phillipps was interrupted by the headmistress. "Sir, why didn't you say something on behalf of Miss Derby?"

Glancing around to make sure they were alone, he frowned. "Mary, I too, have reservations about Miss Derby. After all, she is ... well, you and I have discussed the possibility of offering her a position here as a teacher. If she accepts such a position, what good would the Key do her here? We need a young lady who moves in a higher, wider society to do her works. Maria Collier would be the very one. She will be associating with only the very best of society, no doubt marry an excellent fellow of the highest rank. No, I believe the best good would be gained by having her wear the Key."

"But what if Bobbin does not stay on? What if she chooses to make a new life? She would make the very best emissary.

Imagine an orphan setting such an example for others. It would turn out to be such a miracle, sir."

James exhaled wearily. "A miracle indeed, Mary."

Wringing her hands, she cried, "I find myself in such a twist of fate, sir." She cleared her throat. "I gave Mr John Collier's father permission to write to me. We have been getting along very handsomely. I have been invited to London after graduation." She blushed, twisting her hands. "I do realise his daughter Maria is superior and would make a fine recipient of the Key, but for becoming so very fond of her and my natural affections toward Bobbin, sir, I find myself in a very compromising position."

James pretended surprise at her confession regarding Mr Collier's affections toward her. "Indeed, Mary, I am very happy for you. He is a very good man." He walked to the hearth with a sheepish grin. "Mary?"

"Yes?"

"I, too, have a confession." His voiced lowered, "I have been communicating with Miss Neilson for many months now."

With a not-such-a-surprised look, she nodded. "Oh, I see. Hmm, well then, we are in a pickle, you and I."

Chapter 16 – The Gentleman Dies

One short sleep past, we wake eternally,
And death shall be no more; death, thou shalt die. [40]

It was early morning in the month of June, two months past graduation ceremonies at the Mary Arden Academy, when James Halliwell-Phillipps felt something feather over his body while he slept. It seemed more than a mere dream that stirred him to awaken abruptly. While lying there, wondering about the feeling, he listened as if a particular noise could have disturbed his slumber. He heard nothing out of the ordinary. Dismissing the cockcrow, for it was too early even for a rooster. He assured himself all was well. "No, no need to worry, all is quiet, save Holly's deep slumber." She lay curled at the foot of his bed, undisturbed.

And then a pleasant thought of the very lovely Miss Susanna Neilson moved through his mind. His body relaxed, and he closed his eyes, blaming his yearning to see her sooner than next week the very reason why he awoke at such an hour.

It was the warm morning breeze that floated through his room that aroused him this time. Slowly waking, he thought it to be a beautiful day. There was not the familiar heavy scent of rain in the air. Already the power of sunlight streamed into his room. He thought, again, of Miss Neilson and he missed her. "But all good things come in waiting."

---

[40] John Donne (1572 – 1631) English poet. From *Sonnet X Death Be Not Proud* (1609).

Holly woke and yawned. She glanced up at James and hopped onto the bed. "Good morning, girl." She wiggled and licked his face.

"It is a beautiful morning, girl. Just listen to all the joyous songbirds. You and I will have a very good walk."

He swung his legs off the bed and stretched his way to the window. *Hmm, a carriage I do not recognise, but wait—yes, it is Father's.*

He was puzzled all the more, when who should be escorted from it but Miss Neilson. A cold chill ran through his body; *something is wrong.* He hurried to dress when a knock came. "Come."

"Sir," replied the manservant, "Miss Neilson has come to see you—a most urgent matter."

"I will be right down, Caldwell."

He bowed his withdrawal. "Yes, sir."

James rinsed his mouth, ran his fingers through his hair, quickly put on his shirt, neck-cloth and slipped hastily into his trousers. Leaving the room in his slippers, he called Holly. "Come, girl."

He descended the stairs adjusting his spectacles and met Miss Neilson at the bottom step. She had been crying.

"What is the matter, miss, pray tell? Calm yourself." And he led her to the sitting room. Her hands were like ice. "There you are, sit and warm yourself."

Caldwell bowed. "Sir, tea perhaps?"

"Yes, Caldwell, for both of us."

"Sir, I have terrible news, sir." Her hands shook. "Your father ..."

He gasped. "He has passed, Miss Neilson?" He dropped his head into his hands.

"He has," she said in a quiet tone wiping her eyes.

"I would not have thought such a thing possible. The morning was too beautiful." He remembered waking before dawn and realised it was his father saying good-bye. There was a deep silence. The room was cold and damp. The drapes had not yet been drawn. Walking to the hearth, he rested his hand on the mantle. "Miss Susanna, if I may be so forward as to call you Miss Susanna."

"Yes, but of course." She stammered, "James, but of course you may."

"I am thankful you brought the news."

He took her hands. "Miss Susanna, I need you, you must know that." Tears welled in his eyes.

She removed his tear-stained spectacles as he buried his head on her shoulder. "He died in his sleep, James." She fondly stroked his hair. "It was peaceful. When he did not come down for breakfast, Bobbin went to find him. Lately, she has been making him his morning tea. You know how thoughtful she is."

"Thank you, Miss Susanna. And where is she? Is she too distressed? The poor girl."

"She feels the pain, exceedingly, James. She loved him as a grandfather, we all did. He was more than kind to her. She has remained at the bookstore tending to its business until you come."

"We will leave immediately. I shall pack a few things. If you will make yourself comfortable, I shall not be long. I will have Caldwell prepare a breakfast for you."

"No need, James. Thank you, but I am not hungry."

* * *

James and Susanna arrived at the bookstore a little past three o'clock that afternoon. They found many people milling about. Everyone, rich and poor alike, was grieving for the old professor.

Bobbin was tending the fire when they entered. "Oh, sir," she cried and hurried to him, weeping.

Susanna kissed her forehead. "Come now, you two sit down. I shall make us something warm to drink." Now very familiar with the bookstore's little kitchen, she busied herself preparing a tray while James and Bobbin sat on the small sofa-chair by the fire.

"Miss Derby, Miss Neilson assured me my father did not suffer."

"No, sir, he did not. It was obvious, for he had a smile on his lips. His head rested on his pillow comfortable as could be. His nightcap was atop his head, not lying askew. His blankets were not mussed. There was still a small fire, he had been reading; his candle burned to its nubbin."

"Thank you, Miss Derby. I shall hold that repose in my mind for the rest of my life. It is fitting he should die peacefully, being such a peaceful man. He thought very much of you, Miss Derby."

"And, I of him, sir." She looked away, twiddling her little fingers. "Sir, please, you must call me Bobbin, as he did."

"Very well, Bobbin."

"He is ready if you wish to visit with him, sir. Miss Neilson thought it proper to have him remain lying in his room, until you have come, sir."

"Yes," he bowed his head, "that is very good. Thank you." He stared at the floor. "In a moment I shall go to him."

"Here now, take some tea," said Susanna with a subdued smile. She poured him a cup.

"Sir," said Bobbin, "everyone wishes to come in, bid their respect." She looked at the door. "They have been waiting outside for a very long time."

"Thank you. I shall speak with each of them."

"Sir," she said hesitatingly, "sir, some of them are not— polite society."

"My father cared for everyone, Bobbin. So he did. No, I shall not be offended by touching the sleeve of a beggar, no more than touching a rich man's."

Susanna laid her hand on his arm. "That is good of you, James, wise and good."

Bobbin realised at that moment that the two must be very much in love. She felt relieved, for she had plans now that she had graduated from the academy. There was that calling that haunted her, such a calling deep within her heart. The time had come. She was free to go, free at last to search for her mother.

* * *

The funeral was a very great one. Everyone from the Mary Arden Academy was there. People from a long distance came: beggars, rich men, ladies, gentlemen, royalty, Oxford men, all came to bid their respects and say good-bye. Bobbin stood a little distance, watching the black-robed men and black-netted women of all perspectives of society pass before the modest wooden box where her dear friend lay cold, spent, and forever away.

Watching James Halliwell-Phillipps, as he stood sober and stoic alongside Miss Neilson, made Bobbin weep. It began to rain; the whoosh of umbrellas broke the silence.

Maria, not liking funerals, chose to stand back from the crowd. She spied Bobbin, and thinking it a good diversion, worked her way around everyone to be near her dearest friend.

Bobbin felt something poke her; turning she found Maria standing next to her.

"I am sorry, Bobbin," she respectfully whispered.

"I am happy you have come, Maria. I have missed you."

"I have missed you too, my little dormouse." She cooed. "Papa, Philip and Edward, are standing just a little behind Schoolmaster Halliwell-Phillipps." She motioned with her eyes to where they stood. "You see, and Mrs Aesop is next to Papa."

Bobbin wiped her eyes. "Oh, yes, I see her. It is so good of everyone to come." She looked into the heavens and sighed woefully. "But now it is beginning to rain harder."

Maria opened her umbrella and held it over Bobbin. Those standing near recognised the wealthy Miss Collier and were shocked that she would hold an umbrella for such poor society. The service was near finished when she ushered Bobbin away.

"Bobbin," she whispered, "Papa suggested that you should come back and stay with us for as long as you wish. Edward was very pleased over the prospect. He is very fond of you, but then you know that."

"Maria, that is very kind of your father to welcome me to your home. There is nothing more that would please me as much as spending time with you all. Edward is very much part of my heart, Maria, but," she shook her head, "my station in life is so decidedly beneath yours."

"Come now Bobbin, do not talk so. Times have changed. Those are old, dowdyish ideas, ugly notions of society. You are every bit a lady, and I will defend you."

"Maria," she lowered her chin, "there are things I must do first before I could ever consider being a *real* lady."

"You want to search for your mother, I know. Well, I cannot blame you Bobbin. I only wish my mother was somewhere where I could search for her." She squeezed her hand. "I will come with you, then."

"Oh, that would be impossible, Maria." She glanced over at Mr Collier. "Your father would forbid such a thing, and your brothers would hate me. No, I could not allow it. There is too much danger."

"Certainly there is too much danger, and you cannot do such a thing all alone, Bobbin. You have no money, no resources, what would you eat?"

"Well, as it is, I have no home, Maria. Miss Neilson has been sharing her room at the orphanage with me since the professor died. I have decided it is an omen, Maria. Now is the time to find my mother, dead or alive."

"Oh, such an omen, indeed." Maria rolled her eyes. "Such an omen, Dormouse, and why should such an omen come to you and only you? Could I not have one settle in my head as well?"

Bobbin frowned. "Ah, I think not."

"And then why not, I ask?" She caught sight of a gravestone directly in front of her and smiled. Taking Bobbin's chin, she said, "Yes, Dormouse, right this very minute, I have witnessed such an omen." She pointed.

Bobbin read the etching on the gravestone. 'Parturient montes, nascetur ridiculus mus.' [41] She wrinkled her nose. "I cannot read Latin, Maria."

" 'Mountains will go into labour, and a silly little mouse will be born.' " She lowered her voice as the mourners glared at her. "Certainly that is an omen. Have not I called you my little dormouse since first we met? So, now, it is all quite settled and done with ... I must go along with you, my silly little mouse."

Bobbin eyed the old gravestone and then glanced toward the heavens shaking her head. "But, Maria, what will your father and brothers say?"

Bobbin was actually thankful for Maria's offer. She was frightened at all the uncertainty ahead with only having a little savings in her purse. "I would not want ill feelings to come between our friendship and your family, Maria."

"No need to worry, I shall speak with Father over the matter. I shall convince him that I wish to go on a holiday with you, an extended holiday to travel about and do research—no untruth there."

Spying his sister with Miss Derby, Edward smiled. He had been searching for her the entire service. The vicar ended the sombre ceremony, and everyone began to slowly move away. "Father, I shall be just a moment. I have found Maria."

---

[41] Horace (65 – 8 BC) *Ars Poetica* I. 139. Quoted from *The Concise Oxford Dictionary of Quotations*, by Susan Ratcliffe (2011).

Except for the steady rain and the squish on the soft grass as the people moved away, it was all quietness in the cemetery. The gravediggers stood at a distance behind their carts, inconspicuous as possible, but anxious to fill the hole they had just dug—shovelling wet mud was twice the work.

Catching Edward's eye, Bobbin smiled through her tears.

"Good day, Miss Derby." Edward bowed politely speaking in subdued tones. "I am very sorry for the passing of your dear friend, Miss Derby. Professor Halliwell-Phillipps will be sorely missed, I am sure."

"Yes, sir, very much missed," she replied, lowering her head.

Edward stammered for lack of anything more to say, feeling very shy at being so near her.

Maria broke the painful pause. "Thank you, Edward. I see Papa and Mrs Aesop and Philip are consoling Schoolmaster Halliwell-Phillipps. It is such a sad thing."

"Yes, Maria, it certainly is," he replied, edging closer to Miss Derby. He removed his hat, and raindrops, following the natural path of the limb directly above, dripped onto his head. Such a ridiculous thing; however, such things seemed to happen to Edward, frequently. Wincing, he immediately put his hat back atop his head. "Well then, I suppose we should join Father."

Plop plop plop. Edward glanced up and frowned.

Bobbin covered her mouth in amusement as the steady drip made such a noise atop Edward's hat ... plop plop plop.

Edward smirked at his sister. "Miss Derby finds amusement in all sorts of weather, sister."

"Well, Edward," she scoffed, "you must admit, it is a humorous patter of sorts."

"Certainly it is Maria, as long as it's my hat and not yours."

Chapter 17 – Detective Brown Visits the Academy

> He might be a very clever man by nature, for aught I know; but he laid so many books upon his head that his brain could not move. [42]

Detective Brown, fearful that his ageing gig would not make the journey from London to Wilmecote, rented a sturdier carriage for the long ride to Mary Arden Academy. His coachman eventually got lost, but soon regained his way when Detective Brown interrogated a farmer just this side of the village and learned the exact whereabouts of the academy.

The carriage, now bouncing along the rutted road, entered from the far side of the school, the road that only the servants and farmers used. Though the detective found it ruttier and dustier and troublesome to be sure, all was forgiven when he spied the tall church steeple jutting through the trees and up into the sky. Its shadow now loomed over his carriage. He thought it rather "majestic."

"Stop here," he shouted to the driver, "stop right here."

Brown jumped from the last step with a happy exuberance, but his smile soon faded. All the doors to the church were locked. "Oh, well," and he took in a deep breath, not in the least bit deterred, for it was the graveyard he was

---

[42] Hall, Robert (1764 – 1831) English clergy. Quoted from *The Mirror of Literature, Amusement, and Instruction*, Vol 21, by Percy, Timbs and Limbird (1833).

most interested in anyway. He walked around the side of the church and spied, to his delight, a gate.

Could lead to a cemetery under all those old trees. He stood for a second, eyeing up at the grey stone obelisk steeple and felt a shiver run through his body. He believed in omens. "Perhaps I shall stumble upon something ..." Feeling a chill, he walked along the green, mossy side of the church eager to find a bit of sunlight. A breeze suddenly picked up and near took his hat.

Unlatching the gate's black iron hasp, he pushed it open and gaped in awe. There before him were many, many graves. Graveyards were a source of pertinent information, valuable and necessary for his line of work. However, truth be told, graveyards had always held a morbid fascination for Mr Brown, even as a young boy.

Strolling within the quiet stone walled graveyard, the detective remarked to himself at how old the inhabitants were, some by two hundred years, others by a mere hundred. He tried to imagine what their lives had been like back then and was thankful that he was born in such an enlightened era. *If they could see how we live today, what a shock. Why, they would not believe all the changes in the crown; industrial growth and machinery; the American colonies; Napoleon defeated, and most recently, a vaccination against smallpox; chloroform usage. Nay, it would be altogether too severe. Why, Shakespeare himself would scoff at the very ideas.*

He continued around the well-kept yard, shrouded by huge, ancient trees, and standing on a grassy mound, envisioned the planting of these trees by perhaps the very inhabitants themselves.

And why not? He thought, *they are every bit as old.*

"Sir, may I help you?" inquired Jan, the yard-keeper. Annoyed at finding the stranger taking such liberties—nosing about here and there, uninvited.

"What?" replied detective Brown, as he abruptly turned from Josiah Noble's 1703 gravestone. "Come again, lad?"

"I was wondering, sir. May I help you? Are you searching for someone in particular? I know everyone here."

The detective half-laughed. "Is that so, young man? Well, then, tell me, how did each one die—were it by accident or illness, or perhaps foul play?"

Putting a little distance from himself and the stranger, the young, muddy-handed yard-keeper stammered, "Oh, well now, sir, I, I only meant the living ones, at the academy, sir. The dead ones, sir, I am little acquainted with, but a few."

Brown's eyes narrowed. "What about some Posea's then, yard-keep? Are there any Posea's buried about?"

Jan's face lit up, eager to please the strange intruder and lead him out of the private burial grounds, he nodded. "Oh, yes, sir, many."

"Show me, then," grumbled Brown as he pulled some papers from his pocket. He noticed the lad trembling. "Calm yourself, boy, I am Detective Thomas Brown, from London. I am searching for a Posea." Puffing up, the detective showed his identification papers to the confused looking young man.

"Ah, yes, sir, Mr Brown, right this way, if you please, to the garden." Scratching his head, the yard-keeper held the heavy oak, iron-clasped graveyard gate for the detective to pass through. Reverently closing it quietly, he remembered to lock it this time. "Right this way, sir."

Trudging through the tall wet grass, they soon came to the flower garden adjacent to the Study Hall. By now, curious onlookers peered from the academy windows. Student and professors alike watched the two walk from the graveyard to the flower garden. Everyone surely wondered just who the strange visitor might be? And why were they going to the flower garden?

Professor Barnaby Zany rang for Caldwell, schoolmaster's butler.

Entering the classroom, Caldwell found the professor and his students standing at the window staring down at the stranger and Jan.

"Caldwell, who is that fat man mingling in our garden, our flower garden, of all places?" said Professor Zany.

He glanced out the window. "Why, I have not the slightest idea, professor."

"Well then Caldwell, I think it a very good idea if you found out."

"Very well, professor, I shall." There came a murmur from Zany's students as Caldwell took leave.

The cooks, servants, livery, and stablemen were all watching Caldwell as he strutted importantly to see for himself the matter. He found Jan with a very stupid look on his face and approached the stranger with guarded steps. "Sir, what is the trouble?" Upon closer inspection, he quickly judged the stranger to be a man of the law, though dressed somewhat shabbily and with mud-caked, well-worn oxfords.

"Trouble? No trouble here," replied Brown, who quickly surmised Caldwell to be part of the academy staff, probably headmaster. "No trouble, sir," he laughed, "but the young man here simply misunderstood my question. I asked to see where the Poseas were buried and, he thought I said Posies—imagine that. Ha ha ha, a flower." Brown guffawed louder and slapped his high. "Stupid mistake."

Caldwell did not laugh, nor did the yard-keeper.

It's obvious, thought Brown, *that these learned folk have no sense of humour whatsoever.* "Well then," as he quickly hemmed his lips, "I am detective Thomas Brown. Here are my papers. And, ah, who might you be?"

Taking the papers, Caldwell glanced back at the academy. All the peeping eyes quickly disappeared. He read the detective's identification papers, and when assured of the lawman's authenticity, replied, "Sir, I am Caldwell, butler to Schoolmaster Halliwell-Phillipps, who is, at present, in London. His father died. He is not expected back until noon tomorrow, being Saturday of the week."

Before Brown could question him further, Caldwell added, "I am not at liberty to discuss one thing more, sir."

"Hmm." Thought Brown, years of experience in interrogating this exact sort always turned up most excellent clues—if they could be rattled, that is, but they were hard nuts to crack, these stiff-lipped, manservant types. It was the old-English-servant-loyalty thing—way above bribery, so they were. Realizing the man would not cooperate, Brown teetered a little on his flat feet. "Hmm, so you are not at liberty ..."

Caldwell stiffened. "Sir, Mr James Halliwell-Phillipps is schoolmaster here. I am his butler, and am not at liberty to answer your questions, however trivial they may be."

"Ah-ha, and I suppose no one else would be made available to answer a few questions until he reappears?"

"Well, sir," Caldwell glanced up at Professor Zany, who stood behind one of his students in the second story window, peering over her head, "there is one such man. Perhaps you would have a word with Professor Zany then."

"That should do." Detective Brown finally felt that he was making some headway. He turned, puffed his chest, kicked a little mud from his shoe, and with a moronic air, said, "Take me to him, Kidwell."

"*Caldwell,* sir," corrected the yard-keeper, Jan. "*Caldwell.*"

"Oh, well, yes, yes, so it is, Caldwell," said Brown.

However, the mud-smeared yard-keeper would not let the matter drop so easily and warned, "You are to see Professor Zany? Well then, sir, be prepared. He will not tolerate slurry, slangy mispronunciations of any sort. One is never in doubt about what *he* is saying."

"Right this way, detective, if you will," said Caldwell with a gesture. "This way."

The butler led the way through the sacred Trottoir, walking across the stone path with ease, leaving the detective quickly behind. Early on, he had noticed the man's soles were a bit thin. Reaching the end of the Trottoir, Caldwell stood patiently until the detective caught up.

Calling out in pain, Brown winced, "Slow it down, man, these are sharp little stones here." And the rotund detective stood briefly, resting his bruised feet, his brow beaded with sweat. "What sort of pathway is this anyway?"

Caldwell sniffed the air. "It was built by a very famous Frenchman, sir."

"A Frenchman? Well, say no more, man, say no more. That's the whole of the trouble right off. Never have a Frenchman build anything. They would rather sit and drink wine and make love, but to build a proper pathway? Well, see for yourself." And the detective limped his way to the pebbly finish of it. "I should hope he is still alive, I'd like to tell him my opinion of his work."

"Oh, my no, sir, he is dead, been dead for three hundred years."

"Well, there you have it, Kidwell," he grunted. "Them Frenchies ain't got better in three hundred years, even, nor three hundred more, I suspect."

Caldwell led the limping detective up four flights of steps in the three-story building, down two, and then up one, finally coming to Professor Barnaby Zany's classroom. Tapping lightly, Caldwell entered. "Professor?" he called out. Detective Brown stood at his side. "Professor Zany, where are you?"

His students, all ten of them, tender, sweet young ladies, turned their attention to the window, and there at the bottom of the drape, Caldwell spied Professor Zany's feet.

"Hmm," he uttered, "hiding again, are you, sir?"

"Yes," said the professor suddenly pulling the curtains aside in a huff, "what is it, Caldwell."

Daring not to laugh, his students sat in silence, listening, watching the pompous looking detective, who somehow had found his way into Professor Zany's limerick class, the class of all classes for a stranger.

"Professor," said Caldwell, "this is Detective Brown, and he wishes to ask you a few questions."

Folding one arm behind his back, Zany began pacing and ranting, "Not before I am finished with my limerick, if you please, Caldwell. How many times must I remind the staff that my juices are constantly being drained as through a leaky pipe, or like a mere tap left open to drip into the city cesspool when I am continually being interrupted?"

Brown cleared his eyes and glanced at the young students. *Well, they haven't started running yet.*

"We understand, professor, we certainly do," said Caldwell with a half-bow. Just before he left the room, he nodded to Brown. "Sir, I shall be just outside, if you need me."

Zany spun like a top, now facing the window again, pulling the curtains around him. "As I was saying, students, before I was interrupted, "Count Palmiro Vicarion, when he writes in the foreword of his book of limericks, and quite different from Lear's, please note: '... the limerick is precious, an exquisite thing: like a good Burgundy, it should not be taken indifferently, too often, or in unduly large quantities. Only a fool, I repeat, a fool would gulp down a glass of Chambertin or read this book in a sitting ...' "

Detective Brown scratched his thick head as the professor continued.

"Lastly, let us consider briefly the limerick in the world of 'only yesterday and today, and its future in the world of tomorrow."

The students clapped wholeheartedly as the professor shouted, "I shall recite my very favourite, have it memorised for tomorrow's class, ladies." He began to chant.

His bizarre behaviour would normally have alarmed the seasoned detective, but the young girls remained glued to their seats, obviously entertained. Therefore, he remained motionless. All of a sudden the professor began to hum an indistinguishable ditty, and then he blurted:

" 'There was a fat lady of Clyde
Whose shoelaces once came untied;
She feared that to bend
Would display her rear end,
So she cried and she cried and she cried.' "

Feeding on his student's obvious adulation, he went on:

" 'There was a fat lady of Bryde
Whose shoelaces once came untied;' "

The young ladies shifted in their seats and merrily joined along with the professor. The sing-song chorus thus continued:

" 'She didn't dare stoop (by now they were all chanting in raucous odd humour)
For fear she would poop,
So she cried and she cried and she cried!' " [43]

    Clearly aware that the students were out of control, Brown quietly edged his way out of the classroom. Silly, half-crazed young women could turn very mean and dangerous, betimes. Personal experience convinced him of that fact.

    When he hit the threshold and spied Caldwell's flared nostrils, he brushed him aside with his rotund buckskin belly. "Make way, make way. I can see myself out, thank you."

---

[43] Professor Edward Lear (1812 – 1888) English artist, poet, author, musician, illustrator. *Book of Nonsense*, (1846).

Chapter 18 – Maria Speaks with her Father

If you can keep reason above passion, that and watchfulness will be your best defenders. [44]

Following Professor Halliwell-Phillipps's burial, the Collier family returned to London, Bobbin returned to the orphanage with Miss Neilson. The very next afternoon, Maria sent a note to Bobbin:

My dear friend, I will be speaking with Papa this very day regarding our rendezvous to find your mama. I have not thought of what I will tell him as yet, but upon his answer, I will immediately write to you.
Affectionately, your friend, Maria

Maria's plea to her father began at the breakfast table that morning. "Papa, since my exposure to the Mary Arden Academy, I have such a calling in my heart to travel about England for a very little while, doing research—perhaps for only a month or two."

"Hmm, only two months?" said Mr Collier

---

[44] Sir Isaac Newton (1642 – 1727) English scientist. Quoted from *A Dictionary of Thoughts* by Tryon Edwards (1908).

"Indeed, Papa. I have much I wish to research. The Sir Isaac Newton Foundation has a wonderful new invention with which I would dearly love to involve myself. If you do not mind over it, that is." She set down her fork, holding her sweet pleading face mask.

"Maria," he dabbed his chin, "you call 'a very little while' only one month or two? You forget you are only ten and five. Do you not agree that you are a little young to be traipsing about with the Sir Isaac Newton Laboratory at such an age?"

Philip continued reading the newspaper. Edward shook his head slightly at his father—signalling his disapproval of such a ridiculous plan.

"But, Papa, Edward would chaperone us."

"Us?" Mr Collier set his cup down.

"Miss Derby would accompany us. She has plans of her own on research."

Looking over his spectacles, Collier shook his head. "What on earth is research? A new word you learned at the academy, then? I have never heard it used so frequently, Maria, as I have these past few minutes." He found Edward now smiling.

"Well, yes, Father," added Edward, suddenly thinking about Miss Derby and how Maria's idea had merit after all. "I think that would be just the thing for Maria. I have heard very much regarding Sir Isaac Newton's theory on gravitational, ah, something of the apple sort."

"Gravitational pull, Edward," interjected Maria with a smile.

Nodding, Edward returned the smile. "Yes, that is precisely the word, sister. Thank you."

Glancing at Edward, Philip laid his paper down. "I smell something brewing. I think perhaps since I am the eldest brother, I should be the chaperone for my scientist sister and her friend, Miss Derby." He smirked at Edward.

Maria and Edward dropped their heads. Mr Collier noticed their retreat. "Well, let me think over the matter. I will look into your travel plans, Maria. The bank just donated the Newton Laboratory a considerable sum. Perhaps I would exert a little influence."

Swallowing quickly, Maria sat straight up. "Oh, sir, not to bother, for I want no influence, I assure you. Miss Derby and I … and Edward, will be fine without any help."

"I see," replied Mr Collier, "well, I shall think about it."

"I should hope Papa that a little while means very soon?" Maria was concerned about Bobbin's plight. With nowhere to go and the urgency of her departure, she was permitted only a few days to stay at the orphanage under the care of Miss Neilson—Maria need to act quickly.

Marvelling at the new sophistication of his daughter, Collier considered a little jaunt away from home would do her no harm. She was good, after all, and what evil should come when accompanied by his son, Edward. He was proud of his stalwart son. *I suppose I could spare Edward for a few days.* "Very well, Maria, I shall give you my decision this afternoon; however, a month is far too long. If I agree to your plans, it would be for no longer than one week. I cannot spare Edward from the business, nor could I spare my only daughter from my side for a month."

"Indeed, Papa, I understand." Maria smiled. "Thank you, Papa."

"Sister," inquired Philip, "pray tell, what exactly will Edward and Miss Derby be researching while you are being a scientist?"

Chapter 19 – Mrs Aesop has Lunch with Mr Collier

The flower that smiles to-day
To-morrow dies; [45]

23 June Morning London
Mrs Aesop,
*   In your most recent correspondence, you mentioned
your visit to London to buy material and such for the
academy. I would be most pleased to entertain you for
lunch and a tour of the bank. Do you remember our walk
in the garden at the academy last year? I inquired if you
had ever seen the intimate workings of a bank? Perhaps
not, but your humorous reply delights me still. I am
looking forward to your letter of acceptance.*
*   Yours sincerely, John Collier*

Feeling her face turn warm, Mrs Aesop laid the letter in
her lap. She found John Collier's wit entertaining, charming
and he was a very learned man. She respected a good, solid
mind and found his a worldly one. He was a patient and
tolerant man. She welcomed tolerance. His piercing blue eyes
and shock of grey about the temples reminded her of a similar

---

[45] Percy Bysshe Shelley (1792 – 1822) English poet. Quoted from
Selections from the Poems of Percy Bysshe Shelly, edited by Hamilton
Thompson, (1923).

man, one who had saved her from hell years earlier, a priestly saviour.

Mary Aesop was touched that such a man had recognised, right off, her inner spirit. She knew directly his feelings for her, at first glance his eyes betrayed his heart; he loved her; she loved him. She reasoned without reason that time was not at the essence with their relationship. It must evolve in an orderly fashion. He was an orderly man, and in due time the conclusion would eventually come about. She would be patient while his mind sorted the details.

> *26 June Mary Arden Academy*
> *Mr Collier,*
> *Yes, thank you, Sir. I shall be more than pleased to meet you for lunch. I am very much impressed with the idea of touring 'The Old Lady.' Such a wonderful opportunity to witness, first hand, the inner workings of a bank. I must warn you again, Sir, of my ignorance concerning financial matters. I assure you, however, I shall not wear my old shoe. I shall be arriving in London, 28 June, early morn. I will be staying at the Red Lion. I shall meet you in the lobby at one o'clock.*
> *Most sincerely, Mary Aesop*

* * *

28 June   Red Lion

Standing in front of the room mirror, Mrs Aesop adjusted her hat as the mantle clock struck one. *I must be going*, she thought nervously, *I do not want to keep Mr Collier waiting.* She felt giddy, like a young girl again. Before pulling on her gloves, she sniffed at the Lavender water at her wrist. "Umm, yes, quite nice."

She wore a plain, well fitting grey suit befitting her station and a smallish plumed hat of the same material accented with fluffy black feathers. She wore grey lace gloves. Rouge touched her cheeks with colour; her lustrous thick black hair was twisted up and pulled away from her rather large pensive, intelligent dark eyes.

Descending the stairs, she caught a glimpse of Collier waiting in the lobby. She smiled and extended her hand.

His face coloured lightly. "Mrs Aesop, good afternoon." Kissing the tip of her laced fingers, he seemed briefly mesmerised, perhaps by the scent of lavender or her lovely eyes?

"Sir, good afternoon." She made no attempt to remove her hand from his, nor did she lower her gaze, but met his eyes, wish for wish.

He seemed exhilarated at the sensual meeting of the mind. "I have selected a quiet, beautiful restaurant in which to dine, Mrs Aesop, the Mayfair, Victoria Gardens. Perhaps you have heard of it?"

"The Mayfair, sir?" She politely reminded him, "Sir, I am Headmistress at Mary Arden, one does not frequent such places, I assure you, on my wage."

Collier bit his tongue. *I have embarrassed her.* "Excuse me, I only meant the gardens there are very beautiful, the food very good. Ah, but then the gardens, the flowers ... "

"I love gardens and flowers, Mr Collier. Thank you for your thoughtfulness."

They walked out into the delightful warm London air, his carriage awaited. He slowed, allowing her a half step ahead so as to take in her lovely silhouette.

Collier's footman greeted him. "Sir." He held the door as she situated herself comfortably inside.

"This is a very beautiful carriage, Mr Collier." She noted the flower-filled vase attached to the wall. Spilling over its sides were London Pride's, a delicate flower, one of her favourites, "Lovely idea, that." She smiled. "You are very thoughtful, sir. Indeed you are." Her mind raced with a disquieting thought as she remembered Shelley's verse:

'The flower that smiles to-day
To-morrow dies;" [46]

She sighed, gazing out the window, feeling very much the warmth of his eyes heavy upon her. She felt flushed, light-

---

[46] Shelley, *Selections from the Poems of Percy Bysshe Shelly*, edited by Hamilton Thompson, (1923).

headed, relishing all the feelings that falling in love brings to the mind and spirit. She returned his smile.

She had only read about the Mayfair and the London society that frequented such places. It was more beautiful than she had ever imagined.

As they were escorted into the restaurant, she had not expected the commotion. Everyone turned their attention to her. Immediately she felt inferior, dowdy, and insignificant.

Just then John took her arm, whispering, "You know, you are truly a lovely lady, Mrs Aesop."

"Indeed, sir." She raised her chin, felt full of life, and ignored the busybodies inspecting her hat, gloves, dress, and manners. *Let them wonder who I am.*

She and Collier were seated in a secluded section. Not so secluded, though, that the other diners did not suppose them to be an intimate couple. They seemed curious about her dining with the prestigious banker, Mr Collier, *the* Bank of England Collier. Oh, she was pretty enough, however, her clothes were so ... plain, so cheap.

Mr Collier was rarely seen in public with anyone but his family. Now and again a business associate perhaps; only the well-seasoned society of a few years past would remember his wife, Emily. And then, of course, she would never have dined at the Mayfair, being allergic to the flowers and all. They knew of such intimacies of Emily Collier, *the* Emily Collier.

Mary Aesop loved fountains, and they were situated very near one. "Mr Collier, this is incredibly lovely," she glanced around, "the flowers, greens, ferns and the quaint waterfall. I find it most enchanting." She turned to him to speak again, but his gaze stopped her words, blushing, she lowered her eyes.

I have her. "I am glad to hear it, Mrs Aesop," he said.

Approaching the table, the waiter took Mr Collier's order, a glass of claret for each of them.

"And what would you like to order, Mrs Aesop? I have tried the pates and the cold tongue. Oh, and the game pie is very delicious here. They have every imaginable pastry as well: gingerbread, treacle sponge, seed cakes, fruitcakes ..."

"I see," she murmured, "you must come here often then?"

She tried to read his face. Quite unexpectedly a vision came to her, a vision like those she had experienced very often throughout her difficult life. As if pulled at great speed, she was suddenly awash in warm sunshine. An unexplainable awareness of intermingling within another human's inner soul entered her being. And in the blink of an eye, she was inside John Collier's heart, feeling the depth of his loneliness and despair, as well as a new awakening of a profound love, a love that inexplicably was pouring into her heart. His heart was beating in her chest, and for those few seconds, she experienced the purest joy she had ever known—from this man, this sweet, tender man. Her eyes softened; her face glowed; she was receptive and peaceful when she gave her heart to him, the real one she had been guarding her entire life.

"Oh, yes, I come here, quite often ... alone," he said, gazing at her. "I too enjoy very much the splendid aura of this garden. When financial matters of the bank loom heavy on my mind, I escape here, have my claret and listen to the fountain."

"And take in the magnificent aroma of the flowers here about, yes," she replied. She closed her eyes and breathed in the wonderful humid, moist perfumed air, exhaling softly. "Yes, I understand exactly."

Collier was watching her, smiling. During their meal, he happened to mention his daughter's endeavours with the Sir Isaac Newton Laboratory.

"I see," she replied, "and her most devoted friend, Miss Derby, is to go along, you say?"

"My son, Edward, is chaperone. I understand Miss Derby has a bit of research of her own. They will be engaged for a week."

"Indeed." Glancing at the fountain, she sipped her claret. "Schoolmaster and I are in hopes Miss Derby will return to the academy and teach. She is a lovely young lady, Mr Collier. Do you have any idea what her research is about?"

"No, actually, I do not. However, it does have something or other to do with the Sir Isaac Newton's roving laboratory. Oh, Maria has such an inquisitive mind. She has been, of late, drawn in, fascinated with how apples fall to earth."

"Apples, sir?" She cocked her head. "Oh," she half-laughed, "yes, you mean gravitational pull."

"I suppose so. Though Maria tells me Miss Derby is primarily interested in their experiment regarding human behaviour during a full moon."

"A full moon?" She looked down at her hands. "Well, I have not heard about that, sir, however, I do know Miss Derby is naturally inclined toward thinking about human behaviours." She sighed. "Indeed, for one with such a past, I have long admired her forgiving nature, her own outstanding morals and manners."

"Perhaps, she is trying to find her ... perhaps the young lady is trying to reason why her mother abandoned her. I have heard she may still be alive." He studied Mrs Aesop's reaction carefully as he continued, "Well, it's been many years and her mother is, no doubt, not coming back. It would serve a better purpose, for what sort of woman would abandon her children to run with gipsies?" Finishing the last of his claret, he gazed toward the fountain.

"Gypsies?" She drew herself up with a frown. "Well then," she dabbed her lips, "certainly it would not serve Miss Derby well to learn of such things, gipsies, indeed."

"It was Miss Derby, Mrs Aesop, who told Maria that her mother ran away with gipsies."

Collier gestured for more wine. As the glasses were filled, she glanced at the fountain. Her lips set, her breathing soft and deep, her long thick black lashes glistened in the glow of the candlelight. Turning her gaze to Collier, she smiled. "So, I do hope our dearest Miss Derby finds what she is searching for. I pray the heavens are merciful."

"Merciful, indeed, Mrs Aesop. Perhaps we have judged her mother too harshly." His voice grew soft as she leaned in, listening intently. " 'Nothing will make us so charitable and tender to the faults of others, as, by self-examination, thoroughly to know our own.' " [47]

---

[47] François Fénelon (1651 – 1715) French theologian, Archbishop of Cambrai. Quoted from *A Dictionary of Thoughts*, by Tryon Edwards (1908).

Chapter 20 – Bobbin, Maria and Edward Sojourn

… the good die first,
And they whose hearts are dry as summer dust
Burn to the socket. [48]

Bobbin, Maria, and Edward decided they would begin the search for her mother in London, along Tuppence Lane where Bobbin was raised. As they walked about the poorer section of London, Edward spoke in a serious tone, "Stay close to me at all times, and take heed whatever I tell you."

"No need to worry, sir," said Bobbin, "I was born here. I know very well all the lanes, alleyways, and dark corners. I would wish first off, though, that we should return to the hotel and change. We look very conspicuous." She glanced at their fine clothes. "No one shall tell us anything dressed like this."

Maria nodded. "Very well then, Bobbin." She turned to her brother. "Edward, she does have a point, but Bobbin, what would you have us wear?"

"Come along, I shall show you."

She led them into a modest clothing store and picked out just the things one of low income should wear. The shopkeeper was pleased for the business, but he was puzzled at wrapping such inferior clothes for the three were dressed in such fine

---

[48] William Wordsworth (1770 – 1850) English poet. "The Ruined Cottage" in *The Excursion*, Book I, (1888).

attire, and definitely wealthy. Nonetheless, he was tipped well for his work and dismissed the matter.

* * *

When the three met in the lobby dressed in their plain clothes they were met with glares. They would have been put out, but the hotel manager knew the wealthy Collier family, and though puzzled at their attire, obediently ordered them a coach, bowing as they left.

"I had no idea how strangers look down their nose so stupidly," said Maria in disgust. "Did you see how they looked at me? As if I were ..."

"I know very well, Maria," said Bobbin.

"That is all behind us now, Miss Bobbin," Edward said confidently. "Well, where shall we start?"

"The cemetery—Tottenham Court."

* * *

Arriving at the cemetery, they found the office locked. Edward peered into the window, rubbing against the filthy sill, then stood back, brushing his waistcoat. "Disgusting old place," he mumbled. "I am rather happy no one is here."

Walking alongside the building, he followed the old stepping-stones that eventually led to a gate, near-hidden for the lush vines that grew around its arch. He pushed the old-fashioned latch, and the gate squeaked open. He motioned for Bobbin and Maria.

Bobbin followed Edward, her hands tucked close to her side. She wrinkled her nose at the horse dung scattered beneath the hedges.

"Bobbin, what should we look for?" said Maria.

"Well, first I think we should search out the grounds where the bodies of the poor are buried, the pauper's section."

"Good idea, that," said Edward.

"When we find the section we must search every tombstone for clues," she said. "Look for a death at about 1850 and beyond."

Maria squeezed her hand. "Do you think your mother died? You have never said that before, Bobbin."

"Well, I do not rightly know, maybe she has," she paused, "look for the last name Derby, that is all I know." A few drops of rain hit her. "Dear me, now it is to rain some more."

Opening the umbrella, Edward held it over his sister and Bobbin. "We should have bought sturdy boots," he said, looking down at his expensive, flimsy ones.

"Indeed, but it is a little late now," added Maria. "My shoes are already sopping at the moment."

"Well, we only have a few more sections, look yonder," Bobbin pointed, trudging through the wet grass. When she reached the last section one particular stone caught her eye: *Pauper's Section – felo de se* was engraved on it. "I wonder ... what it means?"

Tree rain dripped from the umbrella Edward held over her. "It's in Latin, Miss Bobbin," he said. "It means ... calculated self-murder. I once read, if the departed made it into the churchyard at all, suicides would be buried face down in a north-south grave on the north side of the churchyard." [49]

Maria frowned at his insensitivity and quickly turned to Bobbin. "Stay here, I will look, there are not that many."

"Nay, I shall," said Bobbin and she moved ahead.

Edward and Maria remained by her side, stone to stone. Many were indistinguishable, old and crumbling; however, when they came to the last row they found a grassy mound with three small stones and a much larger one, shadowing the others. *William Derby father d.1850, Derby-Children d.1850 William, Stella, Jane*

Bobbin stared. "Yes, that must be my father, but who are the others?" Her brows furrowed in thought. "I do not remember them."

Shaking her head slowly, Maria put her arms around her. "No, you could not. You were much too young to remember. They must have all died suddenly, perhaps the typhoid."

Edward, still holding the black umbrella over their heads nodded. "The typhoid struck our mother, too."

"They are all buried in the self-murdered side?" The furrows in her brow deepened. Her little body drew in as if a sudden, shocking recollection seised her. "He burned them to death; he took them to hell with him. I alone escaped."

Maria's jaw dropped. "Your father burned them, Bobbin?"

---

[49] Actual account of suicide burials: 1700-Scenes from London Life, M. Waller, 2000.

"Surely not his children," said Edward. "There must be a mistake." Motioning with his eyes to his sister, "Come, Miss Bobbin, we must go. It is getting late." Rain now poured through the trees' drooping branches.

During the ride back to the hotel, Bobbin didn't look up, nor did she join in their quiet conversation. Her world became soundless and black. She felt a foul sickening chill wash over her body. Her head throbbed. Those terrible, nauseating blinding zigzags came back to confuse her again. She could feel her body floating, and then she felt hot; her throat went suddenly dry, parched. She swallowed hard. Smelling the rain, she thought how wonderful it would be to swim in cool water. She took Edward's hand and brushed her lips. "Edward, are we near the Thames?"

He glanced at his sister. "No Miss Bobbin, we are a long way from the river."

Maria's eyes were wide and apprehensive. "Why do you ask, Bobbin?"

"I am so uncomfortably warm." She ripped off her hat; her thick black hair tumbled loose about her shoulders. She wiped her brow. "I am burning ..."

Edward took her chin in his hand. "You must not go anywhere near water, Bobbin. It is not safe. Promise me."

Turning her face from his grasp, she stared out the window. When they arrived at the hotel, they went straight to their rooms.

Standing outside in the hall, Edward pulled Maria aside. "Come for me when she is settled."

She nodded and led Bobbin into their room where she removed Bobbin's muddy, rain-soaked boots, pulled off her drenched waistcoat, and finding even her frock damp, quickly removed it. Her skin was cold, and Maria quickly covered her body with a thick wool blanket and put her to bed. Gently tucking her in, she put her limp little hand beneath the blanket. "Poor, dear girl." She stood over her for a moment more before hurrying to her brother's room.

* * *

"Edward, she is asleep, but extremely melancholy, and no wonder, she had quite forgotten having a brother and sister, and now she begins to remember them? God in heaven, were they burned to death? What a shock. I do not think it such a good idea to be searching for her mother."

"Indeed, I too, have reservations about going any further with this investigation. We have travelled only three days, and already we have turned up a terrible past. This surely does her no good. What is more, we have found nothing regarding the whereabouts of her mother."

"Indeed, Edward, we will insist that she give up this ridiculous search." She wrung her hands. "But, if we don't go along with her, she will go on alone, and that won't do. I could not bear to have her travelling about unguarded."

"Nor I," said Edward. "So, I will simply not allow her to continue."

She nodded. "Good luck, Edward." With a deep sigh, she stood. "I will look in on her, and then we shall go to dinner."

When Maria entered the room, she found Bobbin sleeping and her breath was laboured and raspy. She ran back to Edward's room. "Edward, hurry, come with me. Bobbin is sleeping, but when I nudged her, she did not stir."

Edward felt Bobbin's feverish brow. He cherished her dear, cherub face and felt terribly sad that she had discovered her family in such a way. Taking her hand, he whispered, *"'Grief is a stone that bears one down, but two bear it lightly.'"* [50]

Maria was touched by his poetics. "Edward, you do have a wonderful side about you, you know."

Looking down into Bobbin's sweet face, he smiled. "I cannot help but feel sorry for her, such a terrible life. I want no more of this sadness to visit upon her. I have made up my mind, Maria. We will return home immediately, and Bobbin will accompany us. She will become the lady she was meant to be. If her mother were at all concerned, she would have searched for *her* long before now." He felt her brow again. "Maria, she looks too flush. Look there at the beads of sweat on her brow." He glanced at his sister. "Is that even normal with a fever? Come, feel for yourself."

Maria touched her brow. "Oh, Edward, she is burning hot. You must go and find a doctor. I will put cold cloths on her brow until you return."

---

[50] Wilhelm Hauff (1802-1827) German novelist. Quoted from *Many Thoughts of Many Minds* by Henry Southgate, (1872).

"Try putting water on her lips, too," he said as he hurried from the room. "I will not be long."

Maria soaked towels in cold water and draped them over her feverish brow. "Bobbin? Bobbin? You must wake up, Bobbin."

She opened her feverish red-rimmed eyes. "Oh, my dearest Maria, do not trouble yourself for my sake." She exhaled slowly, turning her head away, "it is all for nought."

Suddenly the door opened, Edward quietly entered with the house doctor.

Maria glanced at the doctor and then to Edward. "Oh, dear me, we must send for Papa right this minute."

Bobbin smiled up at Edward. "Please, sir," she whispered faintly, "do not trouble yourself, I am not worth ..." she tried to take in a breath, but instead, seemed to gasp.

"Excuse me, excuse me," said the doctor as he ripped the blankets from her body and lifted her into a sitting position, he then patted her back until she took a breath. He laid her back down, positioning her on her side. "Keep her from lying on her back. Her lungs are not clear."

Maria took Edward's hand. "Hurry to Papa, Edward. We will stay with her."

Moving quietly toward the door, Edward looked again at Bobbin. Tears welled in his eyes.

The doctor took Bobbin's hand and shook his head.

Maria glanced up at him, weeping. "Will she survive, sir?"

* * *

Within an hour, John Collier and Philip entered the room finding Maria sitting on the bed, wiping Bobbin's brow. Collier brought his personal physician. Immediately the hotel's attending physician moved aside, acknowledging the distinguished Dr Harris. For what seemed a very long time the doctors conferred as they prodded and poked, lifted and turned her little head, moved her on her side, and then listened intently to her chest by ear and stethoscope. Still Bobbin did not respond; still her fever remained high. Though occasionally opening her eyes, she remained mute.

"Sir," Dr Harris addressed John Collier, "she is very ill, there is no doubt about that. We must remove her to the hospital where attendants will keep her lungs working. If this fever continues longer than twenty-four hours, it could turn ... very nasty."

"She will die, Papa?" cried Maria.

"Let us not think in those terms, Miss Collier. Now, we must move her immediately."

"Certainly, sir," responded the dour-faced John Collier. "You must do all that is necessary, doctor. She is like family to us. Spare nothing."

Maria sobbed, "Please, doctor, spare not one thing. She must live for a very long time."

Edward and Maria left the room and stood silently in the hallway with Philip. "God," Edward whimpered, "it is the very same way Mother died." He buried his face in his hands.

Philip put his arms around his shoulders. "Edward, the doctor will save her. She is young and strong. Believe me, she will survive."

"Her senselessness is so like when Mother was ill, is it not?" Edward shook his head.

"Philip, I know why she is sick. Just before Bobbin took ill, she discovered the most ghastly thing imaginable," said Maria.

"What could possibly be so ghastly?"

"Edward and I were accompanying her to where she lived as a child in hopes we'd discover something about her mother—if she was dead or alive. This Newton science trek was a ruse to fool Father. We began by searching the closest cemetery, and discovered that her father was buried in the self-murdered side, with his children, William, Stella, and Jane. Bobbin stared at the grave, Philip. She recognised her father's name, but not her brother and sisters."

"Oh, God, I fear more than a physical illness has claimed her," said Philip.

"Dear God, Eddie," he shook his head, stunned as well. "I had no idea, the dear girl—God Almighty, what a wretched discovery, indeed." Seeing the anguish on his brother's face, he patted his back. "She is strong, Eddie. You love her, and she loves you."

Maria nodded. "Yes, Edward, you must stay by her side, talk to her, soothe her, and pamper her. She will respond, you'll see."

Edward wiped his eyes. "Indeed, I am more stubborn than she is." He stood. "I shall force her to recover."

Philip and Maria nodded. "Oh, we are quite certain of that, Edward."

* * *

The Colliers left the London Square Hotel in such a flurry that many curious passers-by commented that only the very wealthy commanded such an entourage of at least ten servants and all the hotel managers running about so frantically.

Rushing alongside the doctor, Edward refused to leave Bobbin's side for a moment.

Frightened and worried, Maria remained with Edward at the hospital. Her brother's unusual demeanour awed her—he fussed so with everyone. Tidying Bobbin's covers, her pillow, and he even insisted upon feeding her.

"Miss Derby needs nourishment," he instructed the staff. "Why, she has not eaten a thing since very early this morning." He ordered broth and pudding.

Sitting next to Edward in the small room, Maria dabbed her eyes watching her brother tenderly brush Bobbin's forehead with the back of his hand.

"Oh, Edward, you are very good."

Setting the food tray down, the nurse began preparing a bib for Bobbin. When she reached for the bowl, Edward stopped her. "No need, nurse, I shall feed her."

"Very well, sir."

First touching the spoon to his lips, testing it that it was not too hot, Edward parted her lips, and gingerly spooned the broth into her mouth. "Come now, Bobbin, you must eat. Have a little broth."

Now and again kissing the droplets of broth escaping her lips, he whispered, "You must open your eyes, my little sparrow—well then, perhaps a nod at least, Bobbin." Dabbing her brow, he gazed at her flushed face. "I will not let you escape, Bobbin. I love you too dearly."

Long into the night, Edward continued talking to her listless, feverish body, cajoling her with silly little rhymes, even humming a song now and again. Then in the wee hours of the morning, with exhaustion weakening his spirits, a premonition quietly eased into his heart. Now fearful her soul would soon be swept away, he took up her limp hand, and whispered tersely, "'Sole partner, and sole part of all my joys, dearer thyself than all.' Oh, you must live, Bobbin. You must, Bobbin." He buried his head next to hers and wept openly.

Suddenly feeling her pulse race, he brought her hand to his face. Feeling its coolness, he shouted to Maria, "By God's mercy, her fever is no more."

Groggy and confused in the dark room, Maria rubbed her eyes. "Fever?"

Bobbin turned her head and by the wisp of candlelight that shone on Edward's tear-stained face, brought his hand to her lips, "Yes, Edward, I love you too."

Bobbin had recovered. Indeed, Edward willed it.

Chapter 21 – A letter to Mrs Aesop

He that is down needs fear no fall;
He that is low, no pride;
He that is humble, ever shall
Have God to be his guide. [51]

10 July London
My dear Mary,
Forgive my scribbling, but I regret to inform you
that I cannot be there with you tomorrow – Miss Bobbin
Derby has taken ill. A very bad cold which has settled in
her lungs. Maria is all aflutter with worry… I know you
will understand. I would wish you here, but I am fearful
that you too may come sick, as it is, we are doing well as
one may expect under such sad circumstances.
I am affectionately yours, John C.

Near tears, Mrs Aesop shared her letter with Schoolmaster Halliwell-Phillipps. "Sir," her lips quivered, "under the circumstances, I ask leave for a few days to go to the Collier household. Perhaps there is something I may do to help Bobbin recover. Though I must say, I have constantly been praying for her recovery."

---

[51] John Bunyan (1628 – 1688) English writer and preacher. *The Pilgrim's Progress* (1678).

"There now, Mary, sit down, calm yourself." Handing her a handkerchief, James added, "Of course, certainly you may take leave. I understand exactly, but calm yourself, Mary, colds are not very often fatal anymore."

"One never knows for certain about colds, particularly if they settle in one's lungs. I am certain the Colliers are doing everything necessary for her sake. I wish only to leave at first light to render some bit of aid." She wiped her eyes "As you may well imagine, I am in a very awkward position."

"Please, Mary, do sit down. Let us discuss the situation beforehand." He rang for Caldwell.

"Sir, you rang?"

"Please, Caldwell, bring us some brandy."

"Sir." Bowing, Caldwell removed the keys from his waistcoat, and in his easy, familiar manner, unlocked the mahogany liquor cabinet. "Will it be the peach, apricot, or berry tonight, sir?"

"Bring them all, Caldwell."

"Very well, sir." He removed three brandy glasses lifting each to the light, woe to the glass that was not spotless. Each, one by one, was set upon the white linen cloth placed on the tray. "Sir, would you wish to start with the peach?"

"Thank you, Caldwell, yes. Please, pour the same for the Mary and for yourself, and then join us, won't you?"

He nodded. "But of course, sir." He poured three glasses, each a quarter full. Sipping brandy was an art form, and Caldwell insisted one must do it properly. He held the tray first to Mary Aesop, noting her red nose and weepy eyes. Then he served the Schoolmaster. Taking his own glass, he sat next to Mary.

There was silence in the room save the fire's hissing and snapping.

"This tastes most excellent, Caldwell. It rather soothes my raw throat. I hear you authored the recipe," said Mary.

"Yes, Mrs Aesop, thank you, so I did."

"You're calling me missus again, Caldwell."

"Indeed, Mary." After a few seconds, he added, "but I rather prefer the apricot," he said with great conviction. "It has a particular tang all its own that I find rather satisfying, more so than the others."

"Is that so?" She lifted the snifter to her nose, "Mmm, indeed." And she drank every last drop of the peach. "Now then, I should very much like to try *your* preference, Caldwell, perhaps a little apricot then?"

"Certainly." And he, in his staunch and stiff form, cleaned the sticky residue of peach brandy from her snifter and poured her the apricot. "There you have it, Mary. I do hope you find it to your liking and enjoy it as I do."

"Thank you." Smiling, she noticed that this time he filled her snifter just a little past the acceptable level—over half full. "I will tell you in little time, Caldwell." She brought it to her lips, sipping it slowly, swishing the thick, warm apricot brandy around in her mouth.

The Schoolmaster and Caldwell watched in amused wonder as they waited in anticipation. Would it be the peach or the apricot? They watched her throat's wave-like swallow and then they studied her eyes.

"Hmm," she said, holding the glass up, staring at it, "perhaps to make a better judgment I should try the berry, but Caldwell, please permit me to first finish the apricot. It is very good."

"Thank you, Mary." He looked to James, "Sir, another?"

"Yes, Caldwell." James felt warm inside. "This time I shall try the apricot myself. That is *my* favourite. I assure you right off that apricot is my very favourite." He sat smiling at Caldwell. "Have you ever tried making dandelion wine, Caldwell?"

Mary lifted the brandy snifter with both hands and drank every bit of the apricot and then gently set the glass down. Watching the syrupy liquor as it slowly slid down the sides and pool at the bottom of her glass, she became very quiet. Suddenly tears welled in her eyes, but not so much that anyone would notice.

Hearing her sniffle, Caldwell turned toward her. "Mary, are you taking cold?"

Tears dripped freely upon her hands; her mouth twisted in such proportions that he hurried to her side. "Mary, please, you must calm yourself." He patted her back tenderly.

James filled her empty brandy snifter with water. "There now," he said, "there now."

"I take it you do not care for the apricot, Mary?"

"Oh, hush, Caldwell, will you." She blew her nose. "Your handkerchief, if you please."

Reluctantly he withdrew a clean, white handkerchief from his vest pocket. He hated to hand it over, knowing full well she would destroy it.

She snatched it from his hands. Tears were dripping from her eyes and nose. "Thank you. I shall be just a little while more for crying. I shall give it back, Caldwell."

"Oh, yes," he grimaced, "you always do."

She caught his pained expression. "You are altogether too stuffy, Caldwell. What a face to make at such a moment. You know very well I always bring you back a most perfectly cleaned and well-folded handkerchief—ironed I might add."

"Yes, forgive me." And he stood erect. "It is just the thought ..."

James laughed. "Oh, forevermore, Caldwell, you really must do something about your vivid imagination."

"I am sorry for it, sir, but after these many years I cannot help myself."

"No," said Mary, "it is a lost cause. Forgive me, too much brandy, perhaps, but I must say Caldwell, apricot is the better of the two."

"I thought as much, Mary. Tell me, what has upset you that you cry so? Could it be that Bobbin is ill with cold?"

"Yes, Caldwell." She handed him the letter from Mr Collier. "I just this very hour received it, and didn't even have time to share it with anyone else but the Schoolmaster. And, pray tell, how did you know she was ill even before I?"

"Mary, have you forgotten my nephew, Winfred, is the courier?" Caldwell glanced over the letter as a mere courtesy and returned it.

"I should have known, Caldwell," she exhaled heavily.

"It is my job, Mary, to be in the know. We have discussed that many times, you and I, at the table, with the others in-service here."

"Yes, yes, Caldwell. I know very well. However, I never thought I would be anyone's topic of conversation."

"Oh, rest assured Mary, all of us at one time or another are the topic of someone's conversation." He cleared his throat. "Truth be told, many times over."

"I quite agree, Mary," added James with a laugh, "take it with a grain of salt. It is a small world after all, is it not?"

She nodded. "But one thing amazes me. No one has ever betrayed my deepest secret regarding my dear, sweet Stella Babette."

"Well 'even thieves have a code of laws,' "[52] replied Caldwell. "There are some things people with honour simply do not do, and that is to betray a sacred promise."

"Excuse me, Caldwell, forgive me, you are very right. It is just that I am particularly overwrought this evening. It has been such a year. I don't know exactly what I should do."

James took her hand. "Mary, perhaps it is time you told her. Bobbin is old enough now, and I might add, intelligent enough to learn the truth."

Mary shook her head. "Oh, I don't know about speaking the truth to Babette."

"Mary, she is searching for her mother, for God's sake. Put her mind to rest. We will go along with you for support. If you wish, you could bring her back here and break the news to her with us."

She smiled. "Yes, but of course, I shall bring her back here where my strength is; where my friends are. Oh, yes, that sounds like the very best of plans. When she is well, I shall bring her here. I will speak with Mr Collier and Miss Collier— all the Collier family. She took James's hand. "Oh, I believe I shall need very much help. Am I strong enough for the words?"

"Certainly you are, Mary. Everyone here at Mary Arden will help you. We all understand. We understood the day you came to us. Goodness me, it has been near six years."

"Aye, Mary, no need to worry," said Caldwell, becoming less stiff. "We have all kept the secret these years, and we will not let you down now."

"What if John Collier ..."

"Stops loving you, Mary?" added Caldwell kindly, "then he is not the man I know him to be."

She looked astounded. "Do not tell me, Caldwell, you know him intimately?"

"My brother, Frederick, is his butler, Mary."

---

[52] Cicero (106 – 43 BC) Roman philosopher and orator. *De Officiis*, II, xi, 40. Quoted from *The New Dictionary of Thoughts* by Tryon Edwards (1949) p. 745.

Chapter 22 – A Memorable Evening

For evere was, and evere schal befalle,
That Love is he that alle thing may bynde ;
For may no man fordon the lawe of kynde. [53]

Ambling up the familiar roadway twisting through the lush green summer meadows, the carriage fast approached the Mary Arden Academy. How Susanna Neilson loved this ride, rolling through the open fields, in and around the woods that encircled the academy. Anxious to see James, she kept her mind busy by marking trees, naming shrubbery, watching the village people work in the fields.

It had been near one month since the passing of James's father, and she was relieved that he was now trying to resume his life, albeit a little at a time. She had been invited to hear Bach this evening, and as a memorial to his father, one of the students would be playing his father's favourite: *Jesu, Joy of Man's Desiring.* Afterward, they were to dine on the balcony. All in all, she hoped it would be a lovely, quiet July evening.

It will not be long now, she thought, tugging at her gloves. Glancing around inside the small carriage she found her old purse and worried for looking unfashionable. *I do hope I am presentable. Staying in the orphanage I have been long removed from any sort of proper society...*

---

[53] Geoffrey Chaucer (1343 – 1400) English poet. *Troylus and Criseyde.* Quoted from *The English Poets*, Vol. 1, Chaucer to Donne, by Thomas Humphry (1880) p. 19.

* * *

Whining and nudging James's leg, Holly bolted toward the door.

"What is it, girl?" He stood at his desk, hearing the familiar crunch of carriage wheels just outside, the very one that he had sent for Miss Susanna had finally arrived.

Amid the hustle and bustle of servants, he went to his window. "Ah, there she is. Thank you, Holly. Well done, girl." He ruffled the top of her head. "Come, girl, let's give her a proper greeting."

They traversed the hallway and entered the vestibule just as Susanna was escorted in. The fragrance of summer lingered about her; she smiled.

His heart pounded wildly. Suddenly his mouth became dry, and he blushed. *She has such a profound effect on me.* Regaining his composure, he stood before her. "Good afternoon, Miss Susanna. You must be tired from the long ride, though, I must say you look amazingly fresh."

"Oh, sir, not so very tired now, thank you." Her eyes remained focused on him; she wanted only to remain near him, but she knew she must take time to change, for this evening was a formal affair. "I will be gone a very little while, James, I must dress. Please excuse me."

"I shall be in the study, waiting, Miss Susanna." He smiled and watched as she was escorted up the long spiral staircase to her room. Reaching the top landing, she turned and impulsively blew him a kiss.

Pleasantly shocked at her display of affection, he blushed profusely. Two students, witnessing the event, giggled and continued down the hall. He remained at the foot of the stairs until she was out of sight.

* * *

The concert was to begin at six o'clock, and it was nearing half past the hour of five, and still Susanna had not come down from her room. James paced in front of the hearth when the door suddenly opened. She stood for a moment looking about the room for him. She wore a low-cut, black satin gown, simple and elegant. A very little bit of lace edged the bodice, but not so much as to foil her lovely neckline. She looked stunningly beautiful.

He had never seen her without a cape or bonnet, without long gloves. Her skin looked soft and supple, not a mark or blemish. She was flushed with a sensual pink glow as she slowly came to him, smiling. The room had dimmed, save the fire and a few candles burning softly, he could not take his eyes from her. Wild thoughts raced through his mind; it took all his control not to put his arms around her. His fingers tingled, his breathing quickened; he swallowed hard, "Miss Susanna ... you look beautiful."

"Thank you, sir. I hope I have not kept you waiting long?"

"Oh, no," he lied, "no, certainly no, you have not."

There came a knock, and Caldwell entered. "Sir, the concert begins in twenty minutes. Do you wish to dress for the occasion?"

James, still flustered, stared at Caldwell. "Dress? He looked down at his casual attire. "By George, I must hurry. Miss Susanna, please excuse me; I shan't be long."

She laughed at his absentmindedness. "Sir, I shall remain here and wait for you."

"Please, by all means, go and take a seat in the music room. Seat her in the side open to the cathedral, Caldwell. I shall join you shortly. Miss Susanna, Caldwell will escort you."

"Very well," she smiled.

He stood watching her for the longest time.

"James," she laughed, "are you going to change?"

"Oh, yes, I will go now," he stammered and bowed his withdrawal from the room. Bounding up the steps, he unbuttoned his clothes as he hurried along. When he finally finished dressing, he hastily descended the steps two at a time; he could hear the hauntingly rich grandeur of the pipe organ in the cathedral. A deep power swayed in his heart, his father's most revered music, Bach's *Jesu* ... vibrating, no doubt, every wall in the school, filling every room with his father's presence. *So, they have begun without me?* He glanced at the wall clock. *Indeed I am late.*

He opened the music room door and quietly made way to the seating area. The familiar half-circle now opened, overlooked the cathedral. The heavy, green velvet drapes were pulled back, fastened by red velvet ties. Sitting atop the dark, highly polished backboard cabinet he spied the silver patina of candelabras lending their soft flickering light.

But where is Susanna? He scanned the audience until he finally spied her bright lustrous blond hair, wrapped and curled atop her head. She was surrounded by professors, and not one chair had been saved for him. He dejectedly sat in the back, forced to watch as they courted and smiled at her, smirked and gestured, leaning toward her.

Hmm, he thought, *and she does not move away from their advances. They are most rude to whisper while the students' play.*

There came a short break in the program. When Susanna glanced about the room for James, he casually looked away. She fanned herself, thinking the motion might catch his eye. It did, and he returned her smile, barely.

The gentlemen sitting around her found her so delightful that their idle conversation could not be interrupted, and before she had the opportunity to remove herself from their company, the music began, and she was trapped.

James, at her notice, didn't look her way for the remainder of the program. The recital lasted a little past eight o'clock, and while everyone politely clapped at its close, Susanna anxiously searched for James. When she stood to leave, she had to literally move her chair away from the professors who had hemmed her in. "Please, if you will excuse me."

The other ladies present, no doubt, wondered just who she was as they whispered behind their fans. Susanna finally spied James standing at the hearth; Foss leaning against his leg.

"Well then," she said apprehensively, "there you are." She smiled, "may I cosy by the fire with you and the cat?"

"Certainly." Avoiding her eyes, he moved slightly to the side. He waited for a few seconds before saying, "When I returned to the music room, I could not find you right off. And then when I did ... I could see you were preoccupied with the professors."

He continued to stare into the fire, pouting. She was amused.

"They love to talk, do they not, James?" She held his name, trying to force his eyes to meet hers, but he would not be cajoled. Inhaling deeply, she said, "I tried to hold a chair for you, but a certain Professor Zany, I believe that was his name, acted deaf and took the seat all the same. I am sure I turned a few shades, but that did not deter him in the least. And then the music began, and you arrived. I found myself in a pickle, sir. I do hope you forgive me."

James softened. "In a pickle, indeed." Checking his dark side, he smiled. "Forgive me, Miss Susanna, for being such a bore, will you?" And, in a quiet, intimate tone he apologised further. "I should have realised as much. Indeed, Professor Zany can be quite trying betimes."

"It has been a trying month, has it not?" Smiling tenderly, she added, "We are only human, after all."

He gazed into her lovely blue eyes, and the slight incident was forgotten, "Come, then, shall we have our dinner?"

"Indeed, I am famished."

* * *

As they walked out onto the terraced balcony, that moonlit night, Susanna inhaled the sumptuous breezes scented with night blooming Jasmine. Tables were situated far enough apart for intimate conversation, affording each a hint of seclusion. Their table was centred with a water bowl of fresh flowers, and amidst the floral arrangement sat small floating tea candles flickering.

Starry-eyed, Susanna whispered, "It is all so very lovely. I have never eaten dinner out of doors, at night." Closing her eyes, she allowed her senses to experience the splendour. She felt his lips very close to hers and found his breath sweet ... she kissed his lips.

Chapter 23 – Newpark Orphanage

You will find poetry nowhere unless you bring some with you. [54]

It was near ten o'clock that morning when a courier, sent by the Colliers rang the kitchen bell at the London Newpark Orphanage's side door. Wiping her hands, Moll answered the bell. White puffs of flour floated in the air. "What does ye need, young man?"

"I have a letter for Miss Susanna Neilson. It's important, ma'am."

"Come in then." She looked the lad over quickly. "Wait here." She dusted her hands on her apron and left the fresh-faced young man to eye her warm kitchen.

It smelled heavenly, but nothing was sitting out where he could lift a sweet cake or two. Shortly, he heard footfalls and voices, and then the kitchen door flew open.

"Yes, I am Miss Neilson." She held a book of fairy tales pressed to her chest.

"A letter from the Collier residence, ma'am."

"Have we a penny tip, Moll?"

The young boy shook his head. "Oh, no matter, miss. I knowed this is the orphanage, no matter."

"Is that right?" Moll affectionately tweaked his nose. "Here then, take a couple slices of bread, will ye?"

---

[54] Joseph Joubert (1754 – 1824) French writer. Quoted from *A Dictionary of Thoughts*, by Tryon Edwards, (1891).

"Oh, yes, ma'am, that I will. Thank you." The courier's eyes widened as she handed him two huge slices spread with a bit of lard atop each. He eagerly shoved the slice into his mouth and mumbled a thank you as he descended the alleyway steps.

"What's a slice or two?" said Moll winking at Susanna. "I din' think you'd care."

"No, of course not, but they were worth more than a penny tip, Moll, I assure you."

They both laughed.

"Now then, what could the good Mr Collier need of me?" She and Moll sat down at the kitchen table. She slipped her finger inside the envelope and pried open the wax seal.

"Collier House, London July 18 early morning
*   Miss Neilson, as of this writing Miss Derby is ill with cold and asks if you would kindly come for a visit. She is sitting up now, but still weak. She took cold days ago and talks of nothing but her Miss Neilson. Rest assured she is well looked after. We look forward to seeing you, as well. We have informed the courier to wait for your reply, as we will send a carriage for you—at your convenience.*
*   Yours sincerely, Maria Collier*

"Oh, dear me, Moll," Miss Neilson cried, hurrying to the door, "I must catch the courier." She dashed down the steps and caught a glimpse of him as he was downing the last slice of bread and about to turn the corner.

"Young man!" she called out, waving, "wait just a moment." Out of breath, she scolded him, "Young man, you were supposed to wait for a reply."

"Excuse, miss," he said, sincerely, "I forgot."

"Aye, so you did." She wiped his mouth for the crumbs.

"Return to the Collier residence and inform Miss Collier I will come visit Miss Derby morning next, eleven of the hour." She eyed the young man. "Repeat for me."

"Yes, ma'am, I am to tell Miss Collier you will come on the eleventh hour tomorrow morning."

"Aye, the exact words, and I am very grateful for the offer of a carriage."

"Yes, ma'am, you are grateful for their offer of a carriage."

Satisfied that the young courier knew the message, Susanna sent him on his way. "Go now, but mind the traffic." She affectionately gave him a light-handed spank to his bottom.

His face turned red. "I will, miss, I will."

Chapter 24 – Edward Nurses Bobbin

A crowd is not company,
and faces are but a gallery of pictures,
and talk but a tinkling cymbal,
where there is no love. [55]

"There now, Bobbin," crowed Edward as they sat in the Colliers' drawing room, now converted into a recuperating room for her, "the colour is coming back to your cheeks."

"Indeed, Edward. I feel I am gaining my strength day by day."

Maria looked on, revelling in the fact that her brother loved so deeply. "Edward deemed it so, Bobbin. He willed you from the clutches of death."

Her face glowed as she took Edward's hand. "Indeed."

"You gave us all such a fright, you know," he said, pulling her woollen scarf a little tighter around her neck.

"I am sorry, Edward." She dabbed at her nose.

"Well, you could not have helped it." He gazed at her sweetness. "I have some very good news that will cheer you, Bobbin. Today Miss Neilson will come visit, eleven of the hour."

Bobbin sat erect in her "recovery chair" as Maria called it, propped up and bundled with every spare blanket in the Collier household. She had a coughing fit at the happy news.

---

[55] Francis Bacon (1561 – 1626) English philosopher and Lord Chancellor. "Of Friendship" in *Essays* (1625). Quoted from *Oxford Essential Quotations*, 4th Edition, (2016).

He patted her back. "Easy, now." And he handed her another handkerchief. "Easy." Concerned, he flinched with each cough and sputter. "Easy there, Bobbin."

She protested kindly, "But, Edward, I shall recover. After all, it is only a cold."

"More near pneumonia, I should say, and dangerous at that. Thanks to Dr Harris, you are alive at all."

"Dear me," she replied, amused at his serious demeanour. "I had no idea, Edward that I was at death's very door."

"Well, I know enough about bad colds, Bobbin. You must remain calm and warm. No walking out of doors, no getting overly excited. Your cough is still extreme."

"Yes, it is quite hideous." Lying her head back on the satin bolster, she sighed. "Oh, I am very calm and satisfied here, Maria. The fire is so cheery warm; the air smells so, so healthful. Thank you, Edward, for burning the oil of eucalyptus. I really believe it has helped me to breathe."

"Indeed," said Maria. "So, Edward brought the oil of eucalyptus, did he?" She watched from the corner of her eye as her brother fidgeted.

"Well, I lit it, Maria," he said. Knowing she would brag that the eucalyptus had been her idea in the first place, he quickly changed the course of the conversation.

"Sir," informed the housemaid, "Mrs Aesop is calling for Miss Derby, her card." She held the tray up to Edward.

"Mrs Aesop?" He glanced at his sister in confusion. "We were not expecting such a visit. Well, then, that was a long journey for her. How very kind of her to call." He nodded to the maid, "Very well, show her in."

Straightening her frock, Maria rang the housemaid with the idea of serving tea. Edward fluffed Bobbin's pillows. Within that brief interlude, Mrs Aesop was escorted into the room.

Maria nodded politely, for she so admired the Headmistress Aesop. Edward bowed, knowing how fond his father was of her. Bobbin sat up smiling, but for the excitement, began to cough a little.

"Mrs Aesop, so very nice of you to call," said Maria. "Please, sit here by the fire with us."

Bobbin's eyes glistened at seeing the dear lady. "Oh, how very good it is to see you, Mrs Aesop. How kind of you to call. Excuse my appearance I have recently been ill with cold."

Seeing for herself that Bobbin was really out of danger, Mary's first impulse was to grab and squeeze her. Instead, she smiled warmly while removing her gloves. "Indeed, by your shining face, I can see you are near fully recovered." She smiled at Edward and Maria. "No doubt mending most excellently from the good care of the Colliers."

"Oh, Mrs Aesop," said Bobbin, "tell us, how are Schoolmaster and Holly? Oh, and Foss? Are they well?"

Edward handed Bobbin a glass of water.

Scanning the delightful room, Mrs Aesop thought it to be a fine, cheery place. She smelled the oil of eucalyptus recognising it as an old family remedy. "Well, Foss and Holly are very well, though they miss you and Maria terribly. You two were the only ones who played with them. They still visit your old room, sniffing about."

"Oh, yes, how I remember." Maria giggled. "How mischievous those two were. I miss them. I miss you. I do miss everyone, very much. Bye the way, how is Professor Zany?"

"He is very well, Miss Collier. Visitors are always welcome you know." Her gaze settled upon Bobbin's sweet face. "You are doing well then, Babette?"

Bobbin was taken aback. The name Babette seemed somehow like a secret password stored away in her brain for what seemed a thousand years. The name echoed inside her head ... *Babette? Stella Babette, Stella?* She coughed into her handkerchief. "Excuse me, Mrs Aesop. Yes, thank you. I am very much on the mend from this nasty cold."

"Indeed, I am relieved to see that you are recovering so quickly. Mr Collier wrote, informing me of your condition. I must say I was very worried."

Over tea and sweet cakes, the three exchanged an hour's worth of pleasantries before Mrs Aesop said it was near time to be returning to her hotel.

Maria entreated, "Oh, please, Mrs Aesop; Papa will feel neglected that you did not stay until he returns. You must stay, then, or at least return for dinner. He was called away earlier this morning, but should be returning within the hour."

"Yes, please stay, Mrs Aesop," said Edward. "Where are you staying?"

"Northgate, near the wharf," she replied, leaning very near accepting their most gracious offer. She ruffled the hair atop Bobbin's head. "Perhaps, I shall," she smiled.

"Then it is settled, see you at seven-thirty," said Edward. "Father will be very pleased."

"And so shall I." Bobbin smiled, coughing into her handkerchief.

"Dear me, then, I am most pleased, most flattered by such affectionate attention. I shall be happy to sup with you." Mrs Aesop turned to Edward and Maria. "Thank you so very much for your kind hospitality. I shall see you all this evening then. Good day to you."

Just as she was leaving, Bobbin sat up. "Mrs Aesop, wait ... please, say again, Babette. Do you think Bobbin is a nick-name from it?"

For a paralysing second Mary looked deeply into her dark black eyes, being the very colour of her own. "Perhaps it is. Goodnight, my little Babette." Smiling, she left the room.

It was a very familiar smile, thought Bobbin. *Very familiar...*"Edward," she said affectionately taking his hand, "there is something about Mrs Aesop ..."

Looking down at her, feeling the warmth of her soft cheek against his hand, he nodded. "Indeed, it is quite obvious she loves you, Bobbin, as we all do."

"Mary ... Mary Aesop," said Bobbin. "Hmm." Leaning back in her chair she repeated her name over and over until finally closing her eyes she fell off to sleep.

Covering her legs, Edward felt her brow and sighed contentedly. He was stoking the fire when Maria came back into the room.

Finding Bobbin resting, she glanced at the clock, it was a little past eleven. "Edward," she whispered, "come, I hear a carriage."

* * *

As Mrs Aesop's carriage pulled away, the Colliers' carriage arrived carrying Miss Neilson.

The clock in the vestibule chimed half past the hour as Susanna looked apologetically into the eyes of Edward and Maria Collier. "Dear me, I hope I am not too late. The carriage arrived at the orphanage just a little after eleven. Please forgive me for being tardy."

"Oh, no, Miss Neilson," said Edward, "the delay was no fault of yours. I assure you it was our coachman who left late. No, no, the fault lies entirely with me."

"Thank you, sir." She smiled nervously. "And how is my little Bobbin?" she asked, pulling off her gloves.

"At the moment, she is asleep," replied Maria in a hushed tone. "Come with us, we are to eat lunch. Please join us. Come, come," she urged, "we have a place already set for you."

"Very well," said Miss Neilson, though anxious to see for herself how Bobbin was.

Maria sensed her apprehension. "Of course, you are worried. Come then, have a peek; our little dormouse is fine, really." She took Miss Neilson's hand and led her to the drawing room; quietly she opened the door.

When Susanna witnessed Bobbin's sweet little pink face wrapped in warm, secure quilts, she nodded with a smile. "Thank you, Miss Collier, thank you." She whispered, "I am most relieved."

Maria took her hand. "Come then, Miss Neilson, let us have a bit of lunch."

After they finished a most excellent turtle soup, which Miss Neilson had never tasted before in her life, they were served a very fine assortment of cold ham, beef tongue, potatoes, mixed vegetables and a small glass of wine.

"Miss Neilson," said Edward, "would you care for another claret?"

"Just a little, sir," she replied graciously. "And how are your brother and your father?"

"Both Philip and Father are very well, thank you, Miss Neilson. I took a week's leave from the Bank to chaperone my sister and Miss Derby on a little research project. However, for her catching such a nasty cold, we have been derailed for a time."

"I see," she took a sip and went on, "that is a most generous allotment of your time to be a chaperone, sir. The bank must miss you."

"Thank you, Miss Neilson, but I am the youngest brother, and since Philip has finished his apprenticeship, he will stay close to Father's right hand, so to speak, until I finish my apprenticeship. I shall join them then. I am, at present, in my last year. I graduated from Eton last fall. Philip has a very strong desire to become involved in the business internationally." He paused. "Well now, Miss Neilson, I have bored you."

"Oh, no, sir, no, not at all, I assure you. It is interesting to get a glimpse into the workings of your most prestigious family."

Maria nodded. "Why, thank you, Miss Neilson, Edward and I are more than pleased that you are here."

Just then the dining room door opened, and there stood Bobbin, wrapped like a mummy. "Miss Neilson," she coughed, "so so good to ..."

Edward stood. "Bobbin, you must not exert yourself so. Remember what the doctor said?" He led her back into the sun-filled sitting room.

"Oh, Miss Neilson," she cried as Edward rewrapped her again. "I thought I was dreaming when I heard your voice."

"Well, it was not a dream, after all, was it? So good to see you, my dearest friend." She kissed her forehead.

Edward handed Bobbin a glass. "There now, you must drink your water."

"Oh, yes, yes, I must drink." She smiled at Miss Neilson. "Edward is my nurse, you see."

Susanna was pleased at the mutual affection. *Bobbin would be most fortunate to secure his hand in marriage; such a life of ease with no worries.* "I see you take very good care of her, Mr Collier."

"Oh, my, yes," said Maria, "he is quite the nursemaid to my little dormouse." Smiling affectionately, she beamed. "Actually, Bobbin is very much part of the family now." She tweaked her ear. "Say so, Bobbin, are we not like sisters?"

"Very much so." Her eyes sparkled.

"But, Maria, I do not think of her as a sister, I assure you," said Edward.

Everyone laughed at his honest appraisal. And while he leaned over Bobbin, handing her a clean handkerchief, he smiled. "A little dormouse perhaps, yes, but a sister? No, that would never do."

Flushed, Bobbin beamed. Regaining her composure, she turned to Susanna. "Come, Miss Neilson, please sit here, by me. I have very much wanted to ask how you have been getting along. How are Moll and the others?"

Bobbin coughed now and again, dabbing her mouth, drinking her water, being fussed over by Edward through much of the visit.

When her eyes began to droop, Susanna decided it was time to go. "Well, now, my dear, time is moving along, and you must rest." The chimes on the mantle struck twice. "Dear me, Bobbin, you know very well what that hour means at the orphanage."

"Oh, yes, miss, the reading hour. Someday, and maybe soon, I shall come for a visit, to sit and read to the children again."

"Well, you know very well helpers are always welcome. Everyone misses you so, especially me." Her eyes glistened.

"I know, Miss Neilson, I know, but I have something I must do before I come back. Tell me, before you go, how is Schoolmaster Halliwell-Phillipps? How could I have forgotten to ask about him earlier? Shame on me."

Susanna's eyes lit; she smiled broadly. "We are doing very well, very well, indeed." Her tone softened near a whisper. "We are very fond of each other. I will be making a call at the bookstore this afternoon. There is a bit of business there, and he wishes for me to hear it."

Maria smiled. "How very nice for you then, Miss Neilson, and since the Schoolmaster is in London, please, the both of you should come pay a visit."

Edward, seeing the happy expression on Bobbin's face, nodded. "Indeed, excellent idea, please come for dinner this evening. Father will be delighted at the company, I assure you. And for the first time in days, Bobbin will be eating at the table this evening. At least she should be eating at the table." He looked down at her happy, twinkling eyes.

"Oh, of course, I will, Edward, of course. Oh, I am so happy." She coughed into her hanky.

"Oh, now, see what I am causing," said Susanna. "We shall be very pleased to come for dinner. I will first see what Mr Halliwell-Phillipps has planned. If he has not made prior engagements, we shall come, and be very happy for it, I assure you."

Edward bowed. "It is our pleasure, Miss Neilson."

"Thank you, sir. And one more thing, thank you very much for sending the carriage. It was more than thoughtful."

Maria, impressed with her good manners, replied, "It is nothing, Miss Neilson, our pleasure."

Susanna kissed Bobbin on the cheek. "I shall drop a note to you confirming our plans for dinner. Good day to you all."

"Good day, Miss Neilson." Bobbin waved. "Good day."

"Well," said Maria lightheartedly, "Papa will have a house full for dinner tonight."

Chapter 25 - James, Susanna and Holly

Friendship is the shadow of the evening, which
strengthens with the setting sun of life. [56]

Holly was sniffing the afternoon air as James's carriage
made way through the busy London streets. He, at first, had
not planned to bring her, but her pleading amber eyes softened
his heart, and he gave in, again.

This afternoon James was to meet Miss Neilson and his
attorney, Mr Winston Hughes, at the bookstore. There was one
very important item left yet in his father's will that needed to
be discussed. He was very pleased about it and wanted Miss
Neilson there to hear his father's wishes exactly.

Arriving at the bookstore, Holly jostled about inside the
carriage. Her tail wagged mightily as she sniffed the air,
instantly remembering this part of town.

"There now girl, easy girl, Father is no longer here." He
swallowed hard. "Come, girl."

Holly leapt from the carriage and ran to the store,
scratching at the door, impatiently waiting for the old
gentleman to open it and greet her in his usual kind manner.

James removed the large tangle of keys and inserted one
into the lock. "Wait, now, until I unlock it, and then you shall
see for yourself that he is not here."

---

[56] Jean de La Fontaine (1621 – 1695) French poet. Quoted from *A
Dictionary of Thoughts*, by Tryon Edwards, (1908).

When he turned the knob, Holly forced the door open and dashed in. Sniffing and whining, she ran behind the counter. Not finding the kind old gentleman there, she scampered up the stairs and into his room, into his study, into his library, into each closet. Then down the stairs, stopping and listening on the landing, her eyes wide, her large floppy ears pricked, listening for his footsteps, wondering if he was playing a hiding game.

Feeling a chill from the dampness, James found some kindling and a spurt of oil. He started a grand fire in the hearth. Glancing about his father's store, he heard Holly's nails scratching the hardwood floors as she continued her search. "Come Holly, he is not here, girl."

Holly, having none of it, continued to nose about until, at last, she resigned herself that indeed the old gentleman was not there.

James sighed. "So you think he will be right back, do you?"

Her ears perked. She lifted her head, sniffed the air and whined.

"Well, maybe he will be right back then." James patted her head. "Maybe."

At that moment the door opened, and Susanna entered.

"Miss Susanna, you are looking very well."

"I am feeling well, yes, very well, and for being here, I am excellent." She stroked Holly's head. "Although, my dear little Bobbin is ill with cold."

"Oh, how unfortunate, I was just about to send a note requesting that she visit the store today."

Holly wiggled up to Susanna begging for a pat on the head.

"Go now, Holly," said James in a serious tone. "Lie down, Miss Susanna and I wish to be alone."

"Do we?" She smiled. "And what harm of her sitting quietly near us?"

"She, she never sits quietly, and she demands all your attention."

He is envious of the poor dog. She smiled. "Very well then, James, the dog loses. Send her back to the hearth-rug, and there she shall remain."

"I knew you would agree." He pointed. "Go now, Holly, to the rug." James took Susanna's hand. "Come, I have something I wish to show you."

He led her into his father's study and gestured toward the sofa. "Please, sit here, Miss Susanna, while I light a few lamps." He sighed. "Father refused gas lamps, detested the fumes." He lit a lamp and sat it on the mantle. "Mr Hughes, our family's attorney, will not be here for yet another half-hour." Pulling a small red leather chest from the bookshelf, he smiled. "It rather looks like a treasure chest, does it not?"

She nodded. "You certainly have made me curious, James." Perusing the chest, she nodded. "A very handsome piece with these shiny brass studs fastened all about. Indeed, a very handsome piece."

Taking a small key that hung from a nearby peg, James unlocked the chest. Hearing a noise at the door, he found Holly peeking in at them. "Come in, come in, you spoiled thing."

Holding her head down, she eased her way into the room, tiptoeing cautiously toward Susanna, not looking James in the eye.

"Come, girl," whispered Susanna as she patted the sofa. "Why, I believe she's smiling, sir."

"Gloating is more like it, if you ask me." He shook his head. "She owns you."

"Holly, I think he wants to own me as you do. However, it will take more than a bone to capture my heart."

James smiled. "Well, we'll just see about that, miss. Close your eyes, then." He placed his mother's wedding band in her palm and closed her fingers around it. Bringing her hand to his lips, he whispered, "You may open your eyes now. It was my mother's."

Studying her clenched fist, she asked, "May I now examine what you placed in my hand, sir?"

"Only if you promise to keep it forever."

"I promise to keep it forever and then some." Slowly relaxing her fingers, she found the gleaming gold band. "Why, it is very beautiful." She held it up. "James, it is new, you said it belonged to your mother?"

"It was her wedding band. She died when I was four and had not worn it long. Will you marry me, Susanna?"

Her eyes glistened. "I shall honour and love it as I do you, James, of course I will."

"And I shall honour and love you for the remainder of my life, Susanna."

He leaned over to kiss her, but Holly had wedged her way between the two. Laughing, they heard the ring of the doorbell.

"Come, dear, it must be Mr Hughes."

Mr Hughes entered the bookshop and nodded. "Good day, sir."

James beamed proudly. "May I have the honour of introducing to you my fiancée, Miss Susanna Neilson. She has just consented to marry me."

Hughes arched his brows in delighted surprise. "Good day, Miss Neilson and congratulations to you. I have known the family a good many years. You shall be very blessed, very."

"Thank you, sir," said Susanna. "I did not have the pleasure of knowing Mrs Halliwell-Phillipps. However, I was very familiar with the professor; not a kinder nor more generous gentleman in all of England. I miss him exceedingly."

"As we all do, Miss Neilson. John and I were schoolmates at Oxford. His wife, Jane, was a very dear woman. Well, you have found the crowning jewel, miss—the crowning jewel."

Hughes took James's arm affectionately and squeezed it. Gazing down affectionately at the dog, he teased, "Well, then Holly girl, you have finally met your match." Immediately realising his unintentional insult, he stammered, "Ah, ah, excuse me, Miss Neilson, I meant no disrespect."

"Oh, sir," she said, "no offence intended, no offence taken. I assure you, sir, I do not wear my heart on my sleeve. Being a teacher at Newpark Orphanage, one must maintain a solid sense of humour. Besides that," she smiled, "I rather like being compared to such a sweet, loving creature as Holly." She stroked her head. "But I should wonder if she takes offence at being so closely associated with me?"

The attorney guffawed loudly. "We are a congenial lot, are we not? And he laughed again. "Come now, we have yet a few items that need to be discussed." He looked around the room. "Is Miss Derby here?"

"Oh, dear me, James," said Susanna, "I forgot to mention that we are to sup with Mr John Collier and his family this very night, seven-thirty, with Bobbin. I must send a note immediately if we are to attend."

"Why, certainly, Susanna, I had nothing planned."

"Very well, then. I must send a note this very minute. Excuse me, sir." She hurried away in search of pen and paper.

"The Colliers, James?" Hughes looked astounded. "The Bank of England Colliers? Why, they are the most influential family in London, possibly the whole of England."

"Yes, I know, Hughes. I went to school with Philip and Edward Collier, fine men. We have rekindled an old friendship, oddly enough, through their sister, Miss Maria Collier, a most recent graduate of the academy."

"Hmm." He nodded. "I've heard she can be quite difficult, a handful at times."

"No longer, Hughes. Miss Collier has matured into a very pleasant young lady, I assure you. The sudden death of her mother, I believe, was the catalyst to a most unfortunate disposition, one so extreme that Mr Collier enrolled her at Mary Arden. Though we alone were not responsible for such a transformation, rather, the orphan worked the miracle, Miss Bobbin Derby."

"Ah, yes, Miss Derby, very good then. I have been looking forward to meeting her, so I have. She will be here soon, then, James?"

"Well, no," he replied, "she has taken ill, a bad cold apparently. I just learned of her illness."

"Hmm, well, then ..." rubbing his chin, he glanced around the shop, "all these books will be hers. I suppose you could tell her of your father's wishes, and that she is to inherit the bookstore and all that's within. When she is feeling up to it, bring her to my office; it shall be settled then."

Chapter 26 – John Collier Discovers the Truth

Much rain wears the marble. [57]

At the very same moment, Susanna was sending a courier to the Collier's confirming their dinner engagement that very evening, Mr Collier was climbing the outside steps to Detective Brown's Northgate office on the wharf.

Ringing the outside bell, and with no answer, Collier let himself in. He found a half-dead palm frond propped up by an old broken umbrella, the floor littered with papers stacked knee-high, he frowned at the clutter.

Suddenly jolted awake, detective Brown jumped up and walked from around his desk and out into the small vestibule. "Oh, beg pardon, Mr Collier, didn't hear the bell." He motioned toward an old overstuffed chair. "Sir, take that chair there by the window ... nice view of the Northgate Hotel's wharf, I should say."

The detective sat back down at his enormous, paper-littered desk and gazed at the floor. "I am sorry to say, sir, I hit a cold trail." Inhaling deeply, he looked up. "But I haven't given up. Indeed not, sir. I was on a good line that led directly to a girl's school, the Mary Arden Academy, in Wilmecote. It's a strange sort of school for girls, plenty of strange professors there, too. I wrote to the schoolmaster, Mr Halliwell-Phillipps,

---

[57] William Shakespeare, *King Henry VI*, Act 3, Scene 2.

for an appointment next week. So on that score, sir, I will be back on the trail of Mrs Derby."

"Detective Brown," inquired Collier, "what led you to this girl's academy in search of Mrs Derby?"

"A certain Mrs Waller, from the Oxford Street Tavern, sir. She was the landlady who found the burning house full of the, ah, where the Derbys died. I went back and questioned her some more, so I did. Aye, dropped a few pounds about here and there. Money is an incentive to them types, sir."

"Go on," said Collier glancing out the window.

"The landlady, Mrs Waller, went with her husband to deliver some spirits to this girl's academy about a year after Mrs Derby disappeared. She spied the very woman, Mrs Derby, reading to the students. By her word, unless the lady had a twin, 'twas the very one,' she swore it."

"And what of the inquiry at the academy? Did you not learn one thing more?"

"Strange, that, sir, I learned not one thing, sir, and mighty suspicious for it. They are a strange bunch there, very strange, indeed. For one thing, I never in my life ever heard of such a school, Mary Arden Academy, nor have I ever heard of a limerick. Begging your pardon, sir, have you ever heard a limerick?"

"Tell me, Mr Brown, this landlady, Mrs Waller, from the Oxford Street Tavern, does she imbibe?"

"Well." Gazing into Collier's questioning eyes, he thought, *he thinks I'm daft. I should not have mentioned the limerick part.* "Well, sir, there is a strong possibility that she imbibes betimes. I did smell a wee bit on her breath during the interrogation."

"And you, sir, do you imbibe as well?"

He wilted. "It goes with the work, sir."

"Yes, I thought as much. Thank you, Mr Brown. I shall not be in need of your services any longer. Please, send me your bill. Good day, detective."

Brown stood, near tumbling from his chair. "Ah, yes sir. Good day."

Collier pulled the office door closed behind him and descended the steps. He stopped to view the Thames and pondered the thought that he had heard quite enough to convince him of Mary Derby's whereabouts.

While he gazed into the river, Mrs Aesop stood in her room at the Northgate Hotel. She fretted in front of the mirror, pinching her cheeks, dabbing her brow, wondering if her clothes would be acceptable attire to wear at the Collier's dinner party. Her window was open and being very near the wharf, she heard the passage of boats, navy people, and ship's whistles.

It was a sultry afternoon slowly turning to evening, and the smells, though pleasant, were not those of the country she found so resplendent, quiet and serene. Suddenly a vision of Bobbin crossed her mind. *Dear me.* A difficult feeling entered her heart as she gazed intently into her own French-black eyes. *How shall I find the strength to tell my daughter the story?*

Mary Posea Derby lowered her head. *I must pray and let it go. I have so much to say to everyone.*

She knew John Collier loved her, and that added an immense comfort to her, *but since he knows only a little of my history ... well*, she turned from the mirror, *I shall pray about that, too.*

She paced in front of the hearth. *Dear God, I must make it through this dinner tonight in respectable fashion. I shall be Mrs Aesop for one more night. And why not, I am strong, with your help. I love them both with all my heart. Please, help me to find just the right way in which to bring my daughter home with me.*

The mantle-clock struck a quarter to the hour. *I must hurry now.* She refreshed herself with lavender water. Her hair was twisted up and braided, as she wore it years ago. Against her olive skin and raven black hair, her lovely light green dress looked stunning. She had never thought of herself as stunning, certainly, and never saw the admiring glances of men turned so frequently in her direction.

It had taken her years to sort through the brutality of a sick man that she had once married, William. To trust another relationship never crossed her mind until her heart melted within seconds of John Collier's first warm glance. It had happened so quickly, and with such finality and conviction, this love she felt for him.

With him, it was a quiet passion, one in which she could find shelter, solitude, acceptance, and love. Never before in her life had she ever equated love with tranquillity and peace; that a man could bring such a feeling in her heart that hitherto she had found but only in the quiet solitude of a meadow. Simply being near him was his gift; to touch him was more, and she wondered what his kiss would be.

"There now," she said, daring to look once more into the mirror, "I think I look presentable, though not a new frock, a pretty one all the same." And she nestled, very carefully, her hat upon her dark hair. It was a white lace and linen hat, quite dainty and fresh looking, white netting hung about her face and shoulders. She always handled this hat with special care. White was terribly difficult to keep tidy and only with washed hands did she permit herself to touch it. And so its adjusting was the final touch. As the muffled seven chimes struck from the mantle clock, she was ready.

Mary leaned in to close her window and felt the soft lace curtain blow gently against her cheek. The cool air felt refreshing, and then, a familiar form caught her eye. She pulled the curtain back just a little, leaning out to get a better look, *Dear me, it is John Collier.*

She dropped the curtain. *Upon my word,* she mused. *I should wonder what he is doing in this neighbourhood.* She moved away from the window, her heart beat fast.

There came a knock at her door. Startled she gasped. "Uh? Oh," she exhaled, "yes, who is it?"

"Ma'am, the Mary Arden carriage awaits you," replied the footman.

She spoke through the door. "Very well, I shall be right down, thank you."

Gazing once more into the ageing, speckled hotel mirror, she was pleased with her appearance. She could not judge for herself the handsomeness of her face, but her dress, hat, and white gloves were neat and tidy. She left the room, and finding the footman waiting in the lobby, tipped him two pennies.

Before climbing into the carriage, she inquired of him, "Tell me, young man, just what sort of business is that yonder – up those stairs directly across from where we are presently standing?"

He glanced up at the Northgate Towers. Squinting for a moment, he answered, "Madam, that is the office of a private detective. Ah, I believe a Mr Thomas Brown. He snoops around looking for missing persons, usually of the lowest sort and maybe the highest sort, too—he usually finds 'em, or so I've been told."

"You know these things, then?" she asked, frowning.

"Aye, ma'am. He's a braggart, that fat one."

"I see, thank you." She climbed in, careful to keep her hem from catching filth from the carriage steps.

Before the footman closed the door, he asked, "Ma'am, may I inform the coachman your destination?"

"Oh, yes, please, the John Collier residence. We were there just today. Thank you."

"Aye, ma'am." The pleasant young footman closed the door quietly.

When they pulled away, Mary's face coloured. She was an intuitive woman by nature, her ancient French Gaul heritage saw to that. As she took glimpses of the steps leading up to the detective's office, a sinking feeling took her heart, pulled it savagely down into her stomach, and there it lay churning. *Who was John looking for?*

It began to rain, and the boulevard once vibrant with people was now scant, black, and slimy. Instead of cleansing, the rain brought stench to her carriage wheels and spun the foulness all about her. She found her once spotless, pretty dress now soiled at the hem; her gloves apparently had touched a filthy handle, a doorknob—both now stained and smudged.

Shaking her head slowly, *I am a filthy example of a woman—why in God's name did I choose to wear white? But then*, as she pressed her glove against the inevitable throbbing in her brain, *I deserve every bit of wrongdoing for my own stupidity. Merciful God, I will never learn.*

Her old and persistent haunting devil returned slashing and pummelling her with a vengeance. Weeping, she held her chest. Oh, yes, certainly reminding her of her history, her unworthiness, her shallow, contemptible true self. Then the devil's sickening, shrill laugh enveloped every inch of space within the carriage. *You? You? You cannot be loved by such a man as John Collier or any man, for that matter. Nor will your daughter love you, you fool. Proof enough the beatings you so rightly deserved, and not so long ago that you cannot remember every detail, Mary ... Mary, he laughed with a shriek. Hmm, Mary the dog.*

The voice now drummed deeper and deeper into her chest, she could scarcely breathe. Lowering the carriage window, she lifted her face to the cool wetness, but it was not enough, she sat back gasping and choking.

Wiping her mouth, she shook her head, when presently the right and correct thought crept into her mind. *Oh, for the devil in me. I must not go to that house. I cannot go to that house and sit at the Collier table. Why, I am nothing more than an imposter; a woman who deceives, lies, and now I arrive, a "proper lady?" I cannot claim Babette as my child. What could I have been thinking? God in heaven, what could I have been thinking? She is far better off without me now.*

"Driver!" she cried.

The carriage veered to its left and stopped. Jumping down, the coachman hurried to the door. "Ma'am, what is the trouble?" Finding her with vomit on her lips and bodice, he asked, "Are ye sick, Mrs Aesop?"

"No, no," she cried, "I have changed my plans, Wilfred. Please, take me back to the hotel. I will grab my things, and we shall return to Mary Arden immediately."

"Headmistress, you are all ... soiled with vomit."

She sat back in her seat. "Go now, go now and leave me."

Chapter 27 – The Collier Household

No hand can make the clock strike for me the hours that are passed. [58]

It was a little past the hour of seven, as James and Susanna arrived at the Collier home for dinner. Holly remained in the bookstore, her nose a touch out of joint, but Susanna had left her a treat to ease the slight.

Maria met the two as they came into the vestibule. She was in a cheery disposition exchanging polite conversation as the servants helped James and Susanna with their wraps.

"And how does the evening find you both?" asked Maria.

"We are doing very well, Miss Collier, thank you," replied James.

"You are very welcome, Mr Halliwell-Phillipps and Miss Neilson."

Maria escorted them into the drawing room where they found Bobbin still bundled in blankets sitting in her green-striped, over-stuffed chair by the fire.

"Hello," Bobbin cried, hastily removing the blanket from her lap. She held out her hands. "Come, come." She stood, taking their hands, receiving hugs and kisses from Susanna. "You look so happy, Miss Neilson." She noticed right off the glow on her face. "And you, sir, Mr Halliwell-Phillipps, why, you both are aglow."

---

[58] Lord Byron (1788 – 1824) English poet. Quoted from *A Dictionary of Thoughts*, by Tryon Edwards, (1908).

Edward, coming to Bobbin's side, nodded. "Welcome, so good to see you both." Turning back to Bobbin he shook his finger. "Now Bobbin, remember to be calm, you must not erupt a coughing spell."

"Indeed not." Susanna stifled a laugh at the overly-protective Edward Collier. "Bobbin, please, you may call me Susanna."

She lit up. "Oh, indeed, Susanna."

"Come, Mr Halliwell-Phillipps and Miss Neilson," said Maria, "sit here, by the fire. Papa and Philip will be in shortly. Papa was delayed on business and has just returned home."

James nodded, taking a seat. "Mr Collier, it is most kind of you to invite us for dinner. I cannot tell you how happy I am to see you all again. And you, Bobbin, you are recuperating well?"

"Aye, sir, I am quite recovered, sir, save a coughing fit now and again. Terrible business these colds, but I shall recover."

It was a few seconds more when Susanna smiled broadly, lifting up her left hand to Bobbin. "My dear friend, I have very good news to share with you. James and I are to be married."

Taking her hand, Bobbin stood and hugged her. "Oh, the band is handsome, indeed, Susanna."

"Congratulations," said Maria, "Bobbin and I had discussed, with wishful thinking, your nuptials. Are we not the clever ones, Bobbin?"

"It was obvious," she said, smiling, "we knew, did we not, Maria? Oh, and it was a while ago."

"Is that so," said James, "how long ago exactly?"

Bobbin giggled, "Visitor's Day, to be exact." She glanced at Philip as he came into the room. "Come quick, Philip, Miss Neilson and Mr Halliwell-Phillipps are engaged."

"Engaged? Well, how marvellous for you both."

The room lit up with gaiety and happy conversations. A toast was lifted to the new couple, and everyone joined in with good-humoured conversations. Susanna remarked to James that she did not feel out of place one second in such company as the Colliers. She found them a well-mannered family, never feeling the least bit inferior. Within the hour, John Collier joined them.

"Papa," said Maria, "you will not guess the good news. Schoolmaster and Miss Neilson are betrothed."

"Well, well now," he smiled. "I offer my sincerest congratulations to such a fine couple. Have you set a date?"

James glanced at Susanna. "No, sir, we have not, but I would suppose there is nothing in our way that would preclude marrying sooner rather than later. What say you, Susanna?"

Her face coloured. "Well, no, there is nothing, only that I would worry about the orphans. I must find another teacher to replace me."

Bobbin spoke up. "No need, Susanna, I shall tend them."

Edward frowned. "But, Bobbin ..."

"Yes, Edward?"

"What about your search? Your research? Have you forgotten already? I have only a few days left to help you."

She lowered her head. "I have not forgotten, Edward." The happy sparkle on her face vanished. "Nay, do not think more over the matter, Edward; I have not forgotten. However, I am sure Miss Neilson and Mr Halliwell-Phillipps do not plan on getting married within the week." Quickly regaining her spirit, she affectionately took his hand. "But thank you all the same Edward, you are most thoughtful."

He blushed lightly. "Not at all, Bobbin."

It was near half-past eight o'clock when the butler announced dinner was served. Everyone gathered in the dining room, and the congenial conversation continued.

Susanna admired the beautiful table setting; gorgeous china, hand-cut crystal, ornate silverware, beeswax candles, the cleverly folded napkins and in the centre sat an arrangement of fresh cut ferns amid yellow roses. *Indeed*, she thought, *it is an exquisite table*.

Maria had arranged the table, setting name cards at each place. Proudly standing at her chair, next to her father, she looked over the table with pride. It was perfect. Philip stood at the end. James guided Susanna to the seat next to him. Edward sat next to Bobbin, but of course. Maria smiled graciously as everyone stood waiting for their father to take his chair.

"Maria, my dear," he said, "are we expecting someone else this evening?"

Everyone turned toward the empty chair.

Suddenly Bobbin, Maria, and Edward gasped. "Mrs Aesop."

"Mrs Aesop?" said Collier. "Was she to dine with us this evening?" His face turned pink as he turned to Maria. "Why didn't you tell me she was invited?"

Bringing her hands to her mouth, she shook her head in embarrassment. "Oh, Papa, I forgot about her entirely, I am sorry."

"Excuse us, Father," added Edward, "we were so caught up in the excitement of the engagement of Miss Neilson and Mr Halliwell-Phillipps that we completely forgot all about Mrs Aesop. I am very sorry for it, Father."

"Goodness me," Collier frowned as he glanced at the mantle-clock, "what time was she to be here?"

"Seven-thirty, sir," said Edward. "Perhaps she changed her mind."

"No, Edward," said Maria, "she is much too considerate not to send a note saying she could not be here."

Bobbin dropped her napkin on the table and stood. "I sense something is wrong, terribly wrong."

"Dear me," said Collier, "it is near nine o'clock. What was she doing in London?" When no one answered, he became impatient. "Come now, someone must know what she was doing so close to my home without my having the slightest idea of it."

"Papa," said Maria, "she came to see Bobbin. She said you wrote to her of her recent illness. She accepted our invitation to join us this evening."

James, knowing Mrs Aesop's history, surmised her mental turmoil. "Excuse me, sir. I will go in search of her. She informed me just days ago where she would be staying. "Susanna, I will see you to the orphanage. Come, now."

"I will join you, James," said Collier. He rang to have the carriage brought. "The Brougham is larger, and the horses are rested. It will take little time."

"Father," said Edward, "she told me she was staying at the Northgate on the Wharf. Allow me to come along. I know exactly where it is."

Looking surprised, Collier rubbed his chin thinking of his visit with the detective hours earlier. "The Northgate, you say, Edward?"

"Yes, Father, today while visiting, Mrs Aesop mentioned she was staying there, that's when we invited her to sup with us."

"I see." An ill feeling moved through Collier's body. "Very well, Edward, come along if you wish, I know exactly where the Wharf is."

As they put on their coats, Bobbin took Edward's arm. "Oh, I do hope you find her, Edward. Perhaps she fell ill and is lying down." Twisting her handkerchief, she lamented, "How could we have forgotten her?"

"There now, Bobbin, do not worry so." He pressed her hand. "We'll find her; depend upon it."

Climbing into the carriage, James hemmed. "Mr Collier, if you would be so good as to stop at the Newpark Orphanage and the bookstore, I will see Miss Neilson off and fetch my dog."

"Indeed, Halliwell-Phillipps, no trouble."

James hurriedly saw Susanna to the orphanage.

"I shall anxiously await any news, James. Go now; I will not hold you a moment longer."

He kissed her gloved hand. "I will see you very soon." He ran to the bookstore and hastily ushered Holly into Collier's waiting carriage. She sat at Edward's feet. Sensing an ill feeling, she remained unusually well-behaved.

Edward broke the worried silence. "It is but a little distance ahead, the Northgate, Father. I have been to the wharf many times."

"Yes, Edward and so have I. I was there just today, late this afternoon, actually."

"Really, Father? This is a rough neighbourhood, sir."

Collier sensed his son's inquisitiveness. "I had engaged the services of a private detective, Edward. His office is located directly across the street from the Northgate. For several months now the man has been in my employ, trying to locate a certain woman."

"Dear me, Father, fraud at the bank?" For the blackness in the carriage, Edward could not read the worried expression on his father's face, but his voice was different, very different. "No, no, son, nothing of that sort, I assure you." He sighed heavily, "The story is a complex one."

James knew just how complex the story ... *The wealthiest man in England is not so rich because he was naïve. The man obviously would take no chances with love nor money. Certainly Collier is not a man to be easily duped, but Mary is not that sort. She is only a woman, a mother, beaten by a ruthless, filthy drunkard, father of her three children. And, six*

*months pregnant, beat her into another miscarriage—she
knew if she went back he would beat her for that, too.*

*And because she did not return that fatal night Derby set
the fire that killed her children—no, Mary Derby was not at
fault. And if Mr Collier hired a detective to search the past of
Mrs Aesop, and if her past was all too sordid, well then he
must either love her sincerely and help her, or despise her as
weak and good for nothing.*

The Brougham pulled in front of the Northgate Hotel.

"Please, sir, let me go. I know Mrs Aesop very well."
James stepped out. "I shall be just a little while." Within
minutes, he returned. "She has gone back to Mary Arden,
apparently."

Not sure of Collier's intentions regarding Mary Derby, he
said, "Mr Collier, I will go to the academy by myself if you wish
it, sir. It is, after all, a long ride to the academy."

"I'll not hear of it, James. We'll all go together. Now then,
let us be on our way to Wilmecote."

As the carriage turned and made its way up High Street,
there was sadness in the air. All three men sensed it;
something had gone very wrong.

Collier knew that even with all his wealth and influence he
could not erase Mary's broken life, nor bring back her dead
children. It was finished, done, and complete. He tried
desperately to ward off the sinking premonition that Mrs
Aesop, his beloved Mary, was also now gone. A profound
emptiness lodged in his heart—yet one thin thread of hope
remained. *I must find her, to see her one once more.* He knew
to hold her in his arms would make everything in her tragic,
putrid past but a distant bygone memory. *I just need one
moment with her, just one moment more.*

"Father?" said Edward, "are you going to be all right?"

"I think I shall be all right, Edward, but we must find Mrs
Mary Derby before I can be very certain of it."

"Mrs Derby, Father?"

James closed his eyes. *He knows.* He felt keenly the depth
of Mary's despair. *She is hiding again ... pushing away the
past that she cannot escape, assuming the guilt as hers alone.
I must break that sacred promise I made to Mary Posea
Derby? Posea.* He repeated. *Posea spelt backwards is Aesop. I
swore not to repeat a word of her dark history, but if Collier
thinks he is in love with a woman who has no love for her
children; if he thinks she was aware of Bobbin's survival and*

simply ran away after the fire ... well then, he is very much mistaken. I must tell him the truth. I must not allow him to be misled by a misguided detective who probably knows only half a truth. No, I must explain it all.

Chapter 28 – The House Where her Children Died

> When I wrote that passage God and I knew what it meant; it is possible that God knows it still; but as for me, I have totally forgotten. [59]

Mrs Aesop, now alone with her Mary Derby name and the devil, stopped the carriage. In a sturdy voice, she instructed the coachman: "10 Long Sutton, near Tuppence Lane, that runs along the river."

The carriage pulled directly in front of the house where her children and husband had burned to death. Mary calmly helped herself down, quietly securing the carriage door. For the first time since leaving its smoking, charred remains years ago, she faced the old dwelling.

"It looks the very same."

"Ma'am?" said the coachman.

"It has been rebuilt," she replied, "the same as the neighbours." Walking the full length of the restored house, she looked at it from the bottom to the top story. Stopping a little distance from the carriage, she looked up at the dwelling in wonder. "The very same window placements, the very same door opening."

The coachman nodded at her whispers.

---

[59] John Paul Richter, writing in a London newspaper *Essex (Mass.) Register*, Oct. 9, 1826. Quoted from *Current Opinion*, Vol. 14, by Jewitt and Crane, (1893).

Long Sutton Street was quiet, this being late evening. The house was dark, not a sign of smoke from its lone chimney, and she tried the door—it was unlocked. Knocking lightly, the door swung open.

It was pitch dark as she inched her way in. Rubbing her arms, she felt the dampness and dabbed her nose with her sleeve. The dank, black air was thick and moist as she quietly moved about inside. "It is empty. No one lives here."

Blinking several times, she grew accustomed to the darkness. "The hearth, fancy that, has not changed." Running her hand over the rough surface, she marvelled, "The very same stones when last I lived here." She groped under the secret ledge just inside the hearth. "La, my latchkey and sixpence."

Hearing the familiar sound of rats scurrying about, she tightened her skirt around her ankles and visualised Foss, the cat. "I wish you were with me, clever friend."

She ran her fingers along the worn, chipped stone steps. "How often I climbed them." She fondled the soot-caked latchkey and coins. Their brattle interrupted the dead silence, and she stood motionless, looking about.

Exhaling wearily, she said aloud to the emptiness, "There is nothing more familiar about this place." She turned to leave when a dark shadow entered the room. Her heart jumped in fear the landlady might have her arrested for trespassing. "Who is it?" she whispered.

"It is I, Mama, Stella Babette."

Dropping the key and coins, Mary put her hands to her mouth. She could not speak, for her heart was pounding in her throat; air did not seem to fill her lungs, though she tried desperately to take it in. She could feel her body run cold and her head felt light, "Stella Babette?" she whispered, "my sweetest little Babette? Come then to me, let me touch you if you are not a ghost."

Mary Derby stood in that very spot for an hour more, but her daughter did not come to her, and she finally walked to the open door. The moon was full. She glanced at the coachman, now slumped, still holding the reins. Even the horses stood quiet, their heads drooped. They too had fallen asleep.

"Well, then, there is nothing for me here." She quietly pulled the door closed behind her and began walking the very still, empty streets. Thick fog rolled in as she meandered along, not mindful of where she was going—nor did she give a care.

She felt terribly confused, the foggy air felt cool against her face. She had walked on for a mile more when she realised from the splash against the pillars that she must be on a bridge.

The fog came thicker now, and she did not know from which direction she had come, but still it did not matter, and she walked on. She put a hand to her face and holding it at its farthest distance, she could not see it. "Perhaps if I walk far enough I shall drop off the face of the earth."

And she began to cry, feeling such a relief with tears in the fog. "No one to pat me, or console me, fret over me, or stare in rude wonder at my grotesque face. I am free to cry." And she cried out in shrills and shrieks, sobbing until she felt numb inside. "There now," she wiped her eyes, "I certainly feel the better for it."

Mary wondered at what a miraculous thing she had discovered, to cry all alone in the fog. "I could even scream to the hidden moon, and not a soul should find me." And she laughed aloud at her opaque silliness. If someone should be listening from an open window, one would think me a lost dog or a wayward night-hag."

Still she walked on, no longer hearing the familiar splash against the stone pillars. Now she felt only softness underfoot, not the sharp cobblestones that punished her feet moments ago. "I must be walking on grass. Yes, the only noise being my dress brushing against itself and my breathing. Aah, it is truly a lovely feeling, this—this stunning quietness, the cool fog."

She felt a drop of moisture reach her cheek. "Well, now, yes, the fog." And she removed one glove and felt her breast; her bodice was damp. She adjusted her drooping hat. The white netting sagged, and she smiled. "It is a warm evening, and the wetness shall not harm me."

Continuing on, she heard what sounded like a wagon moving in her direction. "Am I in the middle of the road or alongside? Well, it matters not. It is a mighty thick night; neither they nor I should be out in it. When they pass by, I shall wave to them at our luck, meeting on such a night."

Standing very still, feeling light-headed and giddy, she listened and waited.

"Mama, come here, Mama."

She turned. "Where are you?" she asked, no longer startled at the voice. Moving back a hair, she missed entirely the massive, slow-moving delivery wagon as it lumbered past.

"Mama, I am behind you a little. Please help me, Mama. I cannot find my way in the fog."

She walked toward the voice. "And, pray tell, why have you ventured out on such a night, child?"

"I have been searching for you, Mama."

"Indeed, I have been gone a long time, yes? To which of my children am I speaking?"

"William, Mama."

"Ah, yes." Half-weeping, she closed her eyes. "My dearest, sweetest William, but tell me, child, how is it that you speak to me from afar, yet cannot see through the fog?"

"I do not know, Mama."

"And where is your baby sister, Jane Mary?"

"She is with me, Mama, this very minute I am holding her hand."

"You have not taught her to speak, William, that she might call to me?"

"No, Mama. I have not."

"You have not? Well, perhaps the next time we meet?" And there was no answer. "William?"

"Yes, Mama."

"Have you visited Babette?"

"Oh, yes, Mama. I often visit with her, Mama. She pleads with me to find you and bring you home."

"Home?" She paused, dropping her head into her hands. "Where is home, William?"

Father Macy, returning from his nightly walk, entered the cemetery, homeward; he held a lighted lantern. So absorbed with watching for the usual pathway landmarks to the parish-house, he stumbled. Stopping to regain his balance, he heard voices. The fog, though still thick, was dissipating a little, and he lifted his lantern up higher as if its meek glow should light anything ... or anyone. He remained quiet, listening for the voices to speak again.

"William," repeated Mary, "where is home? I am lost, my son. You must lead me from this fog. Take me with you that I might see again where I am going."

And the old bent-back priest, thinking they were lost was just about to speak, to lead them out of the Tottenham Parish Cemetery, but there was another voice, a sacred voice, a voice he had only read about; had only dreamed of actually hearing once dead. Mary, Mother of God intervened, kissing his forehead, filling him with the grace of God, now pure and redeemed, Father Macy, was allowed to listen.

"Mama, I cannot take you with me. Bobbin will help you, Mama."

"Bobbin?" said Mary Derby, amazed that he called her Bobbin instead of Babette. "Bobbin, William? You call your sister Bobbin? And when did you call her such a name?"

"It was I, Mama, who first gave her the name."

"William, why cannot I go with you now?" Her son's voice was fading fast away.

"I must go, Mama. You must find Bobbin. She will take you home. I love you, Mama."

"Where is home, William?" And she could not hear the words that flowed from her mouth, but she could see them, one by one, floating away, higher and higher on the rolling layers of misty fog that churned and moved up ... suddenly she noticed the soft glow of a light. "William?"

"No, Mary," said the priest, no longer bent-backed and stooped, "it is, I, Father Macy. I have been sent to lead you home, my child."

"Oh, yes, then, it is good, is it not, Father?"

"Yes, it is very good, Mary." He took her hand.

"Did you hear my son, Father?"

"Yes, Mary. He sounds like a fine young man."

Smiling proud, she took his arm. As they moved together along the pathway to the parish-house, she sighed. "Yes, a fine young man—and what age do you suppose him to be, Father?

Just at that moment, they came to the very grave of her husband and three children. She stopped and stared for a very long time. "I must have the stone reworked, Father."

"Aye, Mary, and what would you have done with it?"

"Moved, Father Macy, to another place."

"Yes, Mary, their deaths were an accident after all."

"I want the exact words, "Beloved husband, William Derby, chiselled deeply into the stone, Father."

She stood a little while more in silence, then added, "Just underneath that, I want the word *Forgiven* and beneath that, from our Father's teachings, *In Sickness And In Health.* And my children, Father, *Beloved son, William, beloved daughter Jane Mary, Rest In Peace,* and I will not forget Hester, our most faithful dog."

"I will see to it first light, Mary," said Father Macy. "Now, what say you, we go to the parish-house for a little rest?"

Father Macy no longer needed the lantern light nor his cane to guide Mary through the yard. Though it was still thick with fog, he could see forever—his eyes were once more perfect, his aching back no longer sore; he walked straight and sure.

Chapter 29 – Mary Awakens

Nor deem the irrevocable past as wholly wasted,
wholly vain, if rising on its wrecks, at last to
something nobler we attain. [60]

Awakening from deep slumber, Mary Derby lay for a
moment—adjusting her eyes to the familiar, yet distant
surroundings. She smelled ginger-spice and tobacco. Lifting
herself by her elbows, she perused the room. A delightful fire
crackled. She sat up slowly and noticed a lovely frock hanging
on a peg nearby, and swung her legs over the side of the small
bed and sat up slowly.

"This is the parish-house at St. Patrick's," she said aloud
as she stood and glanced back at her rumpled bed. "The very
one I near died in years ago." She gazed out the window, but
did not see anyone. "I must dress."

Yawning, she moved toward the wardrobe. There hung
her white dress, neat and clean. She remembered the
Northgate Hotel and sighed deeply. "That was so long ago."

She could not remember just how long ago it was, but
thinking no more of the matter, reached for her dress. She
noticed something pinned to it, almost hidden in the folds. "A
brooch, perhaps? But I do not own such a piece." Bringing it
closer, to her disbelief, she saw a miniature portrait of Bobbin.

---

[60] Henry Wadsworth Longfellow (1807 – 1882) American poet.
Quoted from *A Dictionary of Thoughts* by Tryon Edwards (1908).

Unclasping the brooch and holding it tightly, she kissed it several times. Deeply touched, she remained calm as she dressed and fixed her hair. She did not question how such a brooch found its way to her. This morning she felt free and lifted up, and thankful. Holding fast to the painting of her daughter, she left the small parish-house and ventured out into the yard, into the sunshine.

Meandering along the natural footpath to the old section of the cemetery, she was pleased to find her family's tombstone no longer in *that* place, where the self-murdered lie in the eternity of turmoil. She said a prayer, thanking the old priest for his good works.

It was a beautiful day; the sun was full and warm; birds sang their sweet melodies. Happy to be alive, she felt one with every single thing on the earth. Breathing in the fresh morning air, she closed her eyes. "Thank you, my son, dearest William." And she felt a light, airy kiss to her forehead. When she opened her eyes, a beautiful butterfly flitted about her.

Smiling, she resumed her search for the new tombstone. Something caught her eye ... the sun reflected off something lying atop one of the graves. Walking through the tall, unshaven grass to the stone marker, she reached out, touching it reverently. "The Mary Arden Key."

Her immediate recollection amazed and delighted her. "Yes, yes, it is the Key." She fondled it, smiling. "Oh, yes, the Key."

Trying to remember just what its purpose, Mary stood in the warm sunshine, holding the key to her heart. Upon closer inspection, she found the name engraved, "Stella Babette Derby."

She moved to the front of the marker where the key had been placed. There, etched in perfect form:

BELOVED HUSBAND
WILLIAM DERBY
FORGIVEN
IN SICKNESS AND IN HEALTH
Eighteen-hundred and fifty
BELOVED SON WILLIAM
BELOVED DAUGHTER JANE
HESTER
REST IN PEACE

Secluded from Mary's view, Collier sat watching her. He was nervous, his heart pounding; he had been weeping that she finally was up and walking about. Her thick black hair hung about her waist. Beams of sunlight shining through the trees settled upon her head and shoulders, and he knew she was well; her breathing was deep and calm.

Even though he was filled with the urge to go to her, he remained sitting.

Sensing someone near, she turned and found him watching her.

He stood, tears sliding down his face.

"John?"

"Yes, my love."

"John ... have you been waiting for me?"

"I have been waiting for you, Mary."

"For a very long while, John?"

"No, dearest, not for so very long, but, all in all, I have been worried. You have not been eating ... "

"I am terribly sorry, John." She bowed her head, embarrassed that she could not explain what had become of her.

"I would love to hold your hand, Mary. May I?"

"Certainly, you may, John." She felt his soft, warm hand squeeze hers. "Are you alone, John?"

He led her away from the gravestone. "No, my sons and daughter are here. And your daughter, Stella Babette is also here."

She lifted her head and glanced around. "She knows the truth, then, John?"

He nodded and brought her close. "Mary, I love you. I am ashamed for not telling you from the very beginning." He wiped his eyes. "I have known for a long time."

She took his hands and kissed them. "Now, now, my dearest John, what could be so bad that you crying?" And she kissed the tears on his face. "Come now, John, I have sorted out the part of my life that is buried and gone. I do not want to cry anymore. I want to see my daughter and hold her. I want to be forgiven."

"Forgiven? Mary, you have done nothing wrong."

They walked in silence along the path until nearing the Parish-House. She could hear Bobbin's faint call.

"Mama?"

Collier could feel the apprehension in her body. "Do not worry, Mary. Go to her and love her. She has waited long enough."

She kissed him tenderly. "I cannot tell you just how much I love you, John."

"I know, Mary, I know."

"Mama?"

She turned to find Bobbin running toward her with outstretched arms.

"Mama! Mama!" Bobbin cried as she grabbed her and kissed her face over and over.

"Oh, child, how I have loved you." She laughed and hugged her daughter. "I am simply overjoyed. I have no tears left, Bobbin, even for happiness."

"No matter, Mama, I think perhaps you have cried enough." Bobbin clung to her mother, turning when she heard Edward's voice. Taking his hand, she pulled him to her side. "Mama, Edward proposed marriage, and I have accepted."

Laughing excitedly, John took Mary's hand. "Well, well, then. It looks like we will have two Mrs Colliers in our family."

Father Macy stood at the Parish-House door directing the newcomers. "Just there, my children."

"Oh, yes, indeed, Father, we see them now." James and Susanna left his side, waving and smiling as they hurried toward everyone.

Maria and Professor Zany came from the opposite direction. Proudly hanging on his arm, she smiled and waved.

Floss and Holly ran and jumped at the delight of everyone.

There would be a grand and great celebration at the Colliers' home this evening. Indeed, and in the very near future, there would be a grand and great celebration of four weddings—two Mrs Collier's, one Mrs Halliwell-Phillipps, and one Mrs Zany.

Other Great Novels by this Author

Winthrope – *Tragedy to Triumph*
The Arrangement – *Love Prevails*
Bobbin's Journal – *Waif to Wealth*
Poppy – *The Stolen Family*
Sophie & Juliet – *Rags to Royalty*
The Spinster – *Worth the Wait*
Holybourne – *The Magic of a Child*

A Victorian Cookbook

A Novel Victorian Cookbook-Forgotten Gems is the author's latest addition. It is full of authentic Victorian cuisine inspired by the author's colorful and classy characters from each novel. Now you can join them for a tasty meal!

Slipcases

Hand-painted by the author over 70 different impressionist style sturdy Baltic-Birch wood boxes to house her collection of seven novels. Visit KennedyLiterary.com for a look.

Paintings

After encouraging artistic reviews of her slipcases, the author has branched out to painting on canvas and wood, in the style of 19th-century painters. Visit KennedyLiterary.com and visit Carol's Art Gallery.

Links and Reviews

Visit the author's website: KennedyLiterary.com
Like on Facebook: caroljeannekennedy
Follow on Twitter @carol823599

www.ingramcontent.com/pod-product-compliance
Lightning Source LLC
Chambersburg PA
CBHW050931120626
46552CB00001B/156